An End
Where We Stand Now
Book One

Sweet Pickle Books
47 Orchard Street
New York, NY 10002

Brandon Pawlicki

Copyright © 2022 Brandon Pawlicki

All rights reserved.

ISBN: 979-8-9860506-0-7

An End | Where We Stand Now Book One

This work is dedicated to myself, and my future. A special thanks goes to the teams over at Foreword Reviews, BlueInk Review, and Bowker for all of their help and valuable criticism. A special thanks also goes to the team at Polyviou Family Dentistry; not only for their help in fixing my smile, but for their generosity in helping me promote my writing. Thank you all for everything.

CONTENTS

	Disclaimer	i
1	THE PUP	Pg #1
2	AN END	Pg #56
3	WHO WE WANT TO BE	Pg #127
4	LOVE	Pg #163
5	THE WOLF	Pg #219

DISCLAIMER

The events and characters depicted in this work and its sequels to come are of my own creation and are entirely fictitious. Any relation to persons living or deceased and to any other works is purely coincidental and not intended in any way. Additionally, this series depicts fictional scenarios and viewpoints related to political and social issues. None of this is a means of real-life commentary in any way and should not be taken as such. The world that these characters inhabit is also quite graphic. This, too, is not a means of commentary nor is it in any way an endorsement of any kind. In summary…it's all fake.

1: THE PUP

A gentle breeze greeted her in the night, catching with it a waft of incense smoke. With her eyes at rest, Vallerie took a breath and smiled. The scents, both of the night and of the working, mingled pleasantly in her draw. Jaxton looked to her, wearing a joy of his own.

  "It's sweet," she said, her eyes still closed in focus. "That comes closest."
  "That's what I said my first time too," Jaxton replied. The green of his eyes seemed to shine, both from the fire's reflection and from his love. How fond he was of the way her hair tossed with the breeze, blazing orange beside the small bon. How fond he was of her voice, gentle and innocent while holding a subtle edge. A silent moment fell between them, the crickets' song and the occasional crackle from the pit having taken hold of the night. Jaxton looked down to see Vallerie's hands pressed still and firm over the stone slab. He thought to compliment

her on it, but did not, not wishing to break her focus. He turned back toward the fire, closing his eyes and replacing his own palms over the stone. Another breeze came, warm and sweet. "Just follow your gut. When you feel ready, let me know."

Vallerie drew another breath. She listened intently, savoring the scents, and cleared away the passing thoughts as soon as they came. There the two sat before the fire, allowing the time to come and go as it chose. A few minutes later, the decision was made.

"I'm ready."

"Okay. Follow my lead. Keep your focus. Keep your connection to the altar." Jaxton took a deep breath, released it steadily, and began, with Vallerie, following on the perfect mark. "To the Goddess, to the God, the two equal yet opposite, the two eternal that dwell within all, the two eternal that all dwell within, we invite you to join us tonight. We extend this invitation to the elements as well. Of the Earth, graceful in its swaying meadows and mighty in its quakes. Of the Air, graceful in its summer's breeze and mighty in its storms. Of the Water, graceful in its nourishing sip and mighty in its folding tide. Of the Fire, graceful in its warmth and mighty in its burn. We ask that you lend your respective strengths to us tonight to aid us in manifesting our wish."

The two opened their eyes to the altar set before the flames. Vallerie's eyes in particular shone most bright, her sky blues so graced by the flames' light. She observed the items laid on the slab in a way she hadn't expected, as each seemed to hold a power she was unable to describe: the target of the working; the silver-chained pentacle necklace set in the center between their palms; the tall white candles set to the left and right, dripping wax down every so often; the incense sticks wafting smoke on the right-hand side; and the torn brown page held down beneath the midsized cut of pink crystal that sat just below the space claimed by the necklace. Her eyes darted to and fro each object as the fire danced behind. All at once, it hit her. She let out a small laugh as she smiled.

"I can't describe it."

"It's really something, right?"

"Yeah."

"What's the next step?"

"The petition, right?"

"Yup. Remember what I showed you."

"Got it." Moving the stone aside, Vallerie took hold of the paper, and placed it down firmly with her left hand while tearing one edge toward her with her right, careful to do so only along her arm's length. "Clockwise."

"That's right."

She turned the page from its top down to the right, following with another tear along the next edge. She repeated until she was all the way along the paper. Taking the pen from her shirt pocket, she proceeded to write her name, followed by her birthday, three times down the length of the page.

Vallerie Sabell 03/19/2000
Vallerie Sabell 03/19/2000
Vallerie Sabell 03/19/2000

She turned clockwise once more and began writing in threes again, this time with her intent.

I am safe.
I am safe.
I am safe.

Another turn. She wrote further.
I vow to do no harm.
I vow to do no harm.
I vow to do no harm.

After another turn, halfway this time, she signed her signature down, following the three times pattern.

"Now... fold?"

"Yup. Toward you. Turn. Toward you."

"Got it."

Jaxton watched her closely. Her movement was direct and steady, with her eyes never leaving the page.

"There you go. Let's do one more for good measure."

"One more..." Vallerie folded the page a final time, the end result resembling a cramped letter. "All yours."

She handed the page back. Jaxton took it in hand and set it once more over the slab.

"One final piece." He pulled a pin from his pants pocket and held it to the tip of his thumb. After a breath, he forced it in with a grimace before slowly retracting its reddened edge. "To this petition, to its author, and to the object of our spell, to which its intents are soon to be leant, I seal in blood, in trust, and in love, to manifest said intents to the highest effect." He touched the pin's edge to the folded page and signed his name. *Jaxton Tallumn*. He then drew a symbol overtop his signature, a simple star above his name with a curved line dragging downward from behind it. He then set the paper overtop the pentacle necklace laid in the center and placed the pink-colored stone over them both. With hands pressed firmly down overtop, he continued. "I manifest protection to she who shall soon be the owner of this necklace. Let her always be safe from harm. I, too, ask the forces unseen to guide her on her path, to grant wisdom and light as she holds this gift. She alone is to own this necklace and feel its effects."

    He then motioned Vallerie to place her hands down over the spell. As he took his away, she held hers down just as firmly atop the stone.

    "On this night, I declare ownership over this necklace and its effects. On this night, too, do I declare myself a follower of Wiccan faith. I take up my vow with clear mind and open heart. I, Vallerie, Sabell, vow to live freely and at will, and to do so without ill intent. No pain will be bestowed via my name or my hand. None onto myself. None onto others. May I walk with love; with myself; with others; with the land; and with spirit highest, lowest, and middling. So mote it be."

    Vallerie then set aside the stone and took the paper in hand, tossing it into the firepit. The two then, in unison, bade farewell to their deities and ended the working by pinching out the candles' wicks, he with the left flame and her with the right. Together they sat, holding hands while allowing the fire and the incense to continue on. They drew a final deep breath at the scene before Jaxton took up the necklace and placed it around his love. She took hold of the pendant for a brief moment, twirling it in hand and observing its star-etched design, before the two shared a kiss, soft but long, their hearts at a high from their work. She ran her fingers through his dark hair right down to its end at his shoulder before caressing his neck. Jaxton followed the passion for a time before wrapping his arms tightly around her, leaning his head beside hers and speaking softly.

"I love you more than you know. And no matter where life takes us after graduation, after we walk that stage tomorrow, know that I'll always be with you. Whenever you need me."

•••

She reflected on that night as the flat line's hum rang in her ears. She sat seemingly still beside the bed, though a simple glance to her hair, blood soaked and having fallen over the left side of her face, quickly revealed her quivering. Her stare was fixed on her hand held tight to his, the pendant of her necklace resting over her grasp. Her eyes were exhausted, strained from tears, though her expression seemed more that of a deer in headlights. The doctor's hand gingerly came to a rest over her shoulder, jolting her for a moment.

"I'm so sorry."

She didn't respond, merely motioning her head slightly in the doctor's direction before returning focus back to her love's hand. The movement caused a drop of blood to stream down from the gash above her right eye. It rounded her brow and trailed down her cheek. The wound pained her but seemed then no more than an occasional ache. Her only concern was Jaxton. She attempted to speak, but no sound escaped her breath.

"Ms. Sabell, Ms. Sabell, we really need to tend to your wounds."

She hadn't heard the man's words. She made another attempt to speak, only managing a small wheeze.

"Ms. Sabell?"

Another attempt. "I—"

"Vallerie? Can you hear me, child?"

"I vow—"

"Vallerie?"

The ringing of the flat line began to subside as the room faded back into focus. She held tighter to Jaxton's hand, a new tear falling from her eyes despite how dry they had seemed.

"I vow…to do no harm."

Her words came meek and hoarse as she registered the loss.

Another tear.

"What's that? Vallerie? Child, can you hear me?"

"I vow…to do…no harm." Her subtle quivers began to show clearly in her posture. Heavy breaths came between her words. Her sight fell below Jaxton's held hand to her torn blue gown, to the long strand of its fabric hanging down to her sneakers, it, too, having been stained by blood. Her brow deepened as she closed her eyes, causing the wound to bleed further. She drew an unsteady breath as her pulse began to race. "I…vow…to do no harm."

—Two Years Later—

The cabinet's door shut with a slam, revealing her reflection in the glass. She looked, but only for a moment, before turning her attention to the prescription bottle in hand. She uncapped it forcefully and tapped out the dose: two pills. She stood with panting breaths as the faucet ran, the water's steam having started to rise from the sink. It fogged over her reflection in the glass. The image of her messed hair; angry, sleep-deprived eyes; and the knotted scar above her brow soon faded behind the gray mist.

After a moment of thought, she tapped a third pill into her palm, set the bottle down over the vanity, and threw the dose back with a hard swallow. She sighed, hunched down over the sink with cupped hands, and took a long drink of the heated water. She capped the bottle and returned it to its place in the cabinet, once more slamming the door closed. Her breaths still came frantically. She ripped the washrag from its rack, dampened it, and placed it to her forehead. She turned off the faucet and looked to the misted glass of the cabinet once more. She wiped the fog away with her palm before running her hand down through her hair, ultimately brushing it behind her shoulders. Her eyes lingered on the blurred reflection.

"Four hours," she muttered. "Four fucking hours."

She scoffed a laugh, throwing the rag off into the bathtub before turning off the light, opening the door, and stepping out into the hall. The house was still and dark. The only sound present was that of the heat starting to kick on through the vents. For a moment, she breathed a sigh of relief, but that relief faded as the flame of a lighter flashed from the living room. Her brother's smooth yet rough voice soon followed.

"Hey," he called, taking a long drag of his cigarette from his seat on the couch.

"Hey. You hear me?"

"Hard not to. It sounded worse this time.

Ended sooner though."

"Did it?" she asked, rubbing her eyes awake. "Nothing felt any different."

"No? Same dream?"

"It's always the same. No changes."

"Maybe it's another side effect."

"Maybe. I hope I didn't wake you. The dream…or my…agitated…door slamming like I'm still twelve."

"No, no, I've been up. Couldn't sleep for shit. You did make me spill my coffee though. Screaming your ass off like that."

Vallerie nodded, then offered a snarky smile his way as she leaned against the wall.

"Sorry my trauma so inconvenienced you."

He smiled.

"I put a lot of effort into that cup, I'll have you know."

"There any left?"

"Almost a whole pot. Still on."

"Thanks."

As Vallerie started into the kitchen, Allan pulled the string to the lamp on the end table, exhaling a cloud of smoke as the room came to life, the light making the silver dye of his hair seem to shine. Inside the kitchen, Vallerie flipped on the light and pulled two mugs from the cabinet. She poured herself a cup and then one for him, adding double cream and sugar to both. She mixed them well and began back.

"Sis, you didn't have to."

"Yeah, I did. Least I can do for ruining your morning every day."

"You don't ruin shit. And it's not every day.

You know even if it were I wouldn't be upset."

"Most. Here, just take the damn cup before I drink it."

He smiled. "Thanks, Val."

She gingerly held her mug while taking a seat beside her brother, sighing deeply. "When I get there, first thing I'm doing is asking him to change my prescription. I can't keep doing this three to four hours bullshit. Doesn't even feel like I slept."

"Don't suppose my little conspiracy theory comes to mind, huh?"

"It's starting to, I'll give you that. He gave me something that's supposed to work, it doesn't, and now I'm going right back for something else. Maybe it is a fucking racket."

"Ah, the sound of enlightenment," Allan said, cracking a smile.

"Therapy on no meds didn't help either."

He shrugged.

Vallerie's sight lingered on her brother for a moment. He eyed her back.

"What?"

She smiled before returning to her coffee.

"What?" he laughed.

"Just…your hair's getting pretty long. I like it. Suits you."

"You think?"

"Yeah. You should keep it."

"Maybe. Have to see what work says first."

"Another rule? What, movers can't have long hair now?"

"Most of the guys there don't, so we'll see. I've been getting looks."

"Well, if they're gonna keep cancelling jobs on

you, I don't think a hair policy holds much ground. Tell 'em to eat your ass."

"You know I wanna."

Allan hunched over the armrest to put out his cigarette in the tray. His sister looked to him with concern, her brother still focused on grinding out his smoke. She sighed, leaned back in her seat, and rested her head onto his shoulder.

"Yeah. Yeah, I do."

•••

The backpack landed with a thud onto the dining table.

"Badge, pallet gloves, hand sanitizer. Allan, what am I forgetting?"

"Everything. Legit, none of that is in your bag right now."

"Seriously, I feel like I'm forgetting something. What is it?"

"Um—" he pondered, standing with his hair combed to a clumsy part, twirling the remote in hand while observing the weather on TV. The screen highlighted the murky green of his eyes. "Oh, your box cutter."

"Yes! Thank you."

Vallerie dashed down the hall to her bedroom.

"And your umbrella! Looks like you're getting rain!"

"What time?!"

"Bout noon!"

A horn honked from outside.

"Can you—?!"

"Already on it!"

Allan unlocked the door and gave a shout out to the car.

"Trish! She's still getting ready, come on in!"

"Okay!" the girl replied, shouting over music blaring in her car.

"Phone, wallet, keys."

"Your knife," Allan said, handing the switchblade over her shoulder.

"Right, thanks. And boom."

She took her necklace from the nail above her bed and slipped it on around her neck, the pendant metallically sounding as it traced over the zipper of her jacket.

"What up, bitches?!"

Trisha entered the room, sliding across the floor in her socks and barely catching herself on the wall, a strand of her brown hair flying directly into her eye.

"Ow, fuck!"

"You okay there?" Vallerie laughed.

"Yup, just half blind now. You almost ready?"

"Yeah, just gotta run to the bathroom real quick." She scrunched between the two out into the hall.

"Cool, can I watch?"

Allan proceeded to choke on his laugh

"No, perv," Vallerie snickered as she shut the bathroom door.

"Not even if I say please?"

"Off-limits."

"Couldn't resist, could you?"

"Nope. Avery cheated on me, so I happen to be on the market again. I'm dedicating myself to one try a month. Give it a little refresh cycle, you know?"

"You really think you'll get her one day, don't you?"

"I've seen it happen." She confidently looked to Allan with a shine seen in her light, gold-tinted browns. "Everybody thinks they're straight until they have one good night with their best friend. Just a matter of wearing her down."

"This is Val we're talking about. Don't get your hopes too high."

"Yeah, yeah. Hey, you said eight! You're gonna be late!"

"I'm coming!"

"Yeah, if only."

"Goddamnit, Trish, it's too early for this," she replied, exiting the creaking door. "Okay, I'm good to go. Al, you're getting your test back today, right?"

"Yeah… Yeah, I'm supposed to, but I don't think I'm gonna make it. Not feeling too hot."

She noticed the change in his demeanor. It was immediate.

"Don't worry about it, I'll pick it up."

"You sure?"

"Yeah. The school's only a few minute walk from work. I'll call ahead and go grab it after my shift."

"Then I'm picking you up just down the street from work, right? Four-thirty?"

"Yeah, the office is only a block down."

"Okay, cool, cool. Let's go before you're late."

"Yup yup. Later, bro! Love you!"

"Love you too! Kick ass today!"

"Will do!"

•••

"Have a good day, babe."

"I'll try. You know how Saturdays are though."

Trisha nodded quietly as Vallerie grabbed her bag and opened the door.

"Hey, Val."

"Sup?"

"About earlier… You know I was just kidding around, right?"

"Oh, no, I know. If I sounded mad it wasn't you, trust me. Just, um, the fucking nightmares again."

"So we're cool?" she smiled.

"Trish, we're always cool. Hey. I love you. Maybe not… in that way, but you know that, right?"

"Yeah. Yeah," she nodded. "Just anxiety. Forget it. Um, hey, what time again? Four-thirty?"

"Yup. Outta here at three, then picking up Al's tests, then counseling. Should be all set by then."

"Rodger dodger."

"Oh, shit, I'm cutting it close. Gotta go. Safe travels, girl!"

"Blessed be, beautiful!"

Vallerie, after adjusting the strap of her bag over her shoulder, began a jog to the entrance as Trisha pulled off. She stopped short though upon hearing a distant slamming sound. She began walking to the corner of the building and halted before the turn. Another slam echoed from the alleyway.

"Goddamnit." She started walking down toward the back of the building, her stride turning to a jog as she rounded the corner to see a beaten old pickup truck driving off. In its wake stood a large tube television and two tattered and stained mattresses, all set along the side of the building.

"Hey!"

The driver didn't hear her, continuing on down toward the front lot. Vallerie stopped, her sight fixed on the truck as it disappeared into the main road. She looked to her left with a sigh, observing the large array of bulging garbage bags, thrown about clothing and toys, and various unacceptable items, the TV and mattresses included. She groaned to herself before thrusting a heavy kick to a dirt filled vase lain on the ground. It hurled against the building, crashing to pieces. She felt her heart race and her breaths quicken before quickly closing her eyes, tilting her head back, and drawing a deep breath to calm herself. She turned back, her sneakers grinding in their turn over the gravel of the alley, and began her walk back to the entrance. On her way, she noticed another truck pull around, its back being full of large garbage bags. She paid the vehicle only a glance before sighing and continuing on. The driver slowed as he approached her, rolling down his window. She didn't wish to acknowledge him at first.

"Hey, this is where I donate, right? Do I just drop it over there?"

'No,' she thought. Desperately, as she lifted her eyes to the bulky, bearded older man, she wanted to tell him no. She wanted to tell him that dropping it over there was illegal dumping. She wanted to tell him that the donations weren't accepted until nine o'clock and that everything left outside before then was thrown out as it had been left to the elements. She wanted to swear all throughout before finally capping it all off with an exact quote of law. Ultimately, none of this left her breath.

"Yeah, just put it on the right-hand side though if you could so I can get out the door."

"Can do. Thank ya!"

As he rolled his window and continued driving toward the back, Vallerie continued once again, her heart and quickened breaths starting back up.

No. Why didn't she just tell him no? Why didn't she just tell him to wait? She sighed, rounding the corner and approaching the entrance.

"Shut up, Vallerie... Wouldn't have listened anyway." Her hand gripped the door's handle, but, on pushing it, she only managed to throw herself against the window. "Course. Why would it be unlocked?" She turned to observe the empty parking lot and swore to herself. "No manager. No manager, so of course the doors are locked. Why would you think they're open?" She slid her backpack down and took a seat on the curb, setting it beside her. A chilled breeze tossed her hair as her upset furthered A tear fell from her eyes as she watched the distant traffic on the main road. A ticking sound entered her ears. Her watch. She looked down over her wrist, the tick coming seemingly louder and louder each time. Each time. Time. She looked out once more to the traffic across the lot, busy as it always had been. Her next words said to the empty space came hoarse and choked as yet another tear followed. "What the fuck am I doing?"

•••

The hallway sat dim and quiet as she entered

the break room. The lighting brought her peace. She sat down at the computer and began typing her info to clock in.

"And… ten minutes over. Great."

"Hey, Vallerie? Where you at, honey?" her manager's voice called from the hallway. The shrill sound immediately soured her.

"Break room!"

Her manager entered, her knee-high boots clanking with her steps.

"What time you got?"

"I'm ten over, so I—"

"Okay, okay, I'll fix that for ya, don't worry. Listen, Darren just called off, so you're gonna be on your own today."

"On a Saturday?"

"I know. Just do what you can do. If you run out of boxes or collapsibles, either pile things onto a pallet, stuff it all in the corner, or stick it on the flatbed and wheel it to the line. If you get hit bad, come get me and I'll see if I can send someone back to help for a bit."

Vallerie sighed.

"Okay. I've got a mountain of trash out there already, so I'll do that first."

"Yeah, do what you can do."

Her words echoed in a fade as she walked away. Vallerie leaned back in her chair and let her eyes for a moment, the buzz of the overhead lights having come to life filling her ears.

"Couldn't at least leave the lights for a while?" She worked up a plan in her moment's rest. Set up the distributions then start on the mess outside. Mostly, she was preparing herself to work alone. After a time, she stretched, then stood and made her way to her locker, pulling the key from her pocket and hurriedly unlocking it while unzipping her backpack. She pulled from it a small tote with a sandwich inside and placed it into the cramped hold. She then shut the door, snapped the lock tight, and turned to leave to her workspace, stopping short in noticing a leftover bag of fast food over the dining table against the far wall. She walked over and snatched it in hand. "Fucking pigs." She pulled a half full cup from the bag, crumpled the rest and tossed it into the trash before heading to the closet to empty the drink. Upon opening the door, the scent greeted her. Mold. She pulled her shirt up over her nose and hurriedly dumped the cup into the mop's sink before exiting the room with a slam of the door. She tossed the empty cup into the trash and halted on her way a moment more. "Wait…" She turned back and opened the door once more, peering into the dark to study the walls. She scoffed with a smirk. A thin line of calking ran overtop the blackened mold on the walls' edges. She snickered to herself before slamming the door again, more aggressively this time, and heading to the back room, residing pre-set with boxes, collapsibles, and pallets alike. Her irritated laughter settled to a sigh. "Least you did that for me, Dar." She walked to the door and tossed her backpack overtop the desk, then peered over the trash box to find it totally empty. "Cool. Alright, let's do this shit." She pulled the latch aside and slid the door up to see the garbage pile outside having grown by several large bags. Pushing aside the plastic drapes, she found herself greeted by sprinkles of rain. She didn't mind it one bit. She began dragging bag after bag inside, tossing them along the floor toward the truck gate's door. After clearing a path, she started on the TV, pushing her body hard against it in an attempt to push it inside. The set hardly moved. "Come on, you mother fuck." She made another attempt, only successful in moving it a few inches. She stood breathing heavy and smiled, nodding in a stare toward the hulking set. "Have it your way, dude." She left inside, took hold of the flatbed, then shoved it out through the flaps. Returning in once more, she took a pallet jack from beneath a mounted box and threw the plastic aside on her way back out. She set the jack aside and parked the flatbed alongside the TV against the wall, propping the front and back wheels with bags of clothes. She pulled the jack back and rammed it as hard as she could under the TV's raised edges, and began cranking it up fast. With the set on a tilt, she hurried to prop the jack with the mattresses, throwing them down so they sat atop one another behind the wheels. She headed then to the TV, crouched, and pushed it up as hard as she could manage with a loud groan of effort. It just barely fell onto the flatbed, still requiring a heavy few shoves to get it onboard. In standing, she sighted a car pull around as she caught her breath. Thankfully, it was a small one. It stopped beside her. "Hi, there!" she shouted with a smile.

    The elderly woman inside rolled down her window and looked to the piles of dumped items with confusion.

    "My, did you just get all this?"

    "No, no, this is just what I walked into actually."

    "They just leave it like this?"

"Some do, yup."

"Oh, that's awful! And that TV too? Goodness, dear, don't tell me you lifted that all by yourself!"

Vallerie laughed, wiping her hands over her pants.

"I wish. I, um, I improvised."

"Goodness, goodness. Well, please don't hurt yourself, dear. I promise I don't have anything that heavy for you." The woman stepped outside and shuffled to the back door. "Oh, we're getting rain already, huh?"

"Yeah, looks like it."

"Do you have a coat?" she asked, opening the door to reveal a single midsize box.

"Yeah, I do. Got a hood right here, see? Here, I've got that."

"You should have it up, dearie, you'll get sick."

"I'll be fine. I like the rain anyway," she said, taking hold of the box.

"Wow, you're strong! I had to ask my husband to even get it in the car."

"Oh, it's not that bad. All clothes?"

"Yes, yes, it's shoes and, um, and purses, I believe. Oh, dear, could I get a receipt for that by chance?"

"You absolutely can. Come on in out of the rain. I'll fill one out for you."

"I appreciate that, sweetheart, thank you."

"Not a problem."

Vallerie held the drapings aside for the woman as they entered inside. She set the box aside and headed over to the desk, pulling a paper form from the stack along with a pen. As she hunched over to begin filling it out, her necklace fell from its place beneath her shirt, swinging over the paper as she wrote. The woman stood beside her, eyeing the pendant curiously. She smiled.

"Blessed be, young one."

Vallerie lifted her eyes from the page and looked to her. She shyly nodded with a smile of her own.

"Blessed be." She returned to the page. "It's not as long as it looks. Just got a few more things here then you'll fill out the rest."

"That really is a pretty necklace. I can tell it's blessed; the way the light hits it. Was it a gift?" Vallerie continued writing. "I'm sorry, I hope I'm not prying."

"Oh, no, no, you're fine," Vallerie quickly replied, offering a reassuring look to the woman. "I got it from… my late boyfriend. We blessed it together."

The woman's eyes left her for a moment, looking out to the rain as another car pulled up. She sighed.

"That scar. I'm sorry, dear, I should've known not to ask about it."

"You're fine. I don't expect everyone to know. Much less tip toe around me. I just need your name, address, zip code, and town here. Then a description of what you brought down there."

Vallerie set the paper and pen before the woman overtop the desk. She returned her sight, her eyes focusing over the scar. Vallerie averted her sight from the woman.

"Given what you've been through, you carry

yourself awfully well, Vallerie. You're stronger than you know."

"Thank you."

She still didn't meet the woman's gaze, looking shyly off toward the wall. The car outside honked as the rain began falling harder. The woman started on her receipt. The car honked again. The woman looked to Vallerie, now stood against the truck gate with one foot propped back against it. Her necklace was tucked back behind her shirt.

"Oh, you'd better get them, dearie. They seem in a hurry."

"Yeah, well—", Vallerie paused, looking past the woman to the car beyond the drapings. "—they see your car. They can wait."

•••

Vallerie gave the plastic collapsible crate a thrust with an audible effort, launching it atop the one sat full on the floor. It clicked loud as she rotated it to a lock over the one below. She pressed the side bars in and the middle door fell open. She rushed back toward the door as a honk sounded, followed by the rush of water as another donator pulled off. Her brow furrowed as she threw the plastic aside and started out into the rain toward a wooden end table and two large garbage bags.

"Yeah, just dump it in a puddle."

She threw the plastic once more, dragging the items behind her. She stopped to look over the end table, noticing a crack in the middle and the chipping on the corner's edge. She scoffed, nodding her head and gave the flimsy table a hefty kick. It quickly broke and splintered across the back room, smacking into two other large TV sets along the wall, a small mountain of garbage bags sat alongside. She bent down and took hold of one of the hefty bags, ripped it open, and grimaced as the scent of mildew rushed out. "Of course. Know what? All of it."

She tossed the bag into the full box of garbage beside the doorway. The second bag soon followed, with her not having bothered checking its contents. The rush of the day took hold over her as her arms began to feel sore, her legs followed suit. She stood, breathing hard from the effort on the bags, and listened to the rain pattering outside. She sighed, closing her eyes.

"Excuse me? Miss?"

The voice startled her to a twitch before she turned toward the doorway. An older man stood, holding the drapes aside. She knew immediately he wasn't a donator, taking note of his ragged appearance and fearful expression.

"Hi," she replied, her face softening on looking to him.

"I'm sorry, is… is it okay that I'm here?"

"Yeah, yeah, you're fine. Come on in. Get out of the rain."

"Oh… Okay."

The man cautiously stepped inside, clasping his hands together with his sight moving from Vallerie down to the floor.

"How can I help you?"

"This is Lord's Grace, right?" His voice was meek.

"Yeah, this is the place."

"I don't know if you guys do this sort of

thing, but… but I was just wondering if you had any umbrellas and maybe a change of clothes. I don't need food or money or anything. I just, well, as you can see, mine have kinda had it," he laughed, his face soon turning glum again as his eyes continued to flitter from Vallerie down to the floor.

"I'll see what we've got."

He lifted his eyes to her, seemingly shocked at her answer. She smiled.

"Bless you, ma'am."

"Just give me a minute. I'm sure I've got something for ya."

"Thank you."

She gave a nod before turning to check through the row of boxes and bins lined against the wall. She rifled through them, pulling out a large backpack, an umbrella, a poncho, and two sets of clothing.

"How are your shoes holding up?"

"Well… they've seen better days."

"Gotcha. One sec. What size?"

"Um, eleven wide if you've got 'em. If not, don't worry—"

"Eleven wide. Eleven wide, eleven wide, eleven wide," she said, rummaging through. "Where… are… you… eleven… wide? Ah. Boom. This all look like your style?"

He looked to the items and up to her with a light of gratitude in his eyes, appearing exhausted despite their brimming gray-blue.

"Why, that'll all do quite fine. Nicer than most things I've worn."

Vallerie smiled and knelt down, unzipping the bag and folding the clothes inside. She then set it aside and pulled a smaller backpack and a third set of clothing from the bins, matching the colors from the ones packed away. She held the items toward the man and gestured toward the large televisions and stack of bags along the wall.

"Over there, there's a small alcove behind the wall. You can change there. Seriously, get out of those wet clothes. Here's a towel too. It came in freshly washed. You want some coffee? There's fresh in the break room."

He stood holding the items with a look of bewilderment.

"My, my I don't want to impose when you're at work."

"My job is to help people in need. I don't mind one bit."

He hesitated, looking to the floor for a moment before returning his attention.

"Do you have cream and sugar?"

"Sure do. You a fan of cookies and cream?"

"That sounds great."

She gave a nod before starting toward the hall.

"Double sound good?"

"Yes, thank you."

After the man changed, he emerged from the back wall with a bright smile as Vallerie returned, handing him his cup.

"Careful, it's hot."

"Thank you…", he looked to her name badge. "Vallerie. It's been an awfully long time since someone's been so kind. Most of the time they just yell at me to leave."

"Those people can all go fuck themselves." She paused, looking toward the doorway. "Looks like it's gonna rain for a while. You're welcome to stay until it lets up."

"You're sure?"

"Yeah, here, have a seat—"

"I'm sorry, sir, but we actually can't."

Vallerie's manager started at a hurry into the backroom, motioning the man to the door. He hurriedly started on his way with his coffee, seeming frightened.

"No, stop."

Vallerie gave the man a stern gaze. He halted before the drapes. She looked to her boss.

"Vallerie, you know—"

"A helping hand to those in need, that's our motto, right? Let him stay."

"We can't. You can't give away donations either."

"Are you fucking kidding me?"

A confused scowl crossed her face.

"Hey—"

Vallerie scoffed, then took the bags from the ground, and handed them to the man. She then took his coffee and helped him strap on the backpacks before handing it back with a nod and a firm gaze. The man, still spooked, smiled.

"Thank you."

"Vallerie, we can't give away product! He has to pay for it. Now if you let him walk out with it, I'm going to have to write you up again and that'll make three." Vallerie took an umbrella from one of the bags, opened it, and handed it to the man, motioning him to leave. She turned toward her manager with a cold expression as he walked outside. "That's three, Vallerie. I'm afraid I'm going to have to let you go.

Please, take your things and clock out."

Her eyes fixed intensely on the woman.

"You're a disgrace," Vallerie hissed.

"Pack up and leave. Now."

She started toward her.

"How fucking dare you—"

"Security to the dock," the woman called over her radio.

Vallerie stood her ground, staring with unwavering gaze. Hurried steps soon echoed the hall and the guard entered the room.

"You cunt," the girl growled low.

"Miss Sabell is to pack up, clock out, and leave the premises at once."

The man, with hesitation, started toward her as she maintained the cold stare.

"I'll leave on my own. Don't touch me." The guard took hold of her arm. With her other hand, Vallerie pulled her switchblade from her pocket, jerked away, and flicked it open, holding the blade out. The guard backed away, as did her manager. "I said don't touch me. I'm leaving on my own."

"Get out."

"Gladly." Knife still in hand, she stepped around them both, walked backwards toward the break room, closed her knife and returned it to her pocket. She clocked out on the computer, took her things from her locker, and made her way to the doors to the sales floor. The two followed a distance behind. She opened the door and, before leaving through, looked back to them. "You just made me and my brother homeless. All because I gave a damn to help someone."

"Vallerie, please don't make this more than

what it is."

"Rot in Hell."

She started out the doors, throwing them closed behind her as the two approached, and briskly walked down the aisle way with a fury burning in her eyes, the warmth not so long ago present being replaced by what could only be described as a layer of ice.

•••

The soft tick of Vallerie's watch seemed to dominate the silence as she pondered her answer. Her sight was fixed on the graded page folded in her hand, the scribbled note at the top peaking from its edge.

"B+", it read. "Tremendous improvement, Allan! Keep it up and that diploma is all yours."

She flipped it 'round in hand whilst her knee bobbed up and down. The man remained attentive to her on the other side of the coffee table, twirling his pen above an open notebook.

"Vallerie?" he called softly.

"I heard you. I'm just… thinking of how to word it," she replied, still fixed on the paper.

He sat quiet. She placed the paper into her backpack beneath her seat and looked to meet his sight, her eyes appearing tired and dim. Her knee continued.

"When you're ready."

"Hm… I'm feeling—", she pondered further for a moment. "—It's getting worse."

"Did something happen to set it off?"

She nodded slow, her sight facing down.

"Oh, something happened."

"Do you want to talk about it?"

Vallerie sighed, looking off to the side before returning her focus.

"I got fired today."

"What?"

"I gave away donations to a homeless guy. And—", she paused, averting her gaze. Her knee rested still. She looked back with her eyes having turned tearful and angry. "—apparently that was strike three. And now… my brother and I are fucked."

Her physician set his pen down and closed the notebook.

"Any word from your other applications?"

"Nothing. For two months now."

"Are you able to stay with Trisha for a while?"

"I doubt she'd say no, but… I don't wanna put that on her. It's bad enough that I know how she—", she paused with a shaking sigh. "Then to have me hogging up her house too—"

"You know she doesn't hold that against you."

She gave a nod.

"Well, right now, what's most important is to keep to your schedule. Continue with your notes before bed, anything positive that you can write down about the day, your meditations, your prescriptions—"

Vallerie laughed.

"None of that bullshit works."

"Vallerie?"

"I said none of that bullshit works," her voice boomed. The man said nothing, merely sat attentive as she glared onto him. "In fact—", she continued, hurriedly unzipping her bag and pulling her prescriptions. "The new shit you gave me doesn't work. A few hours. That's it. A few more hours is all it did."

She slammed the bottles onto the coffee table.

"It's progress, Vallerie. It's just a matter of finding the right dose." She laughed again. "Okay…", he paused before a sigh. "I can see you're in a sensitive place right now."

"Oh, yeah? What kind of sensitive? What exactly do you see?"

"I see anger. And I see pain. And I want to help."

"You know what I see? I see that, even with your little regimen my anxiety is still a problem. The only thing that helps is my prescription. You know, the one you tried to wean me off of with a sleep pill that doesn't fucking work. I see the same goddamn nightmare every few nights to every other night to sometimes every motherfucking night! I see that I almost punched my boss in her stupid fucking mouth today." The man was taken aback, eyes concerned as he looked on her anger. "And you know what else I see? Your paycheck. I've thought about it for a long time, doc, but today, today it's just rubbing me wrong."

"You know that isn't why I do this—"

"Do I? Have you ever stopped by my house to check in on me? When I've come in here all fucked up in the head, did you ever offer to take a walk with me or something to calm down? No. It's only ever this. Have a seat, Val, let's talk about the same goddamn shit every single week. Do your breathing exercises. Do your meditations. Take this pill. Oh, hey, that one didn't work? Well, let's try another. By the way, make sure your insurance still covers it. Oh, they cut you because of your pay, then make sure you get on that payment plan!"

"Vallerie, please."

"Please what?"

"I'm sorry."

She looked on him at a squint in confusion. "What?"

"I'm sorry. I'm sorry for everything you've been through. And I'm sorry that what I'm suggesting isn't helping."

She sighed, averting her attention once again.

"Fuck." A silence fell between them. Vallerie's attention was caught by her watch's tick. She exhaled deeply, rubbing her forehead with her palm. "Look. I'm sorry. You didn't deserve that. I know you're just doing your job and there isn't a whole lot you're really able to do. You didn't deserve that."

"You're frustrated. And rightfully so. It needed to come out."

She nodded in agreement, her anger subsiding as a tear fell from her eyes.

"Doc, I'm gonna ask you something and I really need an honest answer. Off script."

"I'm all ears."

"Do you think the world is gonna get better? I mean, here we are, the most mentally evolved species to ever walk the Earth and it seems like we're just getting more… stupid. And cruel. Do you think—", she paused, swallowing hard and sighing, fighting back her upset. "—that it'll change?"

"Off script, right?"

"Please."

"I honestly don't know."

"I had a feeling."

"But what I do know—", he continued, Vallerie's eyes meeting him attentively. "—is that the world, especially as it is now, no matter how screwed up it may be, no matter the damage it can cause, it needs people like you to keep doing what you did at work today. I know you feel like it doesn't matter much a lot of the time. I know that… losing your job because of it can feel confusing."

"Putting it mildly."

"But it always matters. Great or small, those good deeds matter. The urge to do good matters even more."

"I just… There has to be more," she struggled, another tear falling as her voice cracked "I just wanna fix it. So many people seem to just not give a fuck; the ones with all the means, all the power to make a difference and all they seem to do is sit on their hands. Then there's people like me that… that see it; that see how wrong it all is; and it feels like we just don't have any power at all."

"But you do. Vallerie, your kindness is that power. And off script, I mean yours specifically. What you've gone through—how deeply things affect you—the fact that you would still even bother at this point is nothing to sneeze at. Look at our exchange earlier. You snapped at me and honestly you were right to. I am limited in what I can do here and believe me that keeps me up at night a lot of the time. But even in your anger, you heard someone out and thought of their feelings over your own. The level of selflessness in you—don't overextend yourself—but please… don't lose that. Don't think you're powerless."

She sat silent, wiping her eyes with her sleeve. The click of a pen caught her attention. She looked across the table to see the man writing onto a slip of paper. He clicked his pen again and looked to her with a smile, sliding the paper her way.

"What's this?"

"Your anxiety prescriptions. A month's supply. Half to keep for when your nerves get the best of you and, only if you really need it, half to hopefully start getting some better sleep until things even out. No charge."

"But… but my insurance cut me, how can it be no charge?"

"Because I—", he paused, pulling several bills from his wallet and setting them over the table. "—am paying for this one, myself."

She was in disbelief, shock overwhelming her face.

"I— Thank you."

"Go home Vallerie. Call Trish and ask if you and your brother can stay for a while. You'll figure something out. You've come too far for me to believe otherwise."

"Now don't go blowing too much smoke up my ass," she laughed.

"No smoke. Just truth. You're capable of more than you know. Much more." She smiled, the pain in her eyes subsiding. "Go on. You helped someone today. And now you're free of a job that you hated anyway. Go enjoy your time off."

"But… what about the rest of our session?"

"Come on, you really wanna be stuck here for another forty odd minutes? Go. Right now you need time with them, not with me."

She gave a hesitant nod before taking up her things and standing to her feet.

"See ya next week, doc."

"See ya next week."

•••

Vallerie took a breath of the dampened air as the clouds began to separate, savoring the scent. It calmed her quite well, knowing the Earth had renewed herself, as she would describe it. The blaring of heavy metal echoed the streets as Trisha's car approached the office lot. Vallerie walked out from beneath the awning and made a jog to the car as Trisha honked.

"Get in, bitch, I ain't got all day!"

"Hey. Thank you so, so much. Seriously. When we get the truck back from the shop, I promise—"

"I got you, don't worry. Quick session, huh? What'd he do, give you some pills and throw you out?" Trisha asked as she turned down the radio.

"No, there just wasn't much left to talk about after a while. He thought I'd be better off at home today."

"That came from a therapist?"

"Yeah, I know. Oh, hey, um, before we get going—"

"What's up?"

Vallerie hesitated with a sigh before she was able to find the words. She shook her head.

"Fuck it. I got fired today."

"What?! That skank actually—?!"

"Yeah. Um, long story short, me and Allan need a place to stay. Babe, I hate to ask—"

"No problem. We'll pack up tonight. Truth be told, I could use the company and living with you guys actually sounds pretty fucking rad."

"What about my… you know?"

Trisha took her friend by the hand and looked sternly into her eyes.

"Hey. I am here for you. For Allan too. You wake up screaming and I will be there to hold you until you feel safe again. Every time. Got it?"

Vallerie gave a nod and smiled.

"Good." She returned to the wheel. "So where we going next, babe? Home?"

"Not yet. I was wondering if maybe you could drop me off at that book store I told you about."

"You mean you're gonna walk from there? You sure?"

"Yeah. I just… need to clear my head."

"Okay. Okay, sure. I'll just go chill with Al for a bit."

Trisha started to pull off into the street.

"Speaking of, I'm gonna text him right now actually." She pulled her phone from her pocket. "Don't want him getting all worried."

...

The overhead bell rang as she entered the store.

"Hi, there!" the cashier greeted.

"Hey."

"Can I help ya find something today?"

"Oh, no, thanks. Just browsing."

"Cool. Well, if you've got any questions, just let me know."

"Will do. Thanks."

The woman adjusted her hair before slouching over the counter and scrolling on her phone. Vallerie observed the space for a moment before perusing the shelves. The store was cramped but struck her as cozy in its limited room. Several shelves sat ahead of her, all filled to the brim with books of varying sizes and colors. Shelving lined the walls as well, all appearing just as full as the ones lined down the aisle ways. As she stepped forward, the scent brought a smile. She ran through the selection, pondering just how many hands before hers had searched the covers and pages as she did, how much knowledge and how many stories must have been shared over time. She eventually pulled one book in particular from the shelf and opened it to the first page. As she read, the faint sound of the radio, previously ignored, caught her attention as the ending of a song transitioned into a news segment. She scoffed, swearing to herself. "Just what I wanna fucking hear while reading."

She attempted to tune it out, focusing on the page's text. She quickly skimmed through before turning to the next page. A distant thud demanded her attention, and her eyes raised to see a man in the far corner. He stood from the floor with a heavy text in hand, a bible. He eyed her briefly before making his way to the counter. She continued reading.

"Breaking news," the radio sounded off.

Vallerie attempted to tune it out once more, but the next moment caused her to listen in.

"Authorities are investigating an apparent

suicide in Grand Park today. An evening crowd stumbled on the body of an older man hanging from a tree. Police say the deceased, identified as forty-three-year-old Walin Marks, was a local homeless man that had occasionally visited the station to check in on the staff."

"Man, Walin was just an all-around swell guy really. I mean, here was this guy that clearly needed help and his only concern was just brightening other peoples' day," one interviewed voice said.

"According to several officers, Marks was offered a place to stay several times, but refused, opting instead to remain on the streets."

"Walin was a stubborn sort. Wanted to get back on his own feet, you know? We'd let him hang out inside, invite him to have dinner and stuff, but that's about as far as we got. Sooner or later, he'd go on his way and nobody could tell him otherwise. But, I mean, he'd always be there the next day. Never thought he'd, well, stop being there one of those days. And now…this. Just…sad. It's real sad," another officer stated.

"Marks was last seen by customers leaving the local donation center of—"

Her heart seemed to stop. A lump had risen in her throat as she fought off tears. She snapped the book closed and began toward the counter, noticing the man had already gone.

"Did you find everything okay?"

"Huh?" she asked, lost in thought. "Oh, yeah."

"Hey, are you okay?"

Vallerie met the woman's eyes, losing the battle against the tears as they began to fall. She quickly wiped them away. "I, um, I met him. The man on the news."

"I'm sorry, I must not have heard it. Is it—?"

"Oh. Never mind. It's not important."

The woman hesitated a moment before going to scan the book. She stopped on catching a glimpse of its cover.

"This is the one you want?" she asked.

"Yeah, that's the one." The woman suddenly became serious, looking sternly toward her. Vallerie's eyes calmed as she found herself confused at the look. "What?"

"You heard about the author, right? What he did?"

She knew at once what the issue was. "Look, I don't wanna seem rude, but can I just buy the book? I'm kind of in a hurry."

The woman shrugged. "I mean, if you're okay supporting someone like that, then that's your business."

Vallerie sighed. "Just because something is alleged online doesn't mean it actually happened."

"Alrighty," she replied, scanning the barcode and hurriedly stuffing the book into a bag. She continued. "So, you don't think he did it? I mean, the book goes pretty in depth for fiction, don't you think?"

"I think that if any of it were real, the last thing any decent person would or should do is harass him over it. Total?"

The woman shrugged once more.

"Ten fifty-three."

"Cool. Here."

"Out of…twenty."

"Thanks. Have a good one."

"Yeah, you too."

As the door slowly closed behind her, Vallerie sighed on her way. Frustrated as she was by the exchange, it was a welcome distraction from the announcement heard over the radio. As it attempted to surface once more in mind, she fought off the tears and buried it down. She drew a deep breath and focused her attention toward the evening sky as she continued down the sidewalk. Distracted, she ran into someone walking her way.

"Oh, fuck, I'm sorry. I didn't mean—"

The man from the bookstore stood tall over her with a judging expression. Before she could find further words, the man grasped the pendent on her necklace and yanked hard against the chain, snapping it from her neck.

"This," the man began, a harsh tone heard in his deep voice. "You a Satanist?"

"Wiccan. Please give it back."

"What's the difference?"

He pulled his hand away as Vallerie extended an open palm.

Her pulse began to race as adrenaline overwhelmed her. She eyed the man sternly, her sight never leaving his. "A big one. Give it back."

"You're her, right? The Sabell girl? You and your brother were the only survivors that day, right? Tell me why, witch? Why did my son die? Did you bring that murderer to the school?"

"He killed someone I loved too. No, I didn't fucking bring him. Give it back."

She made a reach once more for the necklace, but the man caught her arm. The two locked eyes,

Vallerie almost panting with anger.

"I think you're lying. And I think your sins are what got your little boyfriend killed too—"

Vallerie spit into the man's eyes and reached for her necklace with her other hand, her attempt being thwarted as the man slammed his fist across her cheek, a full-on punch, and threw her away toward the wall of the store. Her forehead made contact with the brick, and she fell to the sidewalk in a daze. She held tight to her head as it seemed to pound. She opened her eyes to see blood had begun to fall from her brow. Before she could get her bearings, she felt the man wrap his arms around her from behind, lifting her off of the sidewalk and into the air. She struggled but was too dazed and weak to fight him off.

He whispered into her ear in a hiss. "You never should've survived that shot." He pulled her back further. The motion caused her senses to return, and she acted fast, jerking her head back so hard that it hurt her neck. A small crack sounded as the man groaned. Vallerie managed to wriggle her hand from his grasp. She pulled her knife from her pocket, flicked it open, and jammed it hard behind her, directly into the man's thigh. He moaned in fury and threw her once more. Her hand remained tight to the handle of her blade as it tore from his leg, causing him to scream. In the fall, Vallerie landed hard on the pavement, failing to catch herself in time as the wind was knocked from her chest. She gasped for a breath as she turned to see the man had started fast her way.

"Wait," she wheezed, reaching out toward him.

And then she saw him. A flash of silver. A

flow of black leather. And a raging growl. Within an instant, the man was on the ground, Allan pulling his right arm back in a tight grip with one foot pressed down on his back. He groaned into the pavement. The man still held Vallerie's necklace in hand, the same one held behind his back.

"Stop fighting," Allan said coldly, panting heavily as his silver-dyed curls fell over his face. "Drop the necklace or I break it."

"He'll do it," Vallerie said, rising to her knees on the ground.

"Sinners don't command—aargh!"

The man wailed as a loud snap filled the air. Allan retained his grip over the man's arm as his hand released.

"Sis, get your necklace."

Vallerie stumbled to her feet and jogged toward the two, reaching down and taking the chain in her hand while keeping her eyes locked to the man's hateful gaze below her. She sighed and wiped her sleeve over her brow, revealing a long stain of red, before kneeling down in front of the man.

"Allan, hold his other arm too before he tries something."

"Love to."

The man moaned as her brother did so. She took a deep breath, fixed her gaze to the man's eyes, and held the pendant of her necklace within his sight.

"If I were a Satanist…the specific kind you're referring to at least, or any, and yes, there are many," she began, "then the star would be upside down. I don't believe in a devil. Nor do I believe in causing harm to anyone. You'd know that if you bothered to do even an ounce of research for yourself instead of listening to a bunch of senile morons in church or to your oh-so-holy book that's been rewritten fuck knows how many times by now."

"Blasphemous bitch—"

The man soon held his tongue as she pointed the blade of her knife to his sight, its silver shine stained by his blood.

"That piece of shit killed my boyfriend, shot me and my brother, and massacred an entire school," she growled. "How fucking dare you? Huh? How dare you even assume someone would bring something like that because of a fucking necklace? And, moreover"—she cocked her head—"how dare you piss me off on an already shit day?!"

The man's eyes filled with fear as the blade's edge touched his nose and Vallerie's eyes seemed to pierce him. She drew a breath and exhaled slowly as she retracted her knife, folded it closed, and returned it to her pocket. She donned her necklace once more, clasping the chain locked behind her neck. She looked to her brother.

"Hold him steady."

"Got it."

"No, no, please, you've made your point. I'm sorry, okay?"

Vallerie ignored him as she got up to her feet and walked to her brother's side, taking hold of the man's dislocated arm.

"No, please!"

"Shut up! I'm going to reset it."

"You're gonna what?" Allan snapped, confused. "Are you kidding me, Val?"

She ignored him.

"Now you're gonna wanna hold still. This'll

hurt worse than when it broke. On three, got it?"

The man lowered his head and breathed heavy against the pavement. "Okay."

"One."

Allan sighed, scoffing a small laugh.

"Two." Vallerie adjusted her grip and another snap sounded in the night.

The man shrieked.

"Three. Relax. Just relax. It'll subside." She gently lowered the man's arm and knelt down in front of him. "Hey, you know why I did that? Huh? Because you can't do this to someone else."

The man nodded, crying on the ground as Vallerie's voice rose to a shout.

"Ever! Never do this again! Put down the fucking book and start thinking for yourself!" Her voice cracked as she began tearing up. "No God with love in their heart would want you doing this kind of shit. And neither would your son. Didn't know him, didn't know you, but I know that."

Allan looked off to the empty street and sighed, cracking a smile with another small laugh.

Vallerie eyed him and stood to her feet, backing away from the man. "Let him go, Allan. Let's go home." He looked to her sternly.

"Let him go," she repeated.

He sighed again with a grimace before another scoffed laugh, and then yanked the arm hard. Another horrific snap was heard, followed by a worse wailing than before.

Vallerie looked away, closing her eyes. She was soon met by a soft grasp over her shoulder.

"That one can stay broken. Let's go," Allan declared, starting off.

"You didn't have to do that."

"You know he deserved it. Come on, let's go."

She gave a final look to the man laying whimpering in the road before following her brother's lead.

Loud metal blared before being muffled as an echoing *slam* filled the street. From around the corner ahead, Trisha jogged out.

"Allan, you said you'd be right back, what in the…fuck. Holy shit."

"Don't ask, Trish," he replied, walking to the car.

"Vallerie? Oh, my god, baby, are you okay?"

"I'm fine."

"Come on. We need to go," Allan called.

"Hey!"

As he urged the two on toward the car, Allan looked back to the man.

"What?"

"I'm sorry."

Allan looked to him briefly with cold eyes before moving back toward the car.

•••

"Thank you so much. Seriously, dude."

"Not a problem. Have a good one, miss."

"You too."

Trisha, with the bag in hand, locked the door and went into the kitchen. As she set its contents out over the counter, her attention was grabbed by the TV. She hurried over to the corner's end table and adjusted the volume.

"That incident may be in the past, but its memory continues to reopen the wounds for many parents and staff who still grieve. Behind me, parents, students, and teachers all gather on the front lawn, all paying tribute to those lost with flowers, wreathes, and letters. Though among those gathered, there are two faces in particular not in attendance. Since the shooting, survivors Allan and Vallerie Sabell have been missed by the community, Allan stating that he doesn't wish to relive the incident himself or to further harm his sister."

The report then cut to a younger Allan looking reluctant to face the camera.

"I think it's a great way to honor the victims, but for us it just isn't a good idea. We have graves for those we loved, and we visit often. But the school just…I don't wanna see it all over again. And my sister's better off forgetting it as much as she can."

"Many that attend today honor the brother and sister in their ceremonies as well, in grief for their loss, but also in gratitude, as Allan, only eighteen at the time, was responsible for subduing Malik before he was detained by authorities. In doing so, he suffered a gunshot to the shoulder and a broken nose, while the gunman saw himself stabbed several times in the abdomen by the survivor. Vallerie, before her brother's intervention, saw herself facing the gunman after hiding in a janitor's closet, standing guard over her late boyfriend, Jaxton Tallumn. Her account detailed a chilling exchange in which she simply asked the man why he was doing it, stating that he owed her a reason, only to be met with a smile and the sight down the barrel of a gun. Allan had arrived just in time to tackle the assailant as he fired, saving his sister from what surely would've been a fatal shot."

Trisha sighed, wiping a tear from her eye. The footage cut to the anchors sat at a round table, discussing the incident further.

"In reporting on this, I think it's important to acknowledge that we do so in hopes of encouraging a closeness in our community. The true strength in people is shown in how we band together in times of need and today's ceremony, of the many, is a testament to that. All of these young people, staff, and parents, selflessly paying tribute to lives lost and bonding in the process."

"That's exactly right, and for any who couldn't be in attendance, our hearts go out to you. I mean, my God, the things those siblings had to endure, it's— Well, I can't imagine."

"And we'd like to offer some further news to them specifically if they happen to be watching right now. While I'm sure something like this isn't a wound easily healed, we hope that this at least offers some form of peace for you. The shooter, Cale Malik, was reportedly scheduled for a transfer to solitary confinement late last night after being attacked by other inmates. In the assault, Malik suffered several injuries, a dislocated knee and knife wounds to the face among them. He is currently recovering in the prison's infirmary and, while conscious, is said to be refusing to speak. Well, that's a start, now, isn't it?"

"Good," Trisha hissed, anger in her voice. "Be grateful it wasn't one of us."

"One inmate who was involved in the assault stated the following while recovering from his own unrelated injuries."

"Man, I know they're gonna screw me pretty

hard for what I took part in and all, but the bitch deserved it. I mean, man, I did some bad shit, but I couldn't just stand by when those kids suffered like that. Far as I'm concerned, I was just making good for that girl and her bro, you know? I ain't regret it."

"Speaking of making good for the victims, at this time, Malik remains on track with not one, not two, but three life sentences. During his trial after the shooting, Allan Sabell was present in the proceedings, giving a chilling warning to Malik after being asked by the judge if he had any closing words before the verdict. Quote: 'Even if somehow your sentence changes, technicalities, good behavior, even if you're told one day that you're free, do not leave your cell. Because if you take one step out into the free world again, I'll make you beg for death.' It appears the judge took the boy's words to heart. As should any who dare think to cause such pain to a community ever again."

Trisha wiped another tear from her eye. She was then suddenly startled by a noise from upstairs, sounding to her like a creak. She left the kitchen and stopped before the staircase.

"Hey, Val, you up?" Another sound, like the former, but sharper. "Val?" she called, placing a hand on the rail and stepping to the first stair. A scream, short, but piercing. And then another, longer. "Vallerie?!" Trisha bolted up the stairs, the screaming continuing on. Her heart pounded as it grew louder. She raced down the hall and threw open the bedroom door to find Vallerie writhing in bed, her friend's screams carrying on. Trisha made her way over, knelt onto the bed, and took hold of her friend's shoulders. "Vallerie?! Baby, come on, wake up! Vallerie!"

Her eyes shot open, and, faster than she could register, Trisha was soon grabbed by the throat and staring straight at the point of her knife, the girl's eyes wide and fearful. A moment later, they softened, and she let her friend go, lowing her knife.

"I'm so sorry."

Trisha, pale as a ghost with eyes welling with tears, pulled her into a tight hug.

Vallerie, catching her breath from the episode, returned the embrace. "I'm sorry," she repeated, her voice hoarse.

"You're okay. You hear me? You're okay." She pulled back, meeting her friend's sight while resting a palm over her cheek.

Vallerie closed her eyes and rested against it, now holding a gentle grasp to Trisha's wrist.

"You're okay. It's over." Trisha eyed her with concern, her attention briefly catching Vallerie's lips. She thought to kiss her. She thought about how easy it would be right now to just lean in and tell her in the most powerful way she knew how that the nightmare was over. The thought soon left her mind as Vallerie opened her eyes. Trisha smiled to her, running her hand down her cheek before sitting back and averting her gaze. She gave her a pat on the knee and stood from the bed. "Come on downstairs. I got us breakfast."

"Thanks. I'll be down in a bit. I just need a minute."

"Gotcha." Trisha looked her way before leaving to the door. Before exiting, she stopped and turned back to her friend. She sat in bed with a sigh as she adjusted her hair behind her shoulders. "Vallerie?"

"Huh?"

As their eyes met, the thought returned. It made her smile, her attention again darting briefly down to Vallerie's lips before meeting her sight once more.

"You know if I'd been another, well, an asshole trying to fuck with you…I'd be hella dead right now."

Vallerie laughed, cracking a smirk. "Yeah. Yeah, I've really gone off the deep end. Sleeping with a knife under my pillow. Jesus Christ."

"Hey. I don't see a crazy person, Val." She paused, Vallerie's sight meeting her curiously. "I see a survivor. Now, wake up. This shit was expensive."

Vallerie scoffed a small laugh as Trisha gave her a smirk before leaving down the hall. She looked down to her right hand, noticing she still held tightly to her knife. Her smile faded as she closed the blade. She started to place it beneath her pillow, but stopped, setting it on the end table instead. She pulled open the drawer beneath and retrieved her necklace, tracing the star delicately as she held the pendant in her palm. She raised it to her lips, closed her eyes, and planted a kiss before placing it around her neck and standing from the bed.

As she made her way down the stairs, Trisha glimpsed her while setting plates onto the dining table and hurriedly moved to turn off the TV. Vallerie stopped, looking over to her. Trisha was quick to feign a smile her way.

"The news?"

Trisha sighed, returning to the plates.

"Yeah. Just for background noise. Nothing you need to see just waking up."

"The school, right?"

Trisha's smile faded. She walked over and ran a hand through her friend's hair.

"Don't think about it, okay? It's a bright sunny day, you're in your PJs at your bestest friend's place, and, my dear, you have some bomb ass food here just for you."

She smiled, then looked over to the dining table. "Holy shit."

"I know," Trisha nodded proud.

"How much did this cost you?"

"Nothing you need to worry about. Dig in, babe."

Vallerie, with a small laugh and a cheerful bounce in her step, started over to the table, pulled out a chair, and sat before the array of syrup-soaked pancakes, muffins, fresh fruit, and two large coffees. She looked back to Trisha, forcing a stern face. Trisha, taking her coffee from the bag on the counter, looked to her with worry filling her eyes.

"What?"

"You didn't roofie this stuff, did you?"

Trisha laughed, almost dropping her coffee. Vallerie almost got up to save it before seeing it caught.

"No. No roofies."

"Cool. Just checking." She turned back in her seat and tossed her hair before starting in on her food. "Goddamn, where'd you get this?"

"Little mom and pop place down the street. Good, huh?"

"Very. Thank you. Seriously."

"Not a problem, babe."

As Vallerie took a sip of her coffee, she

turned back once more, the thought striking her.

"Allan still asleep?"

"He's on a job actually."

"He got one?"

"Mhm. He was barely awake taking a piss, then I hear the phone ring, and before I know it, he's pulling on his pants while darting out the door. Must be a big one."

"Good. Good. That's good. Did he, um, did he by chance get to see his test yet? I forgot to show him last night."

"I showed him, yeah. We were up for a while after you passed out."

"And?"

"He was happy. Took a minute, probably just surprised, but oh, yeah, he was happy. First time I've seen him smile like that in a while."

"I'm glad."

"Now enough worrying about shit. Eat your damn food."

"Right. I'm done. Promise."

"Oh, fuck, actually, babe, turn back toward me for a sec."

"What?"

Trisha set her coffee on the counter, walked over, and knelt down, brushing Vallerie's hair to the side.

"Am I bleeding?"

"A little. Should change the bandages. Hang on, I'll be right back."

"Hey, can I finish eating first?"

"While that gets infected? Not a chance. I'll be quick, I promise."

Vallerie sighed as Trisha's voice faded down

the hall. "And leave the TV alone! If I come back and you're watching that shit, you're getting smacked in the tit with the remote!"

She cracked a smile, looking off toward the window as doves called from outside.

"Morning, guys."

Steps began toward the kitchen and Trisha returned with a roll of gauze, tape, and a box of alcohol wipes.

"Alright." She knelt down once more. "You ready?"

"Go for it."

"Okay, quick rip." Trisha reached up and took hold of the tape as Vallerie closed her eyes. A quick tear and it was off, revealing the bloodied gash. "You took that well."

The grimace on Vallerie's face settled as she opened her eyes. "Did I fuck with the stitches in my sleep or something?"

"No, no, they look fine. Well…I don't know, maybe you scratched at it or something. Damn, Al really did a good job on those."

"He's had practice."

"Yeah," she laughed. "Him and his fights… Crazy bastard."

"That, he is."

"Well, my untrained opinion here is that…it's either bleeding for no reason or…you done fucked up in your sleep and picked at the edge or something. Okay, stingy time."

"Ow! Goddamn!"

"I know. I know."

The sound of the front door's lock caught the girls' attention as Allan returned home. He stepped inside, visibly upset, and dropped his work bag to the floor.

"Fucking stupid cuntbags," he muttered.

"What happened?" Trisha called, delicately rolling a piece of gauze over Vallerie's wound.

"They fucked me. Again. Told me specifically over the phone it was a big job. Surprise, surprise, that got cancelled, and we went on to something else. I get up early and get all hyped up and for what? A lousy three hundred." As he finished up taking off his work boots at the door, he looked over to the kitchen. "Hey, you okay?"

"I'm fine. Just had to change it over. My doctor here thinks I scratched at it in my sleep."

"Expert opinion."

"Well, given what I saw earlier, your screaming might've actually been the culprit. Maybe stretched the skin."

"Maybe."

"Bad one?" Allan asked, walking over.

"Dude, she was all sorts of fucked up. Almost stabbed me in the face."

"Yeah, make me feel worse about it, why don't ya."

"Bitch, I'm just telling the truth."

"Reflexes. That's good. Didn't show any signs of a concussion before, so least we know that hasn't changed. Here, I'll take over."

Allan knelt down beside Trisha, tore off a strip of tape, and placed it over the bandage.

"Why do you smell like a doctor's office?" Vallerie asked.

"That bad, huh?"

"Yeah, it's pretty bad. Good description, Val.

I'll just be over here holding my nose."

"It was an old lady's place this time. Guess I need to hit the shower. There, you're done."

"Thanks, guys."

"No prob. As payment for my services though, I'm taking a muffin. Geez, big fuckers, too."

"I better not find pieces of that in my drain, Al."

"Trust me, it'll be long gone before I even get in there."

Allan started down the hall. Trisha moved to retrieve her coffee before pulling out a chair and joining her friend at the table. Vallerie mostly kept to herself, returning to her food.

"You okay?"

"Just frustrated," she replied, voice suddenly weak.

"Hey. Babe, look at me." Vallerie met her attention. "You guys are gonna make it. Allan's working out what to do with the house. He'll find more work. You'll figure things out too. You guys stay here as long as you need. Just take a chill pill, okay?"

Vallerie hurriedly turned away, closing her eyes tight, and nodded.

"Babe, don't fight it. Sometimes we just gotta cry it out."

"No, it's not…that."

"What's wrong?"

"I've got a wild headache all of a sudden."

Trisha's eyes became fearful as Vallerie clutched her forehead. She stood up and shouted down the hall.

"Allan?! Allan get in here!"

He raced down the hall to the kitchen, dressed down to his underwear, revealing his scars over his shoulder. Vallerie briefly looked to him but faced away from the marks.

"Sis, sis, you okay?"

He took hold of her shoulders.

"I…I don't know."

"Trish, call 911."

"No, no, we can't afford it."

"Shut it, you're going to the hospital."

"No! No, we can't! We—"

As Vallerie attempted to stand from her chair, facing them both, she stopped, quiet. Trisha began on the phone with the operator.

"Sis?"

"Am I gonna die?" Vallerie heard Jaxton's voice ask, soft and innocent.

She knew he wasn't there, but, as she closed her eyes, she replied to him.

"No. I promise, you're not gonna—"

She leaned over, holding tightly to the back of her chair.

"Vallerie?" Allan called, voice now shaking.

"No, we don't have that long!" Trisha screamed over the phone.

"—die."

Vallerie's balance gave out and she fell.

Allan rushed over and caught her in his arms.

"Vallerie?! Vallerie?!"

2: AN END

Her hearing came before all else, heavy breathing and hurried steps being the first sounds to drift into focus. She tried to open her eyes but didn't yet have the strength. She heard muttered words between the breathing, unable to make them out, though it sounded like an argument. She went to speak but could not. She felt herself seemingly floating. Another attempt at opening her eyes. She managed, but her vision was blurred. She was moving, that much she could tell. She was being carried, carried by two other people. Her eyes closed again. Suddenly, she felt herself wrapped by two arms, with loud grunts and thuds sounding before her. She looked once more, vision still blurry, but she was able to make out two figures. She squinted to see further, attempting to speak and being failed by her voice once again. A familiar voice was heard from one of the people, the words having come faint, but she was able to make them out. She was unsure if it was who she thought.

"It's safe there?"

"Yes. She looks to be in good shape, but she'll have better odds there. You all will. Just keep close," the other replied.

"Allan?"

She hadn't been heard. She was moving once again, the other figure rushing back to help carry her. Her feet dragged as they continued on. She looked down to her right to see what appeared to be a man laying in a puddle, motionless. Her sight shifted forward, and things became clearer, though still blurred. The other figure was seen walking ahead, looking to be wearing something dark green and patterned, but the pattern was unclear. Her eyes closed again, against her will. Silence. The following moment, she was startled awake again by a loud bang and a ringing in her ears. Another bang followed, muffled. She looked to see two people fall in front of the stranger in dark green. She shifted into an embrace like the one before, and the figure on her right rushed behind the stranger, seeming to hit them in the back. Her ears still rang, but she was sure she heard a scream, muffled, like the words that came after from those carrying her. And then, all of a sudden, silence as she faded out once more.

•••

Her first sight on waking was a rusted metal roof. The faint sound of an elongated siren was heard in the distance, though she couldn't discern where it was or what its purpose could be. It was all still foggy. It took her a moment, but the words finally came, raspy and dry, but clear enough to catch attention this time.

"What happened?"

Her name echoed around her, fading in and out. Soon, Allan came into view, dropping something that sounded metallic and wiping a towel over his face before crouching beside her. He looked to her with a smile and exhausted eyes, seemingly older.

"Hey. Welcome back."

"Mind answering my…question? And what's…what's with the beard?"

His smile left him. Her surroundings cleared up. She was laying under a gazebo. It was a rest stop near a highway. Her head rested on what felt like another towel. The siren wound on, finally heard clear. "Allan, what's going on?"

"Not now. We need to get you somewhere safe. Can you walk?"

Fearful and agitated, she wriggled her hand from his and sat up, trying to stand, but falling to her knees over a spread-out sleeping bag, well-padded, as she barely felt any impact. As it rustled against her knees, she found herself to be dressed in a white hospital gown. She looked back to see her brother and Trisha both crouched around her. Looking past them, she only caught a glimpse of the gray, clouded sky before the two moved in the way.

"Move."

She forced her way through them.

"Vallerie—"

It was too late. Shock and confusion filled her eyes as she saw the city standing small behind them. The highway alongside the rest stop's lot appeared largely bare save for few idle cars, all seemingly abandoned. What was visible of them from the stop saw the vehicles a wreck, rammed against each other with windows smashed. The parking lot itself was littered with suitcases and belongings thrown about. The siren kept on, fading into the distance. Beside her brother, she saw a red-stained towel and a kitchen knife, appearing equally dirtied, both laid on the cement floor. Blood. Frantic, she grabbed her brother by the collar of his jacket. He didn't face her.

"You might be taller. You might be bigger. And I may love you. But Allan, if you don't start talking right now, I swear to God I'll fold your shit right here, whether I fall down again or not."

He still didn't face her.

"Sis," he paused to find the right words.

As she began to speak again, with fear in her eyes, she stopped, noticing the silence. The siren had stopped. She looked back toward the city in the distance. The three of them were then jolted by a loud roar as a plane was seen heading toward the city, spotted high and small through the clouds. They watched in silence as a tense moment seemed to suspend them in time. At that moment's end, a light appeared in the sky above the taller buildings; and then another; and then a third; each appearing and falling after the other before. Vallerie looked on, confused.

"What—"

Allan took action, grabbing his sister and Trisha both, forcing them down to the ground and holding over them tight.

Vallerie fought against him. "Allan, what—?!"

"Stay down!"

A roaring thunder began in the distance, and the rest stop floor shook, the tremor lingering.

"Christ."

Hearing Trisha's voice, Vallerie broke free of her brother's protection and demanded answers, all as the tremor settled and a blinding light enveloped the distant cityscape, never expanding toward them, however.

"Trish, what the fuck just happened?! What—"

She noticed that her appearance was different as well. Her hair was greasy and had grown slightly longer. Her face was dirtied and without makeup. Her eyes were pleading, though not a word left her lips.

"Val."

Allan's hand fell over her shoulder. She looked to him, noticing the fading of his hair dye, his natural brown peeking through.

"How long was I out? At least let me know that much."

"A little over five months."

She squinted, confused at the answer. She was silent for a moment, her eyes locked with his as a warm breeze tossed their hair. She took a breath, the draw having come in a quiver and left just the same.

"Summarize what I just saw, please."

Allan lowered his eyes and sighed. A brief pause later and he returned to calm, knowing that's what she needed to see.

"Something bad is going on."

•••

Vallerie raced onto the grass, knelt down, and vomited. Trisha was quick to sit by her side, holding her hair out of the way.

"Okay. Okay. I've got ya."

Rapid breaths followed by harsh dry heaves hit her next. Trisha looked back to Allan, standing back beneath the gazebo with concerned eyes.

"I…I know it's a lot," he struggled.

"Yeah," Vallerie laughed. "No shit."

She doubled over into another wretch. Eventually, she managed to catch her breath. She leaned back to a seat on the grass, turning to face her brother as Trisha offered an embrace. Her breaths came small and strained as she spoke.

"Zombies," she said, hoarse of voice. "I get

the shit beat out of me, get reduced to a vegetable for five months, and wake up to zombies? Yeah, yeah, that's a lot."

The heaving came again.

"We need to get somewhere safe," Allan began. "You still aren't healed. After that…we'll figure it out."

"We will. Just settle down. Here. Sit."

She eased to a seat once more. Her breaths began to settle. She looked out to the gray sky, a rush of warm air greeting her. A silence fell among the three for a moment. Allan retrieved the items from the ground. He tossed the towel off into the shrubbery and scraped the knife's blade against the grass before crouching down and placing it in Vallerie's backpack sitting beside a picnic bench. She looked back to him, glimpsing her bag.

"We need more," she remarked, forcing a swallow with an agitated groan.

Allan raised his eyes. "What?"

"Backpacks. You're telling me the world ended. We need supplies. As much as we can carry. One pack isn't enough. We have to find more."

Despite Trisha's comfort, she attempted to stand, only to find herself stumbling. Allan hurried to her side, the two helping her to her feet.

"Props for swallowing it so well, but we need to make sure you're okay first. Christ, sis, I don't even know what you had in there to puke up."

"I'm fine. We can't afford to lose time."

"She seems okay to me," Trisha smiled.

Vallerie, eased in her step by her brother's lead, started over to the gazebo, her attention focused on a set of vending machines beside the restroom building.

"You guys tap into those yet?"

"No," said Allan.

Vallerie looked around the small rest area, gestured to her brother to free his aid, and started toward a closet door in between the restrooms. An undone padlock hung from its handle. Allan followed not far behind. She opened the door and grabbed a mop from the room's corner, then went to the machines.

"Val—"

"I'm fine."

Allan eased away cautiously.

"Trish!" she called, seeing her friend quickly position herself before the vendor while readying a kick.

"What? I'm gonna break it."

"Yeah, and you're gonna rip your ankle open doing it. Stand back." Vallerie stepped ahead and positioned the mop in both hands, the draping facing back toward her brother and Trisha with the handle's end pointing toward the first machine. She pulled back and rammed it against the glass. The impact was little more than a dull thud as she stumbled, barely catching herself. "Fuck."

Allan laughed. "'Afor effort, champ. Here.

Give it before you hurt yourself."

Reluctantly, she handed her brother the mop and stood aside. Allan pulled back and jabbed its point, breaking through the glass in one attempt. He knocked the edges of the frame a few more times and set the mop aside to gather what was inside. Little remained save for a few bags of chips. He packed all but one into his sister's bag and handed the last to her. "Boom. Last barbeque in there."

"Oh, I don't think I could keep it down."

"Eat it anyway."

"Why, so I can waste it hacking up again?"

"Sis, you need it far more than we do. Eat the damn chips." Allan took the mop and used it on the next machine.

"Don't suppose they left us anything citrus-flavored, huh?"

"Hang on, Trish, I think there's something here for ya. Aha. Last one too. Here, catch."

"Fucking score!"

"Any vanilla?" Vallerie asked, stepping forward to help her brother.

"All out of luck there. A few waters though, which you desperately need. Here."

"Thanks."

"Looks like that's all I can fit. Guess there's some for whoever passes through next. Okay, so, backpacks; where'd you have in mind?"

"My work. They sold school supplies. They're bound to have something worth grabbing. Like new clothes for one. With any luck they'll have something in their machines too."

"You can make that? It's fifteen minutes by car and, well, we're kinda lacking there."

"Wait. You don't—? How'd you get me?"

"We, um, had Trish's, but by the time we got you out of the hospital it was gone."

Vallerie gave a nod, closing her eyes briefly with an irritated sigh.

"Yup, I know," Allan continued. "Good old united we stand, right?"

"So…we can't just take one from the road? What about those on the highway? They're not looking too hot, but maybe?"

"We checked every one of 'em on the way. If they're not totaled, they're siphoned dry."

"I take it the mechanic never gave ours back."

"Things…happened pretty fast. Everybody had to evacuate. So…yup. Ours is still fucked."

"Right…Walking it is then."

"You guys think we should make a stop or two on the way? There's gotta be something we can grab, right?"

"We can scavenge a few houses, but I think it'd be safer to just go straight there. Coma head here just came to, so the sooner we set up shop for the night the better."

Allan picked up the backpack and unzipped the top pocket. He retrieved his sister's necklace and watch and handed them to her.

Taking the items in hand, she eyed him curiously. "People's houses?"

"Don't overthink it, Val. Anyone in the suburbs left weeks ago."

"And the city?"

"Same thing. Doctors and the army stayed, but they left yesterday."

"So there's still military? Is…is that where we're going after getting supplies?"

Trisha looked to Allan, who now stood silent.

"We"—he began—"aren't headed anywhere near the military. They did a final evacuation yesterday. It was a now or never deal, and we weren't about to leave you."

"They wouldn't take me?"

Allan's eyes met hers. He simply nodded his answer. A brief "no" that chilled her.

"So either leave me to die or you're on your own? Is that the gist here?"

"Well, you were in and out for the last couple days. That's what I tried to argue, but, yeah, pretty much. Couldn't spare the resources, they said. So we stayed."

Vallerie scoffed a laugh, turning away briefly.

Allan knew the motion. "Just…try not to think about it. We are where we are, and we'll figure it out."

Vallerie put on her necklace and her watch, pausing for a moment to check the time. One thirty-seven. She watched the hand's tick.

"And I take it we don't know where they went? No second chances?"

"No."

She sighed, glancing up to the sky and observing the clouds. Her heart started beating fast as she felt the nausea return. She forced it back as best as she could and carried on, a crack heard in her voice.

"Wait, hold on. It's foggy, but…I thought I saw someone in uniform. You said they left already. So who'd I see? Did someone stay to help?"

"They…they were already dead. We crossed through an alley on the way out and I had to take down one of the dead."

She nodded to herself as the breeze tossed her hair. Quiet came again as Vallerie's sight continued over the sky. She began again, pondering aloud.

"Crisis after crisis… Every time the world has the chance to come together for its own good… We finally fucked ourselves."

"You expected different?"

"No. Hoped…maybe. So, what, we just pick at scraps and start our own farms and shit?"

"Looks to be the option at hand."

Trisha, with arms nervously folded, stepped forward between the two.

"It's bad. I'm not gonna try and shield you from that. But…it's a chance to start over, right?"

Vallerie turned back to her, confused.

"Things…how they were before—"

Allan chimed in. "—it's all reset now. Like someone just deleted the save and started a new game. That's what you talked about—"

Their attempts to comfort backfired and Vallerie's eyes grew stern as she released a stuttering breath.

"This is not what I wanted."

Trisha turned away.

Allan sighed. "It's what happened. Like you said, we fucked ourselves," he paused, throwing the strap of her bag around his shoulder. "The woulda, coulda, shoulda doesn't matter. Come on. We've gotta get there while we still have daylight left. I don't want you out here at night." Allan started on toward the parking lot.

"Wait."

He turned back to his sister as she went on.

"The library. It's on the way. We should go there first."

"For?"

"Well, I noticed you didn't hand me my phone, which tells me it's dead, and the internet isn't a thing anymore, so I figure…scrounge up some survival books? Can't hurt."

Allan looked to Trisha.

She agreed. "She's right. I know you've got some skills from your training and stuff, but having a reference is smart."

"Okay. Library first."

Allan set off, Vallerie following closely. She

was stopped by Trisha.

"Watch out."

"What? Oh. Right. Thanks."

"Yeah, you're gonna wanna watch your step these days." Vallerie stepped over a shattered bottle on the ground, aided by Trisha's guide. "Here, take my shoes."

"Trish, no. I'm fine."

"You're taking my shoes," she demanded sternly, meeting her eye.

Vallerie gave a hesitant nod before taking the pair of sneakers and kneeling down to put them on. After tying them, upon trying to stand, she lost her balance, though Trisha was quick to catch her.

"Babe?"

"I'm okay. Just…maybe moving a bit too much too soon."

"You sure?"

"I'm okay." She offered a firm eye. "Besides, if I'm not, what are we gonna do? Go to the hospital?" She cracked a feigned smirk. Neither Trisha nor Allan were amused. "Seriously. I'm okay."

The three made their way across the lot toward the highway's ramp. Vallerie once more looked to the sky. She sighed, her breath leaving uneven. She was nowhere near okay. Far from it.

•••

With a heavy bang, the door swung open.

Allan darted to the side of the doorframe, holding tightly to his knife. He waited, listening. In time, he was satisfied by the silence. He turned behind, looking to the corner of the school sat further down the street. Trisha looked to him from behind the wall's edge. He raised a palm. She nodded in response. Allan returned his attention to the entrance of the library, adjusted his hold over his knife, and started in with a cautious eye. Looking into the doorway, the building appeared empty and dim, with only a faint light shining through the drawn curtains over the windows. He entered inside, quickly grimacing and covering his nose as a foul scent filled the space. Despite looking every which way, he couldn't see an obvious source for it.

His every step was delicate in observing the room. Three closed doors occupied the otherwise open space: one behind the desk to the right of the entrance; one in the far-left corner past all the shelving; and another at the right-hand corner. He started behind the desk first, taking the doorknob in hand with a gentle motion. It was locked. His heart began to race as he stepped back. He faced the door with a firm eye and sighed, readying his stance. He reared back and rammed a kick to the knob. The wooden frame splintered at the edge and the door swung open. It was dark, but he could see it, too, was unoccupied, the space merely a small backroom full of boxes and a wide set of shelves filled with books.

He turned his attention to the corner rooms.

He started toward them, moving behind one of the aisle's shelves to observe any change in the room's silence. No such change came. He went fast to the room on the left, taking the handle delicately as he did the previous one. The door opened without trouble. It led to a small alcove with a restroom on each side. He quickly saw them to be empty, their stall doors left open. Satisfied, he went next to the last room, thrusting an impatient kick to its door to reveal a small broom closet. Inside, it housed only a single shelf of cleaning supplies, and a vacuum stood in the corner. He sighed a relieved breath, sheathing his knife to the belt on his hip.

He left outside and looked down to the building once again before sounding a dull whistle. Trisha appeared first with Vallerie following behind. The two hurried his way.

"Come on. Hurry."

They went inside, hurriedly covering their noses on noticing the scent as Allan watched the street. He backed in, taking hold of the door and closing it slowly. He looked to a cart set beside the desk, stacked heavy with books, and hurried toward it. He rolled it to a rest against the door. Trisha, swearing to herself, paced the room, searching for the smell's origin. Vallerie watched her brother. He adjusted the cart a final time before turning back and facing her.

She nodded his way. He smiled, started over, and roughed a hand through her hair.

"Come on. Let's be quick." He coughed. "Fucking gross."

"What is it?" Vallerie squinted in disgust.

"Yeah, what the fuck? It smells like mold and cum."

"Trish, goddamn it. Please don't make me puke again."

Allan searched the room yet again, heading to the space behind the desk.

"I don't get it, I already—aha."

On turning back to his sister, he noticed a small inner shelf at the bottom of the desk. A foam cup sat inside. He knelt down to retrieve it and made a jog to one of the windows. He threw the curtain, unlocked and opened it with a hurry, and chucked the cup out into the grass. He eased the window shut once more, pulling the drapes back.

"So?" Vallerie asked, lowering her hand.

"Coffee. Really, really old coffee."

"Must've left in a hurry."

"Yeah. Just like we should."

Allan started down the aisles, searching the signs.

"Anything you don't already know, Al. Ways to start a fire. Medical books. Maps. Shelter structure. DIY for water filters."

"On it. How about you and Trish look for some boredom reading. Not like we'll have shit else to do."

Vallerie went down another aisle. Trisha

followed.

"What you thinking?"

"Well," she began, stopping at one row of shelves and thumbing through the titles. "A little occult couldn't hurt."

She pulled a book from the shelf and began browsing its pages.

Trisha stepped forward, eyeing the book curiously. "Thought you knew all this stuff? Just brushing up?"

"I know some, but…it isn't much."

"You thinking of practicing again?"

"I've thought about it before. Buying some crystals, incense, just seeing what I can make happen. But, well, you know the rest."

"Maybe…maybe it won't take you back to it though, Val." She was silent in skimming the pages. "Hey, don't think about after. Just think of that night. What you felt then, not…not what happened later. They're not arm and arm." Trisha placed her hand over her shoulder. She stopped browsing the page and looked to her, eyes pained. "They're not arm and arm. Not if you don't want them to be."

"The whole process, casting again, it might be too much. I don't know."

"So what's the reading about? Is it just…actually doing it that's—"

"…Seems that way."

Trisha watched as Vallerie continued browsing.

"Well, I mean, you know I'm clueless about it. But…for whatever my dumbass perspective might be worth, if you're this dashing just standing here reading about it, I sure would love to see you casting one day."

Her eyes lifted from the text and a warm smile emerged.

"You're a ham, you know that?"

"I do. And that right there would be why. Just…think on it, okay?"

Vallerie nodded, closing the book and looking to the others on the shelf. Trisha gave her a pat on the back and went back toward Allan. As she looked over the remaining titles, her eyes grew heavy. She swore to herself.

"Fuck."

•••

"Wow, you really lucked out with these."

"Yeah, definitely more than I was ever taught in school. I think Val told me about the battery and steel wool method before, but other than that, shit, we're a step ahead for sure."

"You think we'll be able to find what we need though? Like the sand and charcoal for the filters? And the…whatever you just said?"

"Steel wool. And…at least what we need most, yeah, we'll find it. Hell, one hit on a hardware store and we might be golden. Plus, Val's idea for backpacks. We've gotta carry as much of this as possible."

"Speaking of—"

"Yeah, she is taking a while." Allan stepped toward the back of the library, sounding a hushed whistle. Vallerie left out from behind, one hand holding to three small books and the other to the cup thrown from the window. "Val, really?"

"Yup. Really."

She walked past him and set the cup into the trash can at the edge of the sidewalk.

"So next time you say you've gotta go pee, should I, like…expect to, I don't know, find you saving a cat from a tree or something?"

"Maybe. What of it?"

Allan scoffed. "Goody two shoes."

Vallerie continued on toward Trisha, mouthing a silent mock of her brother's comment.

"So," Trisha began, "onward?"

"Yeah. Let's go."

The trio left down the street. Vallerie found herself lagging behind as her attention became drawn to studying the sights in passing. The suburbs seemed to her as more of a movie set than a forgotten town. The homes, some left boarded shut while others had their doors left wide open, stood, appearing out of place. The overgrown lawns, bushes, and flower gardens had an otherworldly nature to them. The lone car with smashed windows and the curious burns over the pavement particularly grabbed her eye.

Trisha looked to her.

"Riots."

"Huh?"

"The black spots. Broken-into cars," she gestured. "People. Police. Soldiers. That's what it's from."

"Jesus."

"Yeah, they needed him. Trust me, you lucked out missing that shit. Especially on the news. Even in crisis they blew it all to hell."

"Anything for ratings."

"Yup."

In passing, Vallerie's sight fixed on the vandalized car as she saw a mysterious brown fabric peering out from behind the back seat. She stopped to get a better look. Allan and Trisha halted their step as well.

"Think we can use it, sis?"

Vallerie hunched over, peering through the driver's side window first.

"It's on E," she sighed.

"Well, can't say I'm shocked." She continued to the back seat, Allan watching with a curious eye. "You see something?"

"I think it's a bag. Like a grocery bag."

"Think it's worth the time? We've got a good walk still."

"Anything they didn't steal might be worth something. Just give me a sec." She set her books down and opened the back door, hunching over the seat to get a better look. She took hold of the back edge and pulled the seat forward. It didn't budge. She looked beneath the seat and felt for a lever. "Gotcha."

She took it in hand, and pulled forward. The seat moved up to reveal several plastic bags in the trunk. As one of the bags fell, a rotten stench caused her to pull back from the interior, covering her face.

Allan laughed.

"Nothing good, huh?"

"I didn't get a chance to look yet. You mind? I really don't wanna puke again. Stomach's sore from last time."

"Hang on, I'll get it."

"I'll help."

"Nah, Trish, I've got it. I've smelled worse at work." Allan slid down his sister's backpack from his shoulder, set it beside the car, and climbed in. He pulled one bag after the other and set them into the street. The girls both looked through their contents, the offending bag going ignored as a tub of ice cream began to leak a stream from beneath. Allan continued searching the trunk. "That looks like it. So, anything good or just all crap?"

Vallerie pulled a can from one bag, holding it steady in hand. After eyeing it for a moment, she smiled, looking to her brother.

"Score."

"What, did you—Oh, fuck. Nope."

"What?" Trisha peered over. "Senior dog food? I'm with your brother on this one. That's a big ass nope."

"Protest all you want. I'll take it then."

She began counting the cans in the bag. There were four in total. She arranged them back inside, placed her books overtop, and tied the bag closed.

"You'll... take it?" Trisha asked, a slight look of disgust crossing her face. "What, as in eat it? You're kidding."

Vallerie continued searching the other bags.

"I told you the shelter story, right? Back when Al and I were kids?"

"Yeah. What, did they... Don't tell me they served you dog food."

Vallerie scoffed a laugh.

"No. No. Once we actually found some work, well, we had a bit saved up and decided we, well, we decided we wanted a dog. A lot of people there came in off the street with theirs, so we kinda just figured they allowed pets. Fast forward: after we'd already bought the food and toys and shit, turns out they actually don't unless they were already with you when you arrived there. We were bummed. Luckily the pups we had our eyes on at the rescue place still found homes, but it still sucked. What didn't suck though, the silver lining, is that we had a whole case of food." She stopped fumbling with the bags and looked to Trisha, sitting attentively. "We had groceries for the week. For half the price of what our regular groceries would've cost. Didn't taste too great, but it worked. He made a bigger deal over the taste than I did."

"Imagine cold chicken and warm beer. Yeah. Not my thing."

"That's pretty much what it tasted like. But," she continued, having stood to her feet, bag in hand, "it was food. And it lasts a long time in the can."

"Wouldn't you rather, I don't know, tuna or something?"

"Allan, do you really think people left any of that in the stores?"

"Hm. Point taken."

"Even if they did, unlit and raided grocery stores seem a little risky. No thanks."

"So...can we go now? Because we really should make camp before dark."

Vallerie went to speak, stepping forward as if in agreement, but stopped, having found herself suddenly lost in thought. She looked back to the car, then to the house behind it, its door left broken open, hanging off its hinges. "What?" She didn't reply, looking silently to her bag. "Val, what?" She sat the bag onto the hood of the car, and raced across the lawn up to the porch. "Vallerie, no!" Allan called, racing after her. Trisha followed suit. Her brother shouted again. "Vallerie, it's not cleared! Stop!" She was already at the front door, looking inside. The living room was completely torn apart. Rugs were turned over and thrown. Marks were seen on the carpeting where furniture used to dwell. A TV with a cracked screen was left on the floor next to a wooden stand, appearing to have been dropped mid-theft. She entered inside, cautious in her step. "Vallerie!" Allan's voice was a roar as he charged up the steps, drawing his knife from its sheath on his belt. He stepped in front of her. "Stay behind me."

"Allan, nobody's here."

"You don't know that," he hissed. "If it's one of them you're gonna get yourself killed."

"If anyone or... anything... were here, we would've known by now."

"Look, just... just wait while I clear it."

"Fine."

Allan sighed a frustrated breath and went ahead toward the kitchen, the sight within revealing cabinets having been torn from the wall and crashed over the floor. Vallerie observed the living room further, checking the drawers of the entertainment stand frantically. Trisha entered behind.

"What you looking for?"

She threw the drawers closed, frustrated, and continued searching the room. In time, her sight caught on a picture hung on the wall with a note seen taped in the frame's corner. She hurried toward it.

"This."

She took the note in hand, the edge of the tape tearing off the glass.

"To whoever may be reading, this home used to belong to us. We're the Peters family. Father, Jack. Mother, Emily. Two teenage twins, son, Raden, and daughter, Jade. And our dog, Leo. We got out in the evacuation thanks to a brave

family friend coming to pick us up. Of course, as luck would have it, our car decided to break down at just the worst time, so they really saved our hides. I'm sure many of you can relate. Anyway, it's doubtful we'll be returning any time soon, so if anything here serves you then please feel free to take it. There's some gas in the car as well if needed. Just, if you can, don't trash the place. Someone could use it. Maybe you. Be safe out there."

She sighed in relief. Trisha stepped forward to read the note.

"What? What got you so riled?"

Vallerie laughed, shaking her head. "I was worried about their dog."

"Gotcha,"

"I just… I was afraid maybe they left him behind."

Trisha smiled, patted her on the back, and began searching about the room.

"Alright," Allan returned, his voice distant from upstairs. Hurried steps descended, and he emerged from the kitchen, sheathing his knife. "It's clear. If you wanna search it, be quick."

"I will."

"This is the last stop, sis. Then straight to the donation place."

"Okay, okay. Got it."

"Let's look around."

"Actually, Trish, Al, do you guys mind waiting outside?"

"You sure?" her brother asked.

"Yeah. I'm fine. I just... I feel like I need to learn how to do it without help, you know? In case we ever have to split up or something."

Allan smiled. "Well, look at you. Sure thing."

He turned to leave out the door. Trisha nodded to her and followed outside. Vallerie looked back to the note and delicately propped it back into the corner of the frame, fitting it as tight as it could go without the tape. She then stepped over toward the kitchen and sighed, observing the broken cabinets and shattered glassware on the floor.

"They ask for one thing..."

She looked right toward the staircase and made her way up. Upstairs, she saw two rooms sat down the hall. One of the opened doors was marked with a hung R and the other with a J. She started toward the daughter's room. Inside, she observed the various band posters and stuffed animals, then noticed the vanity in the corner, lined with boxes of makeup and jewelry. Beside the vanity, next to the end of the bed, was an open closet. She closed the door behind her and began toward it. Inside, she saw a full rack of clothes followed by a soccer bag and a small camouflage backpack set on the floor below. She reached toward the clothes but hesitated. The silence of the room struck her, soon followed by the tick of her watch. She sighed and proceeded to sift through the lineup: various shirts, dresses, jackets, underwear, and few pairs of pants.

After choosing some clothes, she tossed them

over the bed and looked to the backpack on the floor. She knelt down and unzipped the back pocket, finding it to be a camping bag. A glance inside revealed a large box of matches, a thick folded map, and a belt with a fitted loop on one side containing a half-length hatchet. Its design was immediately striking; with a black painted wooden handle and a curious blade, the back end appearing like the face of a hammer and the front as a standard edge save for its curved bottom and the sharp, upward notch in the center.

    She took the bag in hand and stood, setting it over the bed. She untied her hospital gown and took the clothes in hand to change. Her outfit consisted of a plain white t-shirt; a pair of black slim-fits; a pink, metal-studded belt; and a pair of silver sneakers. She went to the vanity's mirror to observe the look, her eyes curiously drawn to the new scar sat above her old one. As she looked on her reflection, she sighed a shaking breath before grabbing a comb from one of the set boxes and fixing her hair. She turned again to the backpack, reached inside, and pulled out the belt. She removed the blade and fit the belt through the double row of loops on her pants, just below the studded pink ran through the row above. She tightened the strap to fit and took another look to her reflection in the mirror. She reached back to the bed and took up the hatchet, sliding it to its hold on the belt on her right hip. After a final gaze to the mirror, she eased a breath and drew the blade. She held it in hand, studying its weight. She scoffed before returning the weapon to its place on the belt. She took the pack from the bed and left back toward the door.

Once downstairs, she headed out the front door, being met by an awestruck Trisha and a cheerful Allan.

"Way to go, sis! Oh, hey, and you found a bag too."

"Yeah. Got lucky," she smirked, starting down the porch's steps. She looked to Trisha, who stood slightly blushed. "What?"

"You just... That's totally your look."

"You think I pull it off? Feels a little too loose and too tight in places.

"Dude, it fits great. All I've got is this shit ass plaid and ripped jeans and you're over here killin' it."

"Thanks."

"Yeah, yeah, you look great. Now we gotta hit the road. Come on."

"Alright. No more side quests. Promise. Oh, Trish, here's your shoes back."

"Thank yee kindly, my dear. Oh! That reminds me," she reached into her pocket. "I have your knife. Here."

"Do you have another on you?"

"No. I've been looking, but nothing yet. Can't even find a damn butter knife these days."

"What about that big ass thing he's got in my bag?"

"Doesn't seem very easy to use. And I can't just, like, stick the thing in my pocket."

"Honestly that's just an emergency backup thing," Allan chimed in.

Vallerie looked to her knife then up to Trisha. "Keep it."

"Are…are you sure?"

She gave a nod. Trisha smiled and placed the knife back into her pocket.

"Sis, what time you got?"

"Almost…four thirty."

"Okay. Not as bad as I thought. Still, we need to book it."

"After you guys. Hey, bro, you take this one. I can carry my bag."

"You sure? I stuck your other bag in there, so it's getting kinda weighted."

"I'm sure. Gimme."

After Allan handed the backpack over, she started off, adjusting the straps over her shoulders with a small grunt.

"You're sure you've got it?"

"Yeah. Let's go."

•••

The sheer emptiness of the trek threw her. As they approached the plaza, she felt especially off in crossing the once jammed streets.

"It's really not what I expected. Hardly any

cars. No bodies littering the streets. No gangs ready to gun us down." Allan and Trisha both continued ahead of her, silent. "Just bizarre."

Vallerie turned her attention from the abandoned roads ahead to the plaza's lot, it too sat empty except for littered fast food bags and thrown over shopping carts. The trio stopped at the sidewalk's edge, just before the parking lot.

"Okay, you two stay here behind the tree line. I'm gonna check around the buildings."

"What about inside?"

Allan retrieved his wallet from his pants pocket and pulled a set of shaped paper clips from within before holding them up with a smirk.

"I'll figure it out." Vallerie looked to him with a worried eye, interrupted before asking further. "Don't worry. I see anyone, I'm out in a flash and we move on."

"How long?"

"If I'm not back in half an hour, you go with Trish."

"What—?"

"Don't look for me. Just go. Trish, take care of her until I'm back."

"I will."

"Alright," he sighed, looking to the three buildings across the lot. "Off I go."

"Allan?"

He was already crossing the lot.

"He's fine. He'll be fine. Trust me."

"Have you guys done this before?"

"No, but he's handled the dead when we got you out. If you'd seen him— Just trust me, your brother's got this. Besides, he's never lost a fight, remember?"

"Yeah, not hand to hand, but what if it's someone with a gun?"

"He's okay. Alright?"

Trisha looked to her and placed a reassuring hand over her cheek. Vallerie turned, looking out to her brother seen heading behind the trio of stores.

•••

Time passed with the two mostly sat quiet. Vallerie's eye remained toward the lot. Trisha observed their surroundings, watchful of anything that may seem amiss. Twenty minutes in, nothing caused her any concern. Over the wait, which seemed to Vallerie like hours, Allan had been seen entering into each store. None, to her surprise, appeared broken into as she'd watched him pick his way through each entrance. He'd most recently gone into the donation center. As she looked on, a tense feeling started in her chest. The occasional breeze tossed garbage about the lot and sidewalks, the disturbance serving as the only sound present in the otherworldly quiet save for her watch, its tick having begun to bother her as she mapped out where her brother was likely to be in the store. In the passing of the next few minutes, the thought struck her. Time.

"He's taking a while."

"Val, he's good. You've seen him already. Don't worry so much."

Her heart continued its nervous pace, each beat feeling heavier than the last as her nerves grew tense.

"Something isn't right. I could get through the whole place faster than this."

Trisha looked to her, observing her stance as she sat crouched on one knee. "Just give it a few more minutes."

Her thoughts raced, every section of the building coming to mind. Another breeze came, tossing her hair and sending garbage further across the lot. The tick of her watch seemed to grow louder. Her heartbeat seemed to grow even heavier.

"Something isn't right." Her voice shook as she started forward.

"Vallerie? Vallerie!"

Trisha's calls were ignored as she headed across the lot. Her pace was a brisk walk at first, but, as her breaths quickened, she was soon off to a jog. Trisha followed behind.

—What Came Before—

She eyed the page as Jaxton looked on, his sight nervously jumping from her spot on the paper to the focus in her eye. Gradually, she sat back, adjusting her seat on the bleachers, and shifted the page over to his view.

"Here. That's what she was talking about."

"This chapter?"

"Mhm."

He sighed, disappointed. "I was afraid I'd have to cut it. Damn."

"No, no, you don't have to cut it. The writing is good. Seriously, babe, it's good. It's just about the pacing and where this part fits in."

"Where else can I put it? I feel like I wrote myself into a corner."

"Well, let's look at it like this. You remember that show we used to watch? Where they phased out the main character after, like, ten seasons and just kept going?"

"Yeah."

"Well, before they did that and we both checked out of things, do you remember how frustrated we'd get? How every few episodes in those later seasons it would be like an entire episode or two with just the side characters?"

"Oh, I gotcha."

"Yup. The character and their piece of the story is good. It's just that you're stepping away from your protagonist to tell it. That disconnect is where you've gotta make some corrections. Maybe see if you can rework it to where your lead is somehow more…directly…involved with this other character's story. Make it weave in with what your main is doing and boom. You're golden."

Jaxton nodded, a smile forming as he looked back to her. "Thanks, baby." He paused, taking the stapled set of pages in hand and looking them over. "It'll take me a bit, but I'll see what I can do."

Vallerie leaned in, took hold of his chin, turning his attention to her, and planted a slow, gentle kiss before running her hand through his hair and resting onto his shoulder. "Don't be too hard on yourself. It's only your rough draft."

"A little frustrated I didn't think about it, that's all. It's whatever. Live and lean."

"Exactly."

"You want me to look over yours?"

"Sure…whenever I actually start it."

"Writer's block?"

"Kind of. I'm just not really sure what I wanna do. Like…the whole topic, not just the essay part."

"You can always ask for a different one. I mean, I don't know if they'll let you for sure, but can't hurt to ask."

"Yeah, I know, but…it's the challenge. I wanna see if I can figure it out."

"Well, if you aren't sure about what you wanna do in the future, then a 'what you wanna do in the future' essay slash example…thing…might not be worth the headache."

Vallerie nodded to herself.

"Hey, we're only sixteen. Don't be so hard on

yourself." He playfully elbowed her.

She looked to him and smiled before her sight fell down to her knees. She folded her hands. "Yeah. But I still gotta figure it out."

A commotion grabbed the pair's attention. They looked to the right of the bleachers, down to the entrance from the gate. Distant shouting was heard, rising in volume. Vallerie stood up. Jaxton followed suit, taking hold over her shoulder.

"Stay behind me," he said.

She nodded in acceptance. He stepped ahead and the two made their way hurriedly down the steps toward the track. They raced past the gate. The shouting continued, pieces of the argument becoming clear. As they drew near the gymnasium, they rounded the corner past the sports shed to see a couple stood there, clearly emotional. They didn't yet notice their presence.

Vallerie whispered to Jaxton. "Is that Trisha Belrave?"

"I think so, yeah."

The boy rubbed his forehead, appearing frustrated, before looking back to her.

The girl was standing with tearful eyes. "Why?" she asked. "Just… tell me why."

The boy sighed.

"This is gonna hurt, but I honestly think you need to hear it."

A sound was heard behind Vallerie and Jaxton. They both turned to see Allan there with them, watching the scene himself while placing his keys into his pocket.

"I'm breaking up with you because I can't take your depression."

The girl closed her eyes, a tear falling down her cheek.

"I know how that sounds," he continued. "But…look. You're the talk of the school, Trish. For fuck's sake, you won the damn lottery. But…you're constantly unhappy, and I genuinely don't see why. You hit the big jackpot, then you got away from your shitty parents, got your own place, a car, and just…everything. But you're always moping around, turning down going out anywhere, always drinking, sleeping the day away. Then last night I saw the pack of razors. You're cutting again. It just…it feels like I just can't do anything to make you happy."

"I'm trying."

"No, Trish, you're not. That's the thing. You're not trying. You're not doing anything. I work my ass off at two jobs. Two. And I still come to school every day. You have more money than I'll ever see half of in my entire life, no reason to ever get a job yourself, and instead of recognizing how fucking blessed you are, you waste it on clothes and liquor and cut yourself? What the fuck?"

His voice grew more aggressive. The girl continued to stand silently, her sight having fallen to the ground. Vallerie and Jaxton decided to step in. Allan made his way ahead of them, anger seen in his stride.

"Hey, that's enough."

"Excuse me, does this concern you?" the boy snapped, slowly stepping up to meet Allan eye to eye.

"When I see a girl standing there broken to hell, yeah. She gets it. Conversation's done. Just leave her be."

"She needs a wakeup call. That's all I'm doing. I'm trying to help her spoiled ass."

"Does it look like you're helping?" Allan gestured to the girl, still standing silently, seeming utterly lost.

"Yes, it does."

Allan's brow furrowed.

"Really?"

"Yeah, really. She hasn't gone through shit compared to a whole lot of other people, man. You, you're Allan, right? You and your sis were on the streets as kids? Bouncing family to family and they all kicked you out, right? That's what I heard. Well, the worst she had were some drug-addict shitty parents. But they never hit her or nothin'. She just…she doesn't care about anything when she has everything."

Allan stood attentively but grew irritated.

Vallerie stepped ahead, Jaxton following. She arrived at her brother's side.

"She's fucking hurt, man," she said. "She heard you. Now let her figure it out and just leave her be."

The boy stepped back, looking over to the girl. She was fiddling with a razor pulled from her pocket.

"Oh, fuck," the boy scoffed.

"Hey," Vallerie called, making her way in front of the boy and taking the girl's hand. She delicately took her blade away. "Hey, that isn't the answer, okay? It isn't the answer."

The girl didn't face her, turning away.

"Maybe it is," the boy said, his tone cold.

Allan glared his way. Jaxton saw and took hold over his shoulder. "Don't. It's not worth it," he whispered.

Allan acknowledged him but returned his attention to the boyfriend.

"Matter of fact"—he continued—"you know what, Trish? If you're really this fucked up, then just do yourself the favor and get it over with."

The boy went to walk away. Allan rushed ahead.

"Al, no!"

Allan tackled the boy to the ground. The two struggled. The boy turned over and called out.

"Get off me, you fuckin'—"

Allan rammed his fist straight into his face, a small crack heard as the boy grimaced, blood pouring from his nose. He groaned as the two began wrestling further, the boy eventually freeing himself from Allan's grasp and standing to his feet. Allan went to stand but was met by a swift kick to the chest. He shouted a growl, holding himself.

"Hey!"

Jaxton joined in, grabbing the boy only to be resisted and thrown a punch to the cheek. Vallerie ran in the middle, guarding her boyfriend with arms outstretched as the boy walked forward.

"That's enough!" she screamed.

The boy laughed. "Yeah, it is. You all started it!"

"You told a crying girl to commit suicide," Vallerie said, anger in her tone. "You deserved a good plow to the face. Now fuck off and leave."

"Know what? That depends on your bro here." He turned to Allan, who was regaining his footing with a cold stare. "So, what about it, man?" the boy continued. "You done?"

Allan squinted as a harsh pain filled his chest. He breathed heavily and looked back to the boy.

"No."

He charged forward. The boy readied a strike. Allan ducked beneath the blow, grabbed to the boy's hips, lifted, and threw him over his shoulder with a roaring growl. The boy coughed as he landed on his chest. He gasped for breath, soon being turned over by a furious Allan and met by another fist, this time striking across the cheek. He followed with another.

"Allan!" Vallerie called.

Her and Jaxton both rushed over and grabbed him, pulling him off of the kid with a clear effort. Allan's shoes scraped over the ground as he was dragged back. The boy coughed on the ground, gradually regaining his breath. But he didn't get up. Allan's breathing was heavy and labored, a slight wheeze heard. He hunched over, holding to his chest. Vallerie threw his arm over her back and held tight. Jaxton followed suit with the other.

"I can walk," he protested

"Don't care," Vallerie said. "You're hurt. Just stop moving or you'll make it worse." He groaned, coughing. The boy remained on the ground, holding tightly over his nose. The trio began off toward the gym building, stopping briefly as Vallerie turned toward the girl, standing just the same, seemingly lost. "Hey!" She was ignored. "Trisha!"

The girl shook before gingerly looking over.

"Come with us."

She pointed to herself, saying nothing.

"Yes, you. Come on."

She started over, cautious in her step.

Vallerie turned back to see the boy still laying in pain before focusing ahead. The four of them continued on. Vallerie glanced to her brother before looking ahead. "You know, I really fucking worry about you."

Allan laughed, grimacing as another pain struck him. "Why? I still won."

"Not that."

"Then what?" he asked, looking to her confused.

She met his eye briefly before looking ahead

once more.

"I'm afraid you're gonna kill someone one day."

—What Comes After—

Vallerie winced, turned away, and snapped her eyes shut as the thunderous crack dominated the space. Allan regained his footing over the grass, breathing heavily and rubbing his shoulder. He stood with blood spattered over his cheek, looking down to the corpse as it lay motionless, blood pooling around the cinder blocks beneath its head. He looked to his sister and Trisha standing just past the trees in the alleyway. Trisha stepped ahead, observing the body. Vallerie sighed, turned away, and stepped back toward the building. On her way, she returned her blade to her belt. Allan closed his eyes after a deep breath, scoffed a laugh, and pulled a rag from his pocket. He wiped down his face and looked to Trisha who met his eye.

"Was that the only one?" she asked.

"Yeah. Everything's clear. I was just about to head back, but I heard something in the woods. Didn't wanna take a chance leaving it."

Trisha nodded, looking down to the gore over the cinder blocks.

"Good thing those were there, huh?"

"Yeah," Allan laughed. "Made things a little easier. Hey, you weren't joking about the trash, sis!

Here, there, fuckin' everywhere."

"Yeah. Doesn't look too different from a normal day."

She faced away in her reply, studying the belongings left behind along the alley. A large pile blocked the door. They watched her closely. Her brother soon stepped over the body to meet her at the wall.

"You okay?" he began. "I, um, I know it's not the easiest introduction to things."

"I will be."

Allan was quiet.

She looked back to him. "I know they're dead. Just…they used to be alive," she paused, turning away to the dumped items. "Whatever. Doesn't matter. You get a chance to go through any of this? Or inside?"

"Neither. But there's a lot in there. Place seems fine."

Allan walked over to the pile before the door and began turning over the bags.

"None of it's worth taking," Vallerie sighed.

"You didn't even look through it."

"I can tell. And smell. Well, unless that's all from…him."

"No, you're smelling the bags. Christ, people really gave you this stuff?"

"Asked for a tax receipt on it, too."

"I don't know how you did it, Val," Trisha said.

Vallerie turned back to see her standing from the patch of woods.

"You find something? On…him?"

"Empty lighter. Figured maybe we can get a spark for a fire and stuff."

"Nice. Good find." Trisha shied away a smile. Vallerie looked to her brother, still sifting through the pile. "Allan, seriously, you won't find…anything."

Allan returned to his feet, bringing with him a sword from beneath the cluster of bags and loose clothing. The blade was housed in a brown leather scabbard, complete with a strap. He smiled brightly with a sharp laugh, like a child getting exactly what they want on Christmas morning.

"Bull! Shit!" he proudly proclaimed. "Fucking dibs, ladies!"

"Is it real?" Vallerie asked, wonder of her own in her eyes as she stepped over.

Trisha followed. Allan cautiously unsheathed the blade. Its edge shined in the light.

"Oh, yeah. My baby's real."

"Please be careful."

"Can I hold it?"

"Trish, if you or Val even try, you'll fall over."

"Oh, come on, it can't be that heavy."

"Trust me, it is. This is genuine steel. Why the hell would someone get rid of this?"

"Same reason they do family photos. Maybe attachment or bad memories. Or maybe just clutter."

He measured the blade's weight a few

moments more before dragging its edge across a dumped loveseat set beside the pile. His motion was gentle, nothing more than a graze across the seat's back. The fabric tore along with no resistance.

"Whoa."

His eyes still shone in wonder. A distant thunder stole Vallerie's attention. She looked up to the grayed sky.

"We should get inside," she said. "Can't imagine getting caught in the rain would be too good for me right now."

Allan sheathed his sword and threw his arm through the scabbard's strap, adjusting it tight to a fit over his shoulder.

"Yeah, that's putting it lightly. To be honest, I didn't expect you to make the trip so well. You didn't even ask to stop."

"Good shoes," she said.

Allan started down the alley, patting his sister over the shoulder. He called to Trisha, now knelt down overturning the bags in the pile. She sprang up, tossing an open bag aside, and followed the two back to the front of the building.

•••

Allan snapped the locks on the door as the girls observed the sales floor. The sky outside grew darker, limiting their view of the space. Vallerie went left toward the manager's office and took hold of the door's handle. It was locked.

"Fucker."

She stepped back and rushed forward, ramming her shoulder against its edge. Nothing.

"Hang on, I'm coming," Allan said with a smirk, walking her way.

Vallerie pulled her hatchet in hand. She turned the handle's bottom toward the door, but hesitated, choosing instead to deal the blow with the blunt end of the blade. She swung hard down atop the handle and attempted to open the door once more. Nothing. "Val, hang on. I've got it."

She ignored her brother and tried again, grunting in her strike against the handle. Still, she wasn't successful. Allan ushered her back.

"Goddamn it," she said, agitated.

"You're still in rough shape. Here, stand back." Allan reared back and jammed four steady shoulders to the door. He stepped back further and hurled a fifth. The door still didn't budge. "Really need a door this heavy at a fucking discount store?" Vallerie laughed to herself, clutching her brow. "Hey, don't laugh at me. It's not nice, you know."

"I'm not. I just…I forgot there's a key. Look under the trash can. There by the bathrooms around the corner."

Allan went over and lifted the can to find a floor tile with a marked slash on its edge. He raised it up and found the key beneath.

"I take it they weren't actually allowed to do

this?"

"Nope. My dumbass manger kept forgetting the office key, so I set up a little hiding spot."

"Your idea?"

She nodded, proud.

"And they fired you?" he asked with a squint. She responded with a shrug. Trisha patted her on the back. Allan moved back to the door and unlocked it. He stopped, adjusting his stance, and scoffed a laugh to himself. "You know I didn't even see this door when I came in?"

"And you're supposed to be protecting me?" she smirked.

"Hey, do you wanna be a vegetable again?" Allan pulled his knife and kicked the door open. All that resided within was a cramped office. He turned and gestured to his sister. "All yours." She stepped ahead and went to flip the light switch on the inner wall. "Val, I already tried the one by the"—the sales floor lights came to life—"door." Vallerie shrugged. "Is that other switch broken?"

"Far as I know it's always worked."

"But I tried it three times."

"Emergency generator maybe? Or the last kick of a power grid? Who cares? We've got light."

Allan stepped away quietly, observing the space. He headed to the door and tightened the lock, already fixed as tight as it could get. "Yeah," he sighed, watching the windows to observe the empty lot.

Trisha wandered the aisles. Vallerie searched about the room for anything they could use. Behind the desk, on the back wall, her eyes caught on a chart for hour availability. She tore it down and ripped the paper in half, throwing it into the trash can in the corner. She searched behind the desk, finding a case of bottled water with around half left.

"Score." She pulled open the desk drawers, but found nothing but the typical office fare: log books, loose-leaf paper, staplers, pens, etc. She thought to grab a few pens or a pair of scissors as a backup weapon, but ultimately deemed them of little use. In leaving the office, she looked toward the entrance, observing her brother as he paced around the windows. "What?"

"Just checking. If I missed the office, then I wanna make sure I don't miss anything else."

"Al, we're fine. Look, the place was never even touched," she gestured to the aisle ways of the sales floor, packed to the brim with clothing, accessories, books, and electronics. "We've got more waters in here too. Keep the bottles for filters."

"Good. That all you found in there?"

Allan turned and started back over.

"That's it. But it's more than enough."

She looked left of the office and paced round the corner near the restrooms, eyeing the two vending machines stood on the wall.

"Holy shit, they're full."

"Finally feeling hungry, huh?"

"Little bit. Must've been that water on the way. Brought my stomach back to life."

"We have food, you know. You could've had something the whole time."

"Didn't feel like chips. A cereal bar though, that seems like a smart pick." She drew her hatchet and rammed the blunt of the blade against the glass. It shattered. She pulled a bar from the machine, tore the wrapper, and bit in. Allan smiled. Mid chew, she looked to him. "What?"

"Didn't think you'd adapt so well to it; what with your whole thing about stealing earlier."

Mouth full, she answered. "That was for random homes," she swallowed "The one had a note from the owner that gave permission to take what we needed. And as far as this place goes—"

"Revenge?"

She shrugged. "Guess you could call it that. Remember when they got real stingy with hours? Guess what they never cut back on; not once? The vendors. Every Friday, half an hour before I left, on time every time."

"Wow."

"Yeah. They couldn't afford to give me a consistent paycheck, me, the one bringing in all their stock, but they could pay the fuckin' vending people. The fuck you need vending machines at a thrift store for anyway?"

"For all the old people that spend their whole day here."

"Fuck that. Take up knitting classes or something. Blowing all their money on recycled crap." She took another bite then went to grab another couple bars from the machine. She tossed one to her brother. "Cookies and cream. Little stale, but they're good enough."

He smirked. "I think that little knock upside the noggin rewired you a bit. I mean, not that I'm complaining. I dig it."

"Just rolling with the shit storm." She looked past her brother to the accessory rack near the double doors. "And we've got backpacks," she smirked. She started down the middle aisle. On the way, her attention was caught by a display of bikes set beside a living room setup. "We're taking these too!"

She continued on toward the back. Trisha, standing beside the double doors glancing at a dress rack, turned to follow. Allan scoffed a laugh to himself.

•••

Vallerie led the way through the double doors into the back hall. As Trisha and Allan followed inside, she pointed to the various sorting areas down the way. Each section was lined with large cardboard boxes set atop pallets as well as a few plastic collapsibles.

"Bric-a-brac; random knick knacks and shit. Then behind that we've got Credential; that's clothes.

Across from that we've got Electronics. Down further we've got Shoe and Accessory, then Linen behind that. Batteries would be in Elec. Belts, handbags, zipper pouches would be in Accessory. Any tools or other shit like steel wool would be in Bric. The latter would probably be in the garbage box. You guys search the sorting line. I've got the break room and the back."

"Oh, so you're the leader now, huh, sis? Fine by me."

"There is no leader. I just don't wanna spend any longer in here than we have to."

"Well, if you were the leader, you're doing a good job," Trisha said.

"Thanks, but a single person leading things just lands you in shit. Not eager to have that on my shoulders."

Vallerie went down the left hall and rounded the corner, the sound of her necklace and backpack's rustling fading in her hurried step.

Trisha watched with a smile. "Fuckin' mommy vibes," she muttered to herself.

Allan crouched before the trash box.

"Hey. You heard the lady. Here, help me turn this over. Fucker's heavy."

•••

Before entering the break room, Vallerie prepared herself, covering her nose. Out of curiosity, she opened the closet door. She scoffed in seeing that the mold remained. She rounded the corner wall, peering through the clear plastic lockers. Nothing inside seemed immediately of use. The table ahead along the wall, too, sat with little in way of supplies. Empty chip bags, half-full drinks, and boxes of paper plates and plastic kitchenware were all that resided over the space.

"Literally like nothing changed."

She left into the hall and started back to the dock. To her shock, it looked maintained, appearing neatly arranged as it would have after a successful close. On her way to the desk, she peered into the boxes, each sitting full. The quiet struck her as her watch's tick filled the space. Occasionally, her brother and Trisha's chatting and throwing of objects would distract her from it, but it came nonetheless; the empty quiet.

She searched the desk, finding nothing yet again. After checking the drawers, in standing, her eyes caught on the schedule tacked to the board on the wall. Three new names were seen for the dock crew. She nodded to herself and sighed. They'd replaced her and her coworkers, and the job seemed of the same quality. The thought stung her. Gradually, her attention went onto another item on her old workspace: a newspaper. Her curiosity took hold as she picked it up in search of answers. The front-page article detailed a report regarding a terrorist group. She paid little attention beyond a glance, choosing instead to seek out further information about what exactly happened. She pondered what it could've been. A virus? An attack? Though, just before starting on the next page, she found herself drawn back to the first, her eyes having caught on the photo of an arrested woman, seemingly in her middle age, smiling in her mugshot. She read on through the article.

"*—a Hell Spawn member responsible for the castration and murder of an eleven-year-old boy was sentenced today.*" She continued to the criminal's words before the judge. "*When all this falls apart soon, just so you know I'm gonna do it again. We like hurting people. It's fun. You'd be all sorts of screwed up if you heard how he cried.*"

Vallerie's grip tightened over the page as fury built within her. After reading over a final piece that mentioned a red wristband that signified the group, she was unable to continue further. She lifted her eyes from the page, sighed deeply, and threw it away over the desk. Her heart pounded as she turned back, rubbing her forehead before proceeding back down the hall. She was met by the others, approaching with backpacks in hand. She choked back her upset.

"Find anything?" she asked.

"Yeah. A few batteries. Some candles and matches. Some other stuff. No wool though," Allan replied.

"Yeah, I was afraid that was asking a bit much."

"What about you?"

"Oh, I didn't get a chance to really go through

anything yet. We might have better luck with the trash back there."

"You okay?"

She sighed.

"They replaced me. And my coworkers. Just…just didn't expect the place to look so good. I'll get over it."

Another distant thunder caught their attention.

"Sis, what time you got?"

"It'll be getting dark soon. We should light some of those candles and cut the power."

"We don't have too many to spare. Maybe we should get some sleep a little early. You need it."

Another rumble.

"Yeah, you're right. There's a box in the back with some bedspreads and pillows in it. We can go upstairs to the storage room. The doors have locks," she paused, eyeing her brother nervously. "Just in case."

Allan nodded. "Okay. Let's grab some and head up. I'll get the lights."

•••

Her eyes shot open. Her breaths were rapid and unsteady. The room was silent as the shadow of the candle danced over the ceiling. She looked to her left to see Allan laying beside her, fast asleep. Trisha was just the same at her right. She sat confused for a moment, but the realization eventually hit. She hadn't screamed this time. She sat up, closed her eyes, and attempted to calm herself. The nightmare remained largely the same, but, she pondered, this time she hadn't seen his face or heard his voice. Why was it different this time? Why didn't she see him? Why didn't she hear him? Why?

She opened her eyes once more, looking to the candle set ahead against the wall. As her breath settled, a further confusion struck her. She could no longer recall his face. She could no longer recall his voice. What happened remained. What happened after remained. But she couldn't remember him. Even his name escaped her. Fear took hold as she wondered what else she may have forgotten. She went over the days before she'd woken up. To her knowledge, no pieces in time were unaccounted for. Everything was there. She just couldn't remember…him. She looked to her brother and thought to wake him but hesitated. If it was her head, what exactly could be done about it? And what would be the use in worrying him?

She knelt forward over the blankets, trying her best not to wake the others. As she woke further, rubbing her eyes, she observed a soft light from the covered window. A full moon perhaps? It was clear to her that she was too ruffled to get any more sleep, and so she went to crack open one of her books to pass the time. She got to her feet and went to the corner of the room where her backpack sat against the wall. She knelt down, unzipped the back pocket, and retrieved her grocery bag from inside. She undid the knot and selected a choice read from the stack. She held the book beside the candle and proceeded to study its cover, dimly seen near the flicker of the flame.

A Solitary Practitioner's Guide to Personal Craft: Pendulums, Divination, and Connecting with Deity.

She turned back toward Allan and Trisha, observing as they lay fast asleep, then stood, taking the candle in its holder, and made her way to the door. Slowly, she unlocked the latch and opened it just enough to squeeze through. She eased the door to a close before holding cautiously to the railing and descending down the blackened stairwell.

She headed out to the sales floor and started up to the office. In approaching the jewelry case, she decided to go behind and observe its contents, setting the candle on the middle shelf. As she studied various necklaces, it wasn't long before her eye landed on a rainbow-colored, triangular pendant, attached to a silver chain. She took the item in hand and was struck at once by the way the candle's flame washed over its colors. She smiled.

"You'll do just fine."

She gathered her things, set her candle atop the cover of her book, and went to the office. Once inside, she set the light atop the manager's desk and closed the door behind her. She seated herself back in the chair and sighed a breath before scooting closer and opening the text. She looked over the chapter guide, then turned the pages until arriving at the section on pendulums. She started to skim the text, holding her sight close as she struggled in the dim light. Time passed calmly as she read on.

•••

She propped her elbows atop the desk and held the necklace between clasped hands. She closed her eyes, focusing on its feeling against her palms. She drew a breath, held to it, and released it steady. She remained still for a moment, allowing the peace within the quiet to wash over her as she focused on the necklace in hand. She began.

"To any who may be present, I'm opening a line of communication now, a line only extended to beings of love and light; spirit guides; wandering souls passing through. If you're positive, then please come forth. Anything negative is not to communicate with me. If you are negative, you don't have my permission to speak to me in any way, and I ask that you please leave. No offense. Just a boundary I need to set. To the positive ones, if you're around, I ask that you communicate with me through this pendulum tonight. I…I'm in search of some guidance. Any you can give," she whispered. "I ask, if you could spare it, that you share your time with me. Allow me to get to know the way you answer first. Reveal a simple swing toward a yes or no." She focused further before continuing. She opened her eyes and coiled her hands around half the length of the necklace's chain, allowing the latter half and the pendant to dangle freely below her grasp. She watched the pendant's sway, allowing it to slow to a stop while holding her arms steady. The colorful point settled still at the end of its chain. "Show me yes," she asked. The object sat still in the air, the light of the candle from behind seeming to envelop the piece over its edges. Around a minute passed by. She maintained her focus. Gradually, the object began to move slightly from its place in the air, swaying in a clockwise circle; a subtle one, but a sway nonetheless. She marveled at its motion, tightening her arms to make sure she hadn't disturbed the process. "Am I…Am I wearing a white tee shirt right now?"

"Yes," The clockwise motion continued, expanding its reach. It swayed several times round before slowing to a stop.

"Am I… Do I have black hair?"

The pendant briefly sat still before starting counterclockwise. It did so subtly before expanding its reach once more, following the same pattern as the one previous.

She watched with wonder. Her heartbeat quickened in her pondering over which questions to ask. One after another they came to mind. One came deep. Another arrived shallow. Others turned up somewhere in between. In time, she decided on her question.

"Earlier today, after I woke up, I was told this could be a new beginning. Is there truth to that?"

"Yes," the pendulum swayed.

Vallerie watched for a while, ensuring the answer. Her arms grew stiff, though she held her posture.

"Am I—" she paused, the question getting stuck on her tongue as her heart kept on. "Am I meant to be a part of that?"

"Yes," the pendulum continued, reaching out further.

As she watched the sway gradually slow, a feeling washed over her that she couldn't put a name to. It was positive, that much she discerned, but no description beyond that seemed to fit. She lowered the object, closing it within her hands.

"Thank you. I now close this communication. May you be at peace. Blessed be."

She sat back in her chair, sighing a breath, before the sound of an approaching thunder called her attention. She looked to her watch, hunching down near the candle to read. It was just past midnight. She sighed, then left from the desk, retrieved the light, and went out from the office. She started toward the main windows, looking out to observe a soft patter of rain visiting the glass from the deep darkness of the night just behind. As she watched the drops continue streaming down the glass, she smiled softly before turning and starting back to the makeshift bedroom upstairs.

Once inside, she returned the candle to its original spot and curiously eyed the window as its light captured her once more. She went toward its glow, peeking around a crudely hung sheet that Allan had ran the curtain rod through. She pulled the corner aside to observe the back alley. Though she saw no moon that illuminated the scene. The light's source was the streetlamp at the building's corner.

She pondered on it, as with the building. How could they have power when she'd been told everything was gone? As she ran over the possibilities, an odd sound caught her attention, a thump. The light was dim, but it revealed the alleyway just enough to tell where the sound came from. On looking right, down the alley, at the corner nearest the building's wall, she spotted a figure standing against the edge. Its head reared back slightly and then knocked forward against the wall. It did so again as Vallerie squinted, focusing further through the dim night. She was only able to make out two distinct details about the figure: a woman with a band fixed tight around her wrist.

A brief flash of lightening captured the sky, illuminating the clouds and the woman further. Soon after, more thunder sounded. In the few seconds of light, Vallerie spotted a bleeding wound on the figure's neck. A dread fell over her as she realized the woman was no longer alive. She'd also noticed the red color of the wristband. Her focused squint soon turned to a glare. Thunder came once more before another thump as the woman repeated the motion.

Vallerie backed away from the window, replacing the sheet, and looked down to Allan and Trisha. They were just the same, lightly breathing in rest.

Vallerie stood with a sigh, looking off toward the candle set flickering on the floor. Another knock was heard as the light patter of rain continued against the window. In watching the flame, a single thought came to her mind. Her chest grew heavy in its arrival. She started toward her backpack along the wall, knelt down, and retrieved her belt and hatchet from alongside. She stood back and adjusted it round her waist as the storm thundered again. Another knock. Setting the blade aside, she took her shoes from beside the makeshift bed, tied them on, and, on heading to the door, took her hatchet in hand and held it tightly. She paused before leaving to look back at the two still sleeping peacefully. The thought repeated louder in her head. She turned back, undid the lock, and began downstairs, closing the door slowly behind her.

"You'd be all sorts of screwed up if you heard how he cried."

•••

With the manager's keys dangling in hand, she locked the front door and turned out to observe the parking lot, quiet and dark. The rain began to fall harder, pelting over the pavement as she returned the keys to her pocket. She stood quietly beneath the building's overhang, looking curiously to the emptiness of the scene. She drew a deep breath and released it steady before looking to her left and starting down toward the corner. On her way, she heard the knock again. She drew her blade from its place on her belt and quickened her pace, leaving the overhang of the roof behind as the warm rain welcomed her in the alley. Her eyes remained fixed ahead as she moved to the back of the building, her brows furrowing as the sound was heard louder through the rain's fall. It echoed the alley. Her heart was pounding. Her breaths quickened. As she reached near the building's edge, the sight of the figure caused her heart to sink. It didn't notice her, rearing back and knocking its head once more against the wall. As it did so, the deceased woman wheezed. Her breath was almost otherworldly; a sickly rasp.

  Vallerie tightened her grip to her hatchet and went to start toward the figure. She was soon stopped by Allan who pulled her back with his hand over her mouth. He caught her arm as she turned with a swing of her blade.

  "It's me. You're alright. It's me," he whispered.

  She looked to him, breaking free of his hold. He was drenched with his sword slung over his back.

  "Go back inside, Allan."

  "You don't know what you're doing."

  "I know I need to learn. It's just one."

  "And it used to be a person. Whatever's got

you all gassed up right now, it's gonna backfire once you look her in the face. And you know what happens then? It kills you. You have no idea what—"

"Just go back inside and let me do this."

"Why?"

Vallerie gestured toward the woman.

"Look at her wrist."

Allan looked over, sighting the red band. He sighed, closing his eyes with a nod.

"An eleven-year-old boy," she continued.

"I heard the story."

"Who knows what this one did… I have to," Vallerie said, starting off. "And you're not gonna stop me." Allan took her shoulder. "Damnit, let me—"

"I'm helping." He released his hold and drew his sword from its scabbard. "I'll be there in case it gets the better of you."

"She's shorter than me with a hole in her throat. How tough can she really be?"

"It's not like the movies, Val. Trust me." The seriousness in her brother's tone gave her pause. She nodded to him. "Do what you were gonna do," he continued. "I'm right behind ya."

She turned back to the figure and took a cautious step forward. It knocked its head once more against the wall before standing still and turning its attention her way. As she looked to its face, her heart seemed to drop. The woman's eyes were missing. Her skin was pale white. A gash bled from her forehead, streaming down into her blackened eye sockets and further to the wound on her neck. Fear struck her for a moment before her sight caught once more to the band on her wrist. She met the figure's face again and adjusted her stance. She charged forward with a growl and struck a hard swing down over the woman's head. The blade caught an inch deep. Vallerie and the deceased woman were now face to face as another flash of lightening took hold of the sky. A roaring thunder sounded as the figure wheezed. Though it did not reach against her, seemingly stunned from the blow. Vallerie attempted to retrieve her blade for another swing, but it didn't budge. At once, as her attempt jerked the figure forward, the deceased seemed to recover and extended its hand toward her. She backed away, releasing her grip on the blade's handle.

"Fuck."

"I told you," Allan said. The figure began walking toward her. With every step that it took forward, Vallerie took two steps back, keeping her distance while holding a firm eye on the woman. "Go for the ankle."

She glanced to her brother before returning focus to the approaching corpse. Its pace quickened as it made a reach toward her. She caught its arms, finding a resistance she hadn't expected. Her breaths came rapid as her heart seemed to beat out of her chest. The figure continued its strained breath as it fought her grasp. Vallerie reared back and delivered a hard kick to its ankle. It stumbled, loosening its grip against her. She backed away and rushed in with another hard blow. The figure fell to the pavement.

Allan charged ahead and held the woman down with a foot placed over her neck. "Get your axe."

She hurried over, taking the blade's handle back into hand. She pulled hard with no result. She used both hands for another attempt. Nothing.

"Goddamn it!"

She slammed a foot down over the figure's face and pulled again. The blade freed itself, dampened by blood.

"Now." Allan ushered his sister away and dragged the woman back to her feet. He jumped back as it made a reach toward him.

Vallerie stood baffled.

"You know how to knock it off balance. And you know you've gotta strike hard. Take it down."

Vallerie adjusted her footing, readying her blade as the corpse approached, wheezing once more. She reared back her arm, readying a strike, but halted. The thought came again. An eleven-year-old boy. She shifted her blade into her left hand and stepped forward, throwing her fist against the figure's cheek. It knocked the undead to the ground. Allan stood by, scoffing with a smile. Vallerie sneered as she loosened her fist. She shifted back to her blade and stepped forward. She looked down to the woman as she attempted to stand. She threw a kick to its face, knocking it back to the ground, and then held both hands tight to the handle of her hatchet. She eyed the corpse for a moment before rearing back and striking the blade down with an aggressive shout. It penetrated deep, reaching down between the figure's brows. At once, the wheezing stopped, and the dead woman remained still. Vallerie planted her foot and shoved it forward while pulling hard on her blade. It retracted and the corpse fell motionless. She lowered her weapon and stood with unsteady breaths. Her brother came forward, planted the end of his blade to the pavement, and looked down to the slain corpse. He smirked once more, scoffing a laugh, and looked to his sister. She looked past him, her eyes softening as another flash of lightening illuminated the woods behind the alleyway. Allan's smile faded and he quickly turned to see two taller, bulkier figures lumbering forward. They wheezed in their stride. He lifted his sword. Vallerie stepped to his side.

"Allan?"

"Lesson's over, sis. Go back inside."

She squinted, confused.

"You're taking them by yourself?"

"They aren't passives, I can't leave 'em."

The terminology seemed of little importance as she watched the two continue forward. She readied her blade.

"Not by yourself."

"Vallerie, no—"

"Make up your mind; either I learn or I don't."

She started forward.

"Vallerie!"

She stopped fast as the closer figure quickened its pace her way, its head shaking violently. Allan ran ahead of his sister and struck with his sword, making a sideways slash toward the figure's neck. The corpse dived under his swing and rushed, tackling him to the ground while grabbing at his head. He released his sword to the ground and attempted to hold back the figure as it hovered over him with its rotted eyes fixed to his. He pushed hard against it but made no progress as it pushed just as hard back. He was soon met by a spray of blood as Vallerie reached over and pressed the edge of her blade deep into the undead's throat. She pulled back, dragging the corpse away from her brother. Having an edge, he was able to free himself. Vallerie darted back away from the figure, soon being charged herself by the second. Allan took his sword from the ground and, as the figure went to charge again with blood pouring down its neck, he delivered a swift strike, slicing its head clean off. The body dropped to the ground with a thud. He readied a strike to the one that fought against his sister, but she protested.

"No!"

Vallerie gritted her teeth as she held off the body, the face of her blade propped sideways into its mouth as she held both hands tight to the handle. Allan stood ready as the figure pushed back against his sister. But, to his shock, she remained on her feet.

The corpse wheezed aggressively, its hands held tightly to Vallerie's head. She groaned, grimacing as she struggled to hold her footing. Her pulse raced. Her eyes were locked with the deceased, its pupils gray and faded, illuminated by the streetlamp overhead. Allan stepped forward, worry written in his eyes.

"Vallerie!" Trisha called, rushing toward the scene with knife in hand.

"No! I don't need help!" she shouted again.

The figure pushed further. Vallerie held her ground as a fuse ignited within her. She breathed fast and heavy, rage filling her eyes as she stared down the creature in an effort to push back. As adrenaline fueled her, she shoved hard, driving the figure's footing back, and screamed into its face. She drove it back toward the woods. It fell backward through the tree line, with Vallerie following suit as the two tumbled down.

"Vallerie!"

Allan and Trisha both rushed after her. She tumbled down the hill, pelting her chest against the face of an old, discarded television as the corpse fell just past it onto the ground. As she planted her hands into the moist grass, she struggled to catch her breath, coughing. A faint light was all that offered clarity down the hill. She fumbled in the grass for her hatchet but was met instead by the force of the undead corpse as it held her down on her back. It rushed toward her with an open mouth, the stench of rotten breath bombarding her. Thinking fast, she slammed her forehead against the creature's face with great effort. Its balance faltered, and, fighting through the pounding in her head, she kicked hard against it and swerved herself away from the body as it fell into the grass. She managed to overpower the figure, turning it over and pinning it down onto its back. As it attempted a reach her way, she jammed her thumbs into its eyes and pressed hard with a vicious scowl of effort over her face. Blood spattered against her cheek as the pressure collapsed the figures eyes. She didn't relent, digging further into the skull. She forced her nails deep, feeling the tissue tear within. She pressed further, baring gritted teeth in her strength as the figure remained motionless, pulsating blood out over her hands. Allan pulled her away. She fought his grasp.

"Hey! Hey!"

Her eyes met him and her expression softened. Her breath came in hurried quivers. Her eyes were strained, reddened and tearful. Trisha, too, now stood at their side. The two looked onto her as if she were almost a stranger, her face spattered by blood, trickling downward as the rain continued. Her shirt, too, was stained by it.

Allan held gently to her shoulders. "You had that in you all this time?"

Her breaths began to settle as she swallowed hard, facing away back down to the body. "This… I don't—" She closed her eyes and started to cry. "It's not who I wanna be."

Allan rested his hands beneath her chin, turning her to face him. The two looked into each other's eyes.

"What you just let out, that's what's going to keep you alive. Use it."

She closed her eyes as another tear fell down her bloodied cheek.

"Hey."

She looked to her brother once more, her eyes appearing exhausted.

"Where do you stand right now?"

She squinted, confused.

"What?"

"Right now, mentally. Where are you at?"

She averted her attention, sighed, and shrugged before facing back to him. "I…I don't know. I'm alive, I guess."

Allan sat back, took her hatchet from the ground beside him, and offered the handle her way. He smiled. "That's all that matters."

She looked to his hand, took the handle of the blade, and stood to her feet with an effort. He followed.

Trisha stepped over, placing a gentle hand over her friend's back. "You okay?" she asked.

Vallerie looked down to the blade, closed her eyes, and returned it to its place on her belt. The rain's fall lessened to a mere sprinkle as she looked next to the body on the ground.

"Yeah. Yeah, I'm okay."

3: WHO WE WANT TO BE

The door swung open with a crash, revealing Vallerie stood with her blade raised in hand, a tense expression on her face. Her arm lowered as she observed the empty room. She relaxed and called back to the others.

"Clear!"

"Same this way!" Trisha responded.

"Here too!" called Allan.

He stood facing toward the wall with an anger in his sight and fists trembling, tightly clenched.

"Hell hath no mercy."

The sentence was written in red above the array of shattered glass enclosures. Behind them, the wall was riddled with bullet holes and blood spatter. Below, on the floor, several once-alive animals, now unrecognizable, though the listings on their former homes revealed what they might've been, laid still:

fish; snakes; lizards; mice; guinea pigs; rabbits; birds; all slain. Allan sighed an unsteady breath and turned to leave the room, closing the door behind him. Down the hall, he met back with the girls.

"Anything?" his sister asked.

"No." Vallerie noticed the crack in his voice. He met her worried eye and spoke firmly. "Don't go in there."

•••

Vallerie looked off toward the overcast sky, the breeze lightly tossing her hair as she sighed.

"I didn't listen. Thought maybe…maybe exposing myself to whatever it was would make me stronger. I guess ultimately it will. In the long run, you know? But—" She looked down to Jaxton's plaque, the edges overtaken by grass. Her palm rested over his name. "But I think I should've dialed back. I should've just left it."

She closed her eyes.

•••

Vallerie left the room, wiping her wrist over her eyes.

"I told you."

"Yeah, you did."

She closed the door behind her.

•••

"No pros at all. I thought maybe, maybe the place would be left alone. Maybe at the very least we'd have some more food. The story didn't change much on the way. Time after time, we'd come up with a game plan, clear the store, and it'd be picked clean. Always with the same message." A tear fell as she opened her eyes back to Jaxton's grave. "I miss you. Now more than ever," her voice broke. "But I'm glad you don't have to see any of this. Fucking sadists…"

•••

Vallerie exited the store carrying a studded purple collar in hand. She met the others outside. Trisha glanced to the item and seemed to blush, holding back a smile. Vallerie took notice.

"What?"

"Nothin'."

Allan looked between them, eventually cracking a laugh. "Christ, that's a thought I didn't need."

"What? Oh."

"Sorry." Trisha began to laugh, turning away.

"Sorry to blue ball you, babe, but no. It's um, it's me just…thinking for the future."

"Good to see you with some hope," said Allan.

She shrugged. "Lot of critters out there

without a home."

•••

Vallerie sat quietly for a while before the grave, twirling her necklace in hand. A dread fell over her.

"This might be the last time I get to see you." She released the pendant from her grasp, allowing it to dangle freely from her neck. "We're leaving soon. Somewhere farther north. Away from…whatever…whoever might be here. Allan thinks Michigan would be a safe bet. Lots of woods. Cabins by the lakes. Try to scrape together some kind of life."

•••

The engine revved. Allan shouted, his hands tightly clutching the steering wheel of the pickup.

"Yeah! Listen to that baby fucking purr!"

•••

"We found something that runs. We've got bikes, backpacks, enough food and water for the trip. Nothing all that healthy, but it's food. Clothes, bedding, some weapons."

•••

Allan set the trio's bikes, backpacks, and supplies into the back cabin and shut the window, snapping the lock tight.

"Road trip!" Trisha shouted, climbing into the back seat. "Come on, bitches, let's go!"

Allan turned, looking to his sister.

"New beginning, right?" she said.

He stepped over, resting a hand over her cheek. He nodded.

"New beginning. Come here." The siblings shared a lasting hug before getting inside the truck, Allan in the driver's seat and Vallerie beside in the passenger. He looked to her, holding his palm over hers, the two then holding tight to each other's hands. "We'll stop by the cemetery before."

"Thank you."

•••

She flattened her palm further over the plaque, taking the pendant of her necklace in hand once again and holding to it tightly. "I love you." She returned to her feet and gave a parting look to his grave. "Rest easy, sweet boy."

•••

The sights in passing continued to perplex her. Ghost towns would be her go-to name for the majority. Occasionally a bleak sight of devastation would come along—a burned down house, a store with shattered windows, the odd car wreck in a left-behind traffic jam, a still body left forgotten—though, for the most part, many areas passed in the drive came and went with little to see beyond overgrown lawns. She watched them go by with her chin rested over her palm as her arm sat propped on the door's edge. Allan remained focused on the road while Trisha leaned forward cycling CDs through the player.

"Country, country, and more country. I can't headbang to this shit," she sneered.

"I mean, technically, you can," Allan chimed in. "All music has a beat."

"Well, not all music makes me wanna beat my own head in. I don't know how people listen to this yee-haw crap."

Vallerie smiled, her sight still fixed out the window.

"Last page. Come on, gimme something." Trisha looked over the discs held in their respective slots of the binder, gradually landing on the second to last. "Huh. Not what I had in mind, but—"

Allan and Vallerie both glanced over.

"Nice."

"Don't think I've heard 'em," Vallerie commented. "But as long as it's not country."

"What?! Dude. Here, I know just the song to start you with. Boom. I dedicate this to the three of us."

"What's it called?" she asked.

"Celebrate The Hooligans."

Vallerie listened as the track played, gradually turning from the window and sitting back against the seat. "Hm. I'm feeling it."

"Knew you would."

As the trio traveled on, the road began to stretch through rural terrain.

"We heading into farmland?" Vallerie asked.

"Definitely looks like it, doesn't it? Hey, maybe instead of a dog we can adopt a cow."

"You'd just turn him into burgers when I'm asleep."

"Damn right I would," Allan smiled.

"Sorry, Val, but I'd take his side there. Fuck, I miss burgers."

"Hey, speak of the devil. See up there? Good old Calhoun's."

Allan gestured to an approaching restaurant with a large red C perched on the roof.

"Hey, we should check it out."

Allan scoffed.

"For what, Trish, food poisoning?"

"You'll see. Just pull over."

"Yeah, we should stop," Vallerie agreed, now hoarse of voice.

"You good, sis?"

"I was. Starting to feel nauseous."

"Gotcha. Figured a long drive might be hard on you. Hang on, I'm stopping now."

Allan pulled to a stop along the edge of the road, just before reaching the restaurant. Vallerie was quick to leave the truck, heading off into the grass and heaving hard.

"Oh, fuck. Hang on, babe, I've got ya," Trisha said, hopping out and shutting the door. Allan undid his seat belt and followed. "Here. It might be greasy, but your hair's still too beautiful for puke."

"Thanks. It'll be over soon."

"Take your time. Here, just take it easy."

"She okay?"

"Y-Yeah," Vallerie struggled, kneeling down over the grass. "Just gotta get it…out. Give me a minute."

Allan stood, looking over to the restaurant as crickets sounded along the road.

"No rush. We've got time."

"Here, lay back."

"Fuck. I thought I got over motion sickness years ago."

"It happens, babe. Surprised that's all you're going through."

She laughed, easing back into her friend's arms. "Yeah, after being vegatized. Ugh. Thanks."

"Anytime. Here, actually, lay over sideways. Like in my lap."

"Trish, goddamn it."

"I'm not trying anything, I swear. Seriously, it'll help."

After a hesitating glance, Vallerie sighed and

rested her head back, looking up to her friend as she ran a gentle hand through her hair. She smiled down her way. "See?"

"This actually does help a bit."

"And you thought I was perving. Rude."

"For all I know, you are. But if I sit up, I'll just puke again, so whatever. Just keep doing what you're doing with my hair please. It's nice."

"Rodger dodger."

"So what's this thing you wanted to show us, Trish?" Allan asked, walking over.

"Oh, it's nothing important. I was just being stupid. There's this thing I heard last year about how fast food actually doesn't rot. Always wondered about it."

"Ah. Well, that is indeed stupid, but now you've got me wondering too. Preserved burgers… Like, just the meat doesn't rot or the whole thing? The cheese and stuff has to go bad, right?"

"Allan, I swear to God, if you make me puke again, it's going on your shoes."

"What, I'm just asking. Because, you know, normally there's mold and stuff."

"You know your balls are in punching range too, right? Seriously, shut it."

Allan looked off to the distant road with a snicker. Though it gradually faded.

"Map says there's a college not far from here. Could be a good place to stop on the way."

"You trust it?"

"Not sure. But it's a long trip still and I think you need a break before we go on."

"I'm fine, Allan."

"Mentally maybe, but your body's what I'm worried about. Since you woke up, you've been in go mode. I meant what I said that first night. But you're pushing yourself too hard right now."

"He's right, babe."

Vallerie looked from her brother up to Trisha, soon averting her sight to the sky.

"Besides, can't be that unsafe, right? I mean, what are people gonna stay there for? Not like there's anything to take but books."

"Shelter's shelter. If there's dorms then you can basically have a little town," Vallerie said, sitting up. "Food too, depending on what's left behind."

Allan continued watching the distance, observing the spaced-out buildings and signs down the road. He drew a deep breath, exhaling with visible frustration. "I just want you to be okay," he said with a slight break in his voice.

Vallerie looked to her brother, his tone striking her.

Trisha embraced her, resting her chin over her shoulder. "Same here. Even badasses need a break once in a while."

She smiled, resting her hand over Trisha's. She looked down to her friend's grasp, observing the faded white scars on her arm. She traced her hand over them. Trisha held her tighter.

"Okay. I'll slow down for a bit," she agreed.

"I'll head on by myself to check it out. You two stay here."

"That's out of the question."

"Sis, you just puked up whatever energy you had. Stay with Trish. I've got it. I see anything sketchy, I'm out and we move on."

"Fine," she agreed, meeting her brother's eye. He walked over, pulling a folded map from his pocket. He opened it, knelt down, and showed it to the girls.

"While I'm gone, stay off the main road. There's a creek nearby, past the tree line here behind Calhoune's. Grab us some water with those filters. Maybe stay busy catching frogs or something."

"Take my hatchet with you."

"I've gotten better with my sword. I'm good, don't worry."

"You need something close range too."

"So do you. Keep it." Allan stood and left to the back of the truck. He unlocked the door of the cabin and retrieved the trio's backpacks before going back to the girls. "Follow me," he said, starting ahead toward the trees.

"Easy does it, champ," Trisha urged, guiding Vallerie as she got up.

They followed Allan's path, ducking under branches and weaving through brush. Shortly, they reached the creek. It wasn't large, merely a thin stream with mild depth. Allan set down the bags beside a tree, his included, and looked to his sister.

"If anything happens, and nothing will, but if, I'd rather no one rob me. What time you got?"

"One-thirty."

"I'll be back by three. Clean sweep. Any trouble, I'm out. Promise."

Vallerie nodded, unsure. "Okay."

Allan rested his palm over her cheek before starting back through the wood. She watched him leave with a sigh. Trisha took her by the shoulder.

"Come on. Let's do the filter thingy."

•••

Allan heaved himself up into the driver's seat and shut the door. He sighed, looking out to the road, then hunched down with a reach beneath his seat. He retrieved a solid black pistol secured in a camouflage-painted holster and looked to it with a stern gaze. He placed it into the compartment between the seats and closed the lid with a snap. He looked back to the road. After a moment, he pulled and locked in his seatbelt, revved the engine, and gripped tightly to the steering wheel.

•••

"So how exactly is this supposed to give us clean water? Looks like it'll only make it worse," Trisha grimaced as Vallerie retrieved the bottles from her bag.

"The idea is that the water passes through the different layers and they basically catch and trap all the bad shit that might be there. That's why you've got more than one in the bottle. What one layer might not catch, the next one will."

"What, like bugs and germs and stuff?"

"Yup. It isn't perfect though, so we'll still need to boil what we come out with."

"But it gets most of it?"

"It should, yeah. Here," Vallerie motioned to Trisha who sat beside her, observing the bottles in her hands. "So, if you look, the bulk of the bottle is the filter part. The bottom was cut off and we've got the cap end of the rest facing down. From the cap end up, you got your tissue stuffed down, then charcoal powder above that, sand above that, then the pebbles last. Then you've got another bottle that had the top half cut off, and we just set the filter down into that. Bam. That's where we'll get the good stuff from."

"So what's with cutting the little bottom piece off the filter?"

"I made something called a baffle. It's just a cut of the middle piece set on top of the pebbles. Supposed to direct the flow and prevent eroding the rock. Or something like that. It's been a while since I saw the video."

"You taught yourself this?"

"A little. Got some from Al and a bit of reading too."

"So, what, we just dunk it in the stream and wait?"

"Nope. First we get yet another bottle, fill that, and wait for all the gook to settle to the bottom for a couple hours. Then we pour it into the filter, you know, without letting the settled stuff go with it. We wait for it to do its thing, then boil it, and it's good to go."

"So if you're dying of thirst you should still wait?"

"Yeah. Not worth taking a chance. What if one of them trudged through that water? Or a rabid squirrel or something? You want rotting toe fungus and rabies suds in your water?"

"Valid points," Trisha smiled. "Alright, gimme. I wanna help."

Trisha grabbed two empty bottles and started toward the stream. Vallerie retrieved a book from her bag, a guide on edible fruits.

"While you're doing that, I'm gonna check"—she paused, thumbing through the pages—"to see if that tree over there is what I think it is."

"You spot some nummy nums?"

"I think we've got some mulberries growing over there, yeah. But I don't know shit about wild berries, so I gotta make sure. Um…come on. Yup. We got mulberries." She snapped the book shut, placed it back into her bag, and jogged over to the tree, hurriedly picking the fruit until her palm was full. She picked a few more to snack on and went back.

"Dude, I haven't had these in forever. Here."

"Thank you, love."

Vallerie once more noted the scars over Trisha's arm. She sat down beside her at the stream, stretching her legs out down the pebbled slope. She glanced over briefly before looking out over the wood with a sigh.

"Hey, I've been wondering about something," she began.

"Sup?"

"Back when we first met, when we got Allan to the hospital, we were talking in the waiting room, and I asked about the cutting."

Trisha shied away, setting the filled bottles over a level stretch of grass.

"You told me you had a hard time dealing with the pressure, just of life; always paying bills, doing things you don't wanna do but have to. Told me you wondered if it was all really worth it."

Trisha snickered to herself, still avoiding her friend's sight. "I was quite the mess back then, huh?"

"Look, I'm not trying to…stir anything, but I just—" Vallerie sighed, her sight fixed to the foliage beyond the stream. Trisha looked to her, meek of eye.

"What's up?"

"Earlier, I thought I saw some new ones. I thought maybe I was wrong, but…then I noticed again. Just a second ago."

Trisha hesitated, gradually looking away from her and down to her shoes. She busied herself in retying their lace. Vallerie looked to her. "Did you start again?"

She saw a tear fall from her friend's eye as she distracted herself on the laces.

"I thought maybe you'd never wake up," she replied, tying the laces tight and looking back, eyes welling with tears. "It wasn't because I was afraid of life anymore. It wasn't all that existential shit like before. I just… I slipped because…because I didn't want you to go."

Vallerie nodded, becoming emotional, herself. She looked down to her hands, clasping them over her lap.

"It felt like…like that night all over again; stuck in traffic on my way to see you graduate and I get that text from your brother, that same…fucking dread." Trisha stopped to wipe her eyes.

Vallerie looked back to her with a stern eye. "I'm not going anywhere," she said. "I just wanted to make sure you weren't either."

Trisha shied away a laugh and sniffed with another wipe over her eyes. "Don't worry, I'm good now. All that old stuff doesn't really apply anymore anyway."

The two sat beside each other watching over the stream, the soft sounds of the wood washing calm over them. All of a sudden, Vallerie scoffed a laugh.

"Goddamnit…"

"What?"

"I just realized. Dude, we have running

water."

"And? Oh. Oh, fuck."

"Right?!"

Vallerie sprang to her feet and started toward her backpack. She unzipped the front pocket and took out a few small hand towels, tossing one over.

"Any soap in there too?"

"Gonna be a no on that one."

"Shit."

Vallerie closed up her bag and went back.

"I'm headed down a ways. No peeking. Seriously."

"Psh. Party pooper."

She started down the stream toward the thicker wood. Trisha watched with a sigh. As her friend disappeared from her immediate sight, her good spirit followed suit, her smile fading. She knelt down before the stream and dampened her rag. A weight began inside her chest. She hissed to herself.

"Stupid..."

•••

Vallerie sat at the bank, tying the laces tight on her shoes. Her shirt was splotched by her dampened hair falling loose down her shoulders. Finished with her shoes, she knelt down and began another rinse of her hair. Trisha was laying down beside the tree behind her. Her eyes peeked open briefly before closing once more as she smiled, adjusting her backpack beneath her head.

"You don't need to wash it a million times, ya know." Vallerie was silent as she rang the water out. "Val, seriously, you're good."

"I need to get the grease out. Felt like the nurses didn't even take care of me."

"Last few weeks they stopped going the extra mile. For everyone."

Vallerie sat back and stretched. She relaxed, laying back into the grass. Trisha reached out, running her hand through her hair. The two were quiet for a time, enjoying the singing crickets in the distance and the afternoon heat beneath the shade of the tree.

"So, if it's safe—" Vallerie began.

"Which it will be."

"If…it's safe, there anything you think you'd wanna study?"

"Hm. Gimme a sec."

"No loans. No debt. No distractions."

"That does sound nice. Hm…definitely something music related. I mean, I don't know what classes teach what, but something about music. I guess it'd be cool to start that one label that doesn't screw bands over. Like, an indie group could sign with me and actually make money."

"I'm sure there's something."

"What about you?"

"I've thought about a few things. Mostly law stuff. Nothing specific though."

"What about a lawyer? Can do plenty of good

with that."

"It's come up. Problem is the profit aspect feels pretty gross. Like, sure, I'll help prove you're innocent. Just pay me more money than you probably have right now and hope that the judge and jury listen to me."

"Yeah, there is that. Oh, I've got one. What if you went for biology? Or medicine? Who knows? You're smart. Maybe you'll be the one to find a cure for this thing. Well, if…whatever happened has a cure."

Vallerie scoffed with a smirk. "I'm not that smart. From what you guys told me, things going so bad so fast, doubt I could do anything the big shots haven't tried already."

"Well, maybe you not being a big shot is an advantage. You're not on anyone's payroll, and there's no ticking clock. Just sayin'. Never know."

"Maybe."

"I wonder what your brother'd go for."

Vallerie closed her eyes as her nerves tensed. She tried her best to shake it off.

"Probably"—she started—"something he can do with his hands. And on his own. Nobody that'll get in his way. A mechanic or electrician or something—"

The approach of a truck halted their conversation. The two hurried to their feet. Vallerie went for her backpack and retrieved her hatchet. Trisha pulled her knife. The two stood by each other's side beside the tree, looking out from the trunk's edge. The truck slowed to a stop and a quiet moment took hold after the shut of the door. Allan's voice calmed the girls' nerves.

"It's clean!" The two breathed a sigh of relief. Allan approached through the brush, being met by his sister's embrace. He returned the hug. "I'm okay."

She eased back and covered her nose.

"Good. But you stink."

"Yeah, I should probably dive in there, shouldn't I? I see you guys took a bath already. Nice to know I won't be smelling rotten fish again for a while."

"Oh, as opposed to sticky ballsack?"

"Or dry cum," Trisha interjected with a cough.

Vallerie sneered, sticking her tongue out and facing away.

"Trish, fuck, come on."

"Alright, alright. Point taken. I'll cleanse myself before we go. Which bag has towels and shit again? Yours, Val?"

"Yeah. Just be thorough please. You are actually getting pretty bad," Vallerie said, pinching her nose tighter as Allan passed down the stream.

•••

"Wow. Is this it? Just a few buildings?" Vallerie asked, undoing her seatbelt as Allan parked behind the main building.

"Yeah, that's it."

"I thought colleges were supposed to be like little towns," Trisha said, leaning forward in her seat to get a better view.

"I know. I expected more too. But it's a college. And it's got student housing. Oh, and an art studio. Think that'll be up your alley, Trish."

"Recording studio?"

"Yup."

"Sweet tits."

"It's pretty open," Vallerie mentioned, peering around the campus.

The grounds were sizable, though the buildings appeared cramped with little distance between them. Only a handful of trees occupied the property, with open lawns and trails dominating the campus. The parking lot itself was open, with only a handful of light poles peppered in and no gates present at the approach.

"Yeah. Not as secure as I'd like, but it is what it is. Best I can do is pull behind the housing."

"Let's back up to the main doors. We'll scavenge the classrooms first. Load anything we find, then we can hide the truck after. Get it all done first, then we can rest."

"Sounds good."

"We just looking for textbooks?" Trisha asked.

"Textbooks, class guides, and student notes.

We've got a free education here. Can't waste it."

"Are we taking everything? You think we'll have room?"

"Lord knows she wants to."

"Just what we can use. Dental, nursing, agriculture, engineering; anything like that. Fuck the rest."

"Well, keep in mind, this, to my dimwitted understanding, is a community college, not a university. So they might not have a whole lot. Didn't really look yet."

"They'll have enough. And if you call yourself that ever again, I'm smacking you." Allan backed the truck close to the main doors and pulled to a stop. The three got out, taking with them their backpacks.

Vallerie was the first to step forward, observing with wonder the structure's height and its large windows. "Three floors…"

"Yup. Three floors.

"Is it as untouched as it looks?"

"Unfortunately not. Lunchroom, vending machines, hell, even the dorms, all raided as far as food goes. Other than that, it's civil. Probably students evacuating."

"What about anything else? Books? Bedding?"

"At a glance, there's plenty of both. Library's spotless. Most beds are fine. Actually, speaking of the dorms, I found something I think you'll like quite a bit. I'll have to show ya later."

"Right now let's just get this done before we

lose light."

"Yes, ma'am." Allan stepped ahead, pulling a ring of keys from his jacket pocket and unlocking the doors. The trio entered, their steps echoing in the vast, empty halls. Allan closed the doors and locked them before starting ahead. The inside stood dimly lit by the windows' light. "Pretty crazy, ain't it, girls?"

"Yeah," Vallerie said, gazing up to the glass-walled balcony from the staircase. "Never thought I'd see the day. What with the price tag and all."

"Yeah, well, it's all free now."

"It's fucking huge, dude," Trisha shouted. "How are we supposed to… Oh, right there."

"Yeah, that map definitely helped."

The three approached a mounted sign with a directory of the building posted inside the frame. Vallerie read through the various classrooms.

"Jesus, they taught everything. Biology, psychology, fucking every type of med course." She turned to the others, bright in the eyes. "About as good a head start on things as you can get."

"Mhm. Just be quick about the sweep. One night, that's all we're staying for."

Allan started off down the hall.

"What's on your list?" she called cheerfully.

"Engineering. That's useful, right?"

Allan continued with a hurried step. Vallerie watched her brother with a smile as he began up the stairs before returning her attention to the map. Trisha leaned over her shoulder.

"And now we know."

"Yup. He'll have a degree before we know it. No more struggling through tests to get it either."

Trisha looked on her friend's focus over the map.

"Where you thinking?"

"I think…nursing, then dental, then go from there."

"And those are…second floor. Cool. Last one up sucks dick!"

Trisha bolted off toward the stairs with Vallerie not far behind.

"Hey, no running in the hall!"

•••

She sat a final textbook onto the pile, its weight causing the cart to sound a metallic clank as it shifted downward.

"Think that about does it," she said, looking to her brother.

"Damn. Overdid it just a little, don't ya think?"

"Nope. Most of it is med stuff, and there's a lot to learn there. Besides, what else are we gonna do, play checkers?" She hesitated, soon turning with a slight grimace. "Where'd you get this thing?"

"Lunchroom. Should've seen what I took off of it."

"Really getting bang for your buck here,

huh?"

Allan laughed.

"Oh, hold up, guys. One more."

Trisha hurried beside the two and added a binder overtop.

"What's in there?" Vallerie asked.

"Some more lecture notes. Found it in the office in lost and found."

"Nice."

"Alright, I'm gonna get these put away and start behind the housing."

"I'll meet you. I wanna look around for a bit."

"Me too."

"Don't be too long."

"We won't." Allan went outside with the cart. Vallerie stepped over to the wall, observing the plaques of graduates' names from throughout the school's history. Trisha seated herself beside the doors, sighing while stretching out her legs. "It's bizarre," she remarked.

"What is?"

"Just…all these kids. They all worked so hard. Probably balancing a job the whole time too. And here we are just raiding the place for free."

"When opportunity strikes, right?"

"Yeah." She took a final look over the plaques. "Hopefully it struck for them too."

•••

Trisha dropped her bag on the floor and threw herself onto the bed, which appeared neatly made.

"Oh, yeah," she squeaked while giving a stretch. "This one's mine."

"Wow. Never expected such clean rooms," Vallerie said, entering the dorm.

"Seriously. You think college, you think parties; beer, orgies, cops getting called."

She scoffed a laugh while adjusting her hair behind her shoulder.

"Don't know if I thought of that. Maybe a little like Allan's room. At least a pile of dirty clothes or something. Kids actually gave a shit."

Trisha continued stretching and tossing about on the bed as Vallerie studied the space. She made her way to the computer desk along the wall. A stack of sketch art sat overtop.

"So what's this thing your bro wanted to show ya? Just the clean room?"

"Nope. It's this," she said, taking the top page in hand. "Gotta say, that is pretty cool."

"What?" Trisha sprang up and went over to her side. She handed her the artwork. "An elephant and a donkey arm wrestling?"

Vallerie laughed.

"No. Look at the title. Bottom right.

"Unity? I'm confused."

"Democrats and Republicans. They're not arm wrestling. They're joining forces. Not sure what you'd call that hand-in-hand thing, but that's what it means."

"Oh! Gotcha. Hm... Guess that is pretty cool."

"Very. If we had more of that before, maybe things wouldn't have gone to shit."

Vallerie eyed the picture further.

"You can keep it, you know," Trisha said.

"Yeah. We've taken a lot to still feel weird about it, but…still." She took the sketch and went to the room's corner, sliding her pack from her shoulder down to the floor and seating herself on a beanbag chair. "Holy shit," she said excited, looking down to the seat. "So that's what they feel like."

Trisha smiled, glancing back to her before becoming distracted in thumbing through the artwork on the desk. She landed on one piece that particularly caught her eye. It depicted a couple holding hands on a beach. "Follow your heart," the title read.

Her eye lingered on the image for a moment. Gradually, her smile faded. She replaced the other pages overtop and turned back.

"Hey, babe, I'm gonna go check out some more rooms, okay?"

"Sure. I'll come with."

"No, no, don't get up. Sit your ass down and rest."

"You sure? I'm not tired or anything."

"I know. But you should be. You've got your first beanbag. Chill out for a bit."

Vallerie nodded.

Trisha gave her a smile before grabbing her pack and turning to leave the room.

"Hey. When you're back, we'll go check out the studio."

"Cool."

Trisha closed the door and started down the hall, her eyes quickly becoming heavy as she sighed an unsteady breath. The familiar sinking in her chest started again.

Vallerie leaned back and closed her eyes. The tick of her watch was the only sound present in the room. At first, the stillness brought her calm, but she found herself unable to fully relax. Something felt off. She opened her eyes once more and stood to her feet, starting over to the desk. Curiously, she sifted through the artwork, eventually landing on the one Trisha had been looking at. She sighed, replaced the pages, and stood with her palms overtop the desk, becoming lost in thought. Her watch ticked on, each second growing heavier along with her nerves.

"Goddamnit." She took a deep breath, exhaling while looking to the door. A few tense moments later, she took up her bag and left out into the hall. "Trish!" she called. No response. She began a jog around the corner. "Trisha!"

"Huh? What's wrong?"

Her friend peeked out from one of the further down rooms. Vallerie stopped, breathing a sigh before starting toward her.

"Look, I'm sorry if you're trying to have some space, but I just had to check—"

"I'm fine. Don't worry about it."

"No you're not." Still shaken, Trisha looked away from her friend's sight. She fought back her tears as her eyes grew heavier. A silent moment fell between them. "Trish?"

"I'm trying to give…you…space," she said, meeting her eye again.

"I don't need space from you." Trisha's tears gave way. She was quick to shy away, wiping her eyes over her sleeve. Vallerie continued. "I… I know it's hard to feel it, but…just because it isn't…like that…doesn't mean I don't still wanna be with you twenty-four seven."

"Yeah," Trisha nodded, still shying away. "I know."

"Hey. Let's go check out the studio. Come on."

Vallerie took her by the shoulder. She followed out of the room with a nod. The two started down the hall.

"Thanks for putting up with me," Trisha laughed.

Vallerie pulled her close as they walked, running her hand over her hair.

•••

Allan shoved the last stack of books toward

the back of the cabin and lowered the tailgate. He took a seat on its end and looked out to the campus, watching as the girls rushed up the stairs to the building.

"Have fun, kids," he sighed.

He adjusted his jacket and noticed something thump against his side. He reached into the inner pocket of his leather, retrieving his wallet. He eyed it curiously before scoffing with a smirk. He looked to the back pocket and pulled out the few bills inside, holding them in hand while setting his wallet aside. He observed the image of the presidents, the numbers, and the text. Soon after, he scowled with a sigh and tore the bills in half, tossing them into the grass.

•••

The door unlocked and the two entered inside. They were greeted by an expansive foyer, lit by a large round skylight pane. A double-row spiral staircase sat at the end. A banner was draped across the ceiling.

"Center for the arts…" Vallerie read.

"It's gorgeous."

"Yeah. Fancy for such a small place. There's the directory." Vallerie led the way over toward the left-hand wall; Trisha followed eagerly. "Boom. Audio production. Looks like just a few hallways and we'll be there." Barely finishing her sentence, Vallerie saw

Trisha hurry down the opposite hall. "Hey, wait up!"

•••

The pair entered the recording studio. Inside, another smaller skylight illuminated the room. To the left sat an open seating area and a mixing station. On the right was a separate recording room, housed behind a single door and large window. Seen inside were several instruments, a microphone, and various other pieces of sound equipment, as well as another door toward the back end.

"Whoa," Vallerie said, observing the space.

"Yeah, no shit. Dude, we could make an album in here."

"Well, could've. Sorry, Trish, but doesn't look like there's any power."

"Who said we need power?"

Trisha started toward the door to the recording room.

Vallerie laughed. "What are you doing?"

"Just play along. Trust me, it'll be fun."

Vallerie sighed with a smile and went toward the mixing station. She heard the door to the other room close. She eyed the elongated desk curiously, looking to the various soundboards and monitors.

"Hey, babe, I don't really know what I'm supposed to do with all this—" She turned and her heart dropped, a tense heat rising inside as she looked on.

Behind the glass, Trisha was thrown against the wall by two large men, grizzled, in tattered clothes, with not a sound escaping the recording room. She slid down her backpack and hurried with the pocket, pulling her belt and taking her hatchet from its hold. She held it tight in hand and bolted for the door. It didn't open. She rammed it with her shoulder. The door remained shut. "Leave her alone!" she screamed, her voice breaking in its pitch. She rammed the door again, grunting hard in her attempt. It was to no avail. She slammed the blunt end of her hatchet against the door's edge, making several attempts before striking next against the handle. The knob was forced loose, but the door didn't budge.

She headed to the glass to see Trisha had bitten the hand of one of the men. She was met by a hard blow across the face, followed by a knife into her gut. She silently screamed before being thrown to the ground. "No!" Vallerie raised her blade and threw its edge against the glass. The act was to no avail, as the hatchet bounced straight back, jolting her shoulder. She did so again, her eyes furious and tearful.

Trisha tried to get up and looked to her friend from behind the glass. She cried, mouthing her name. The two men approached from behind, grinning as Trisha pulled her knife from her pocket. Vallerie looked to them, sighting the red bands across their arms, and screamed against the glass as they met her eye. "You're gonna die!" She continued rapidly slamming her blade against the glass. "You're gonna fucking die!" Over and over, she repeated it, all to no avail as the men forced the knife from Trisha's grasp and held her to the ground. One knelt down on her back while the other started to pull off her jeans. Vallerie screamed on, hammering both ends of her hatchet against the glass.

As the man undid his pants, the door at the back of the room swung open and Allan aimed his gun. In an instant, blood splattered against the glass as the man closest to him fell. She saw another shot go off, landing into the other man's throat. The force knocked him off of Trisha. He was down, grasping his throat. Allan rushed ahead, pulling a knife from his belt. He viscously stabbed the man on the ground. All the while, Vallerie continued against the glass.

After several hard blows with his knife, Allan stood, noticed his sister, and went immediately to check on Trisha. Pain filled his face as he lifted her bloodied shirt. He looked back to his sister beyond the glass, and stood, hurrying to the door. He dragged away and tossed over three tall amps with an effort as his sister pushed from the other side. She rushed through the door, going to her friend laying bleeding and crying on the floor.

"Trisha?" she called, kneeling down beside her. "No… Baby, no."

Trisha began to speak, but ended up in a coughing fit. A grimace crossed her face as she cried further, the blood over her wound expanding.

Vallerie looked to the wound and quivered. "Baby, hold on, okay? You hold on!" She began taking hold of her back but was stopped by her brother. She looked to him frantic. "I'm not letting her die!"

"Vallerie… You'll only make it—" he trembled in tone, pausing before continuing. "She can't walk with that."

Devastated by the words, Vallerie sat with loss in her eyes. She looked to Trisha, now meeting her eye.

"It's okay," she said, placing a hand over Vallerie's wrist.

Tears began down her face as she nodded, resting her friend back down.

"Allan," she said, looking to her brother. "Please do something," she plead "We have to have something." He was silent, closing his eyes with a tear of his own. "Allan. Please."

"Val."

She looked down to Trisha. Her eyes were more serious than she'd ever seen them.

"Allan," she said with shallow breaths. "You need to know."

"Trish, please don't," he said.
"What?"
"She needs to know."
"What?" Vallerie asked, leaning closer.
Allan looked away, his hand over his face.
"When you were in the hospital, and things

were getting bad, there was a draft," she struggled in her speech. "He didn't go."

"A draft?"

"He stayed with you. They—" she coughed again. Vallerie took her hand, holding it gently while her other palm rested to her cheek. "They want him. They're looking—"

"Hey. Hey. Don't force yourself. It's okay, I heard you," Vallerie struggled to say behind tears. "I heard you."

Another tear came from Trisha's eyes. She held tighter to Vallerie's hand.

"Please."

"What? Baby, what?"

"One kiss. Just to know what it feels like."

Vallerie closed her eyes tight as further tears fell.

"Whatever you…call it. A last request or…whatever. That's mine."

Vallerie nodded and forced a smile. She traced her hand down Trisha's cheek and leaned in, planting a soft, lasting kiss to her lips as Trisha, too, closed her eyes. She felt her friend's hand reach back to caress her as well as the two shared the moment.

At its end, as Vallerie eased back, Trisha opened her eyes, looking weak yet bright, and smiled to her. "If only you knew…" she said.

"I know. I know. You…know—" Vallerie struggled, holding tighter to her friend's hand. "I love you. I love you so much."

"I know." Trisha looked to Allan, who stood facing away. "Al."

He looked back, silent and desperate in the eyes. "Come here." He stepped over and knelt down at her side.

"What— What do you want us to do?"

"Just stay with me."

Vallerie lay down beside her, still holding her hand, this time with both of her own. Allan sat, taking hold of her other.

"You got it."

4: LOVE

Vallerie traced her thumb over her necklace's pendant, holding to it delicately for a moment before resting it back over her chest. She sat beside the tree, spattered by blood. Streams fell down her cheek. Stains smeared over her shirt, now appearing a worn gray. She looked out to the hill ahead, her eyes cold. The occasional rustling of foliage and the tick of her watch kept her company in the stillness. She glanced to it, observing its ever-moving hands. In watching them, before long, an irritation crossed her face, and she undid the watch's strap from her wrist. She held it in hand and rested her arm down over her lap.

    She returned her attention to the hill ahead, and to the two corpses laying still at the slope's end. She sighed, reaching beside her to a wallet sitting alongside her hatchet in the grass. She took it up and pulled a small white card from inside. Tossing the wallet aside, she stared curiously at it. Her attention was soon turned to the distant crunch of jogging over the railroad tracks atop the hill. She looked to see Allan approaching fast. He stopped atop the hill, breathing heavily while looking down to her with stern eyes. She glanced his way and returned her eye to the card.

"Future reference," he began, "when I tell you something's a bad idea, listen."

Vallerie sighed, resting the card to her lap and looking to her brother.

"I wanted to be alone for a while."

"Yeah. I read the fucking note. Next time, wait until we're back home and take a walk around the lake. Go out on the boat. Don't just fuck off somewhere we haven't cleared."

"Am I dead or are they?" she snapped, gesturing to the bodies.

"Your point? Judging by your little, um, gore fest there, guessing they didn't go down so easy—"

"They went down!" she shouted. "I'm fine, alright?! God, give me a fucking headache."

She returned to the card in hand. Allan started down the hill. As he approached, Vallerie remained distracted. He knelt in front of her, pulling the sleeve of his shirt down over his fist.

"Here, let's get some of that off before you get sick." He rubbed some of the stream away from her cheek. She didn't protest. He sat back, looking on her firmly. "I'd rather give you a headache than a funeral."

She looked to him, his tone causing her to soften her gaze. She looked down once more.

Allan took a seat beside her, picking up her hatchet and looking to its blade. It was wiped clean of blood. "You've got a real attachment to this thing, huh?"

"It does its job."

He looked to her hands. "That from them?"

"Yeah." She looked over, gesturing the card up to him. "Open carry license. Got his address on it. Could be a lead on guns."

"Happy accidents."

"That's one way to put it. If we don't find anything there, he might…I don't know…might have a receipt or something for a source."

"Where at?"

"1143 Chaffeurville Ave. Remember anything like that on the map?"

"I do, actually. Fancy name like that sticks in your head. It's not too far away. Seems like a small town. I mean, the whole area is small towns, but shouldn't give us much trouble."

Vallerie placed the card into her pocket.

"Let's go then."

She retrieved her blade as her brother handed it her way and rose to her feet; Allan followed suit.

"Sure you don't wanna keep resting a bit?" He looked to the bodies. "They were pretty big guys."

"No. Like you said, we need firepower, and I

need to practice more. Get in, get out, and head back."

"Okay," he paused, looking back to her. "You're getting better." He patted her on the shoulder and started back up the hill. "We can follow the tracks most of the way."

Vallerie returned her blade to her belt then twirled her watch in hand, observing its tick. She drew a breath and followed her brother up the slope, observing the power lines set along the far edge ahead. He started right down the path, his shoes crunching the pebbled rock of the track. Reaching the top, Vallerie stopped with a pondering eye to her watch. After a moment, she started after her brother and tossed it to the rail's edge on her way. As the two trekked down the path, the watch remained ticking in its rest overtop the wooden plank.

•••

Vallerie followed behind her brother, looking to the open notebook.

"Basement of Joe's Pawn Shop, right-hand side… Oh, there."

"I see it." Allan smirked. "Basement of a pawn shop… See, if I was a cop, that'd be the first damn place I look."

"Yeah, it's not the smartest place. Then again, we are in the sticks."

Vallerie looked back down to the notebook

and soon noticed her brother's steps come to a stop. She looked up to see him stood still before the window of the shop.

"What—" As she stepped aside, she saw several flyers taped to the window, all with the word "wanted" printed in bold at the top of the page. A symbol was stamped in the upper right corner, the silhouette of an eagle midflight from the end of a branch. She stepped forward and observed the black-and-white photographs in the center of each flyer. Allan's was third in the arrangement of five. She looked back to him. He was white as a sheet, uneasy in eye, with his hand over the holster of his gun from behind the end of his jacket. She looked to the holster's camouflage pattern before returning her eye back to the flyers. "The Bastion. So this is them, huh?"

"Yeah," Allan's voice trembled. "Yeah, that's them."

She read on.

"Reward of firearms and rations if the traitor is turned in. Option to join the cause in restoring our great nation. To any surviving Americans passing through within the next few days after this notice is posted, we will be pulling our patrols from the area and the state. At present, resources and manpower cannot be spared. Please, stay safe, and don't be shy to work with fellow survivors if you can. Before long, our nation will be renewed. For those who seek refuge, or to turn in one of those named in this notice or suspected members of the Hell Spawn group, head to our base in Columbus, OH. Further

directions will be given by patrols upon entering the city."

Vallerie's pulse began to race as she glared toward the text. Allan rushed ahead, reaching toward his flyer. She stopped him, hurriedly grabbing his arm.

"No. They don't need to know we were here. Best thing we can do is just leave it."

Allan looked to his sister with complete fear in his eyes. "If they catch me with you"—he subtly shook his head—"I don't know them. I don't know what they could—"

"Stop. Look, they said they've pulled their patrols. And there, bottom corner. See the print date? That's—" Vallerie paused, eyeing the flyers once more, then turned to her brother. "You said I was out for five, right?"

He nodded. "About. Yeah."

"It's already been a month…" She paused in thought. "And…when I was in and out, what I saw, that guy was actually alive, wasn't he? In the camo?"

"…He was."

"Okay," she said, turning back to the flyers. A quiet moment passed between them. "Bastion," she scoffed. "These guys aren't actually military. The real deal gave you an out and dipped when you didn't take it. Them, the guy you took out…they're just some backwards-ass extremists thinking they're patriots."

"Look, I know I was a little…vague…about what exactly happened. Wanted to avoid scaring you any more. But how things started, I think maybe it's time you heard the rest."

"When we get home. Come on. If there really are guns in there still, then we should get them before someone else does." Vallerie started toward the door, tossing down the notebook and retrieving a makeshift picking kit from her pocket. She started on the lock.

Allan looked out to the streets of the town, wary in eye despite the calm.

After some effort, the lock clicked. "We're in." She went to grab the handle but felt taken by her brother's hand. "What?"

"Me first." He handed her notebook back and drew his gun. His hand was delicate in its grasp over the door. He looked through the glass, between the various signs and text. The room appeared empty. Still, his nerves remained uneasy. His heart began beating hard as his grip tightened over the handle. He threw the door back and dashed inside, sweeping his aim across the space of the room. He started fast to the glass-case counter, pausing with his aim to the back door. As the moments passed, no disturbance was seen or heard. Vallerie entered behind, closing the door and locking it. She immediately went toward the bathrooms on the right and threw the doors open with her blade drawn. "Vallerie!" Allan shouted in a hush, again white as a ghost.

She was out just as quickly as she'd gone in. She left the rooms and went to the counter. "Go. I'm right behind ya," she said.

He turned and, with cautious step, went around the counter toward the back room door. His sister followed closely. He threw the door to find a short empty hallway leading to another doorway. Opening it, he looked onto a stairway leading down to pitch black. He moved to the side of the doorway, holding his position and listening closely for any disturbances. Vallerie sneaked his lighter from his jacket, jolting him briefly, and flicked it alight in her stance at the opposite end of the doorway. Allan scoffed before a failed reach as his sister jerked her arm away. He protested in a hush.

"Hey, come on, it's all I've got—"
"Light or no light?"
He sighed. "Light. Gimme."

Vallerie handed the lighter over as Allan aimed his gun down to the basement. Taking up the flame, the light was just enough to see, though the two still found themselves squinting to focus. Allan started down, his sister close behind with her hand at her belt. The quiet came over them as they observed the various boxes from the end of the stairs. The only direction to go was to the right through a narrow hallway lined by large stacked boxes, all labeled. At the hall's end sat a gate to another room, sealed by a simple padlock. On peering through, the siblings smiled in unison.

"Feel safe yet, bro?"
"Certainly helps."
"I've got it."

She went to work on the lock. Allan scoffed, impressed. She opened the gate and the two entered.

Two rifles lined the back wall. An array of pistols lined the one on the left. To the right was a single shotgun and an assault rifle. Boxes of ammunition rested beneath each wall.

"Well, at least they've got bags for the rifles," Allan said, looking to each weapon.

"You think you'll be able to manage those with your sword?"

"It'll be heavy, but I can do it. I'm more worried about the ammo."

Vallerie peered behind a stack of boxes in the right corner and found a large camouflaged pack.

"Don't be," she said.

"What?"

"Check this out."

Allan smiled. "Thanks, Santa."

"Yeah. Seriously."

"Alright, so I'm thinkin'… I grab the shotgun, one rifle, and as much ammo as I can carry with that pack. Don't quite know how I'll arrange it all, but I'll figure it out. You take the assault and the other hunter. Should be pretty light, so just strap 'em over your shoulders. Think you can manage a couple pistols too?"

"Yeah. I'll just clip the holsters on my belt."

"Good. Let's get these loaded before we take 'em. Just in case."

"Right." The two rifled through the boxes, finding the appropriate magazines for each firearm and loading them to their limits, then making sure each was set with their safety on. Vallerie threw her arms through the straps of the rifles, adjusting their position over her back. She then took her pick of the pistols. "Wow. Way lighter than I thought."

"Good. Let's lock up and head back. We'll make a second trip for the rest."

"Yup."

Allan grabbed what he could and the two headed back upstairs, closing and locking the gate on their way and doing the same to the other doors. Once upstairs, Vallerie looked back to the display counter as Allan hastily closed his lighter and headed to the entrance. He turned back to her.

"You see something?"

"Just…one sec."

On the left end of the counter sat a small arrangement of stones, all rough in shape and varied in color. Each was labeled and individually priced. She headed behind the counter, her eye then being drawn to a box on the floor which was half-full of grocery bags. She laughed. Allan looked on curiously.

"What?"

She sprang up with a bag in hand, jimmying it with a bright smile.

"Wow."

"Yeah. Here, go back and grab whatever you can. I'll be down there in a minute."

"Yes, ma'am."

Allan took a few bags and went back downstairs, sneering as he once again pulled his lighter. Vallerie opened her bag and delicately placed every stone inside. She then set it inside of a second bag and tied the two tight before grabbing several more and following her brother.

∴

She closed the door. It stopped short, the lock catching against the frame.

"Fuck."

"Won't shut with the lock?"

"No. Damnit. I can try to lock it with my pick. That'd work, right?"

"It'll be fine. Just leave it unlocked and close the door."

Vallerie scoffed, turning to her brother while throwing a hand. "I'm not just gonna leave it unsecure."

"Leave it. If we hurry it won't be a problem."

He turned and began back down the street. Vallerie undid the lock and eased the door to a close before jogging to catch up to her brother. She caught sight of his gun still drawn in his hand and called out.

"Hey."

Allan continued on.

She stopped ahead of him, taking him by the shoulders. "Hey. Look at me."

"Val, we need to—"

"Look!"

He raised his eyes to meet hers, their

sternness catching him off guard. "What?"

"They aren't gonna get you. Al, look around. Think about how we've been moving since we got here. Nobody's coming to take me away from you. And nobody's coming to take you away from me."

Allan took an unsteady breath. "You don't know that for sure."

"I do."

"How?" he asked, his tone meek.

"Because of where we stand. That's how." Vallerie's eyes softened toward her brother as she rested her palm to his cheek. He closed his eyes and gave a nod, sighing a breath. "Just relax. Besides, we're fuckin' strapped, bro."

He scoffed, smiling while looking back to her. "You're right. You're right. Just—"

"I know. I know. But you know what, it's my turn to keep you safe now. First step in that is to calm your ass down."

She paused, looking behind her brother to the town.

"What?"

"Second step… We've still got a few stops to make."

"For what? I don't see much around. A dinky little hardware store, but that's it."

"There's a party store too. Saw it on our way in. We'll hit both for just a couple things then we'll tear ass back home. We've got daylight left to get it all done."

"What are you after exactly? I can see the hardware, but a party store? What, you thinking of grabbin' some booze?"

She smiled, patting him on the shoulder and starting back down the street.

"It's a surprise."

•••

"Firecrackers… You made us detour for firecrackers?"

Vallerie retrieved another one of her bag's contents as the two walked down toward the hardware store. She raised the item to her brother's view.

"And this."

"Hairspray?"

"Mhm."

Allan eyed the can curiously before she replaced it in her bag. It took a moment, but the idea became clear. He smiled. "Well, well."

"Surprised?"

"Where the fuck did you learn that from?"

"The interwebs were a wonderful place. In small doses."

"And you, what, just happened to pull this all outta your ass at the last second?"

"Yup. One of those things. The spark came and I followed it."

"So what's next? Bear traps?"

"Duct tape, fishing line, more steel wool—um—razor blades, glue, and hopefully some nine volts. If they work for a fire, then they'll work for this."

"So we got a homemade bomb and fishing line. Trip wire?"

Vallerie stopped before the door, peering through the shop window. She pulled a pistol from her hip, flicking the safety off.

"That's the idea," she said, standing before the door with a raised aim.

"And the razors?"

"That part I'd rather not spoil yet."

Allan scoffed. "You know it's honestly adorable watching you hold that thing like you know what you're doing."

"You know you did actually give me lessons before."

"Yeah, years ago."

"Oh, fuck off. It's close quarters. I don't think I'll need to be a fucking sniper to land a shot."

"Whatever you say, champ. I've got your back just in case."

He readied his aim as Vallerie adjusted her stance toward the paint-chipped wooden door. She reared back and delivered a hard kick that immediately broke the latch from the frame. She stumbled, having expected more than one attempt, before starting through with her aim to the left while Allan followed to the right. They observed the space, their grocery bags rustling over their shoulders as they swung from the motion.

"I think we're good," Allan said, setting down his bags and closing the door. "I'm not seeing any other doors. Geez, not even a bathroom."

"Well, it is a small town." Vallerie set her supplies down and holstered her gun before starting down the aisles. "I'll be quick."

The store's small size made it easy to find each item. With little effort, she gathered the components, unfolded another bag from her pocket, and stuffed everything inside.

"All of it?"

"Yeah. Found it all."

The pair grabbed their things and went back outside, Allan with a tight hold over his firearm. They exited out to the street, Vallerie easing the door shut as much as possible given the damage to the old worn frame. The two started on their way out of town.

"Okay, let's head back, drop off, and hurry this up. By nightfall, if we're lucky, we'll have dinner in one of the snares."

"Fuck, Al, I'm still not over that."

"I know. I know. But we gotta eat."

"Yeah, it's just…somehow killing undead people seems easier. The thought of a bunny or something—"

"Dude, you've been eating animals since forever," he laughed.

"Yeah, but I never had to kill them, myself.

Top-tier human hypocrisy, as long as I don't see it, but this is a whole different thing."

"Well, think of it this way. Either we catch it and it passes away quick or one of them gets it and it might be…not so quick." She grimaced. Allan smiled, looked to her, and turned back with a snicker. He looked back to his sister, who was still visibly disgusted, shaking her head with a sigh. "What? It's true!"

"Yeah. Yeah, I guess it is." He looked ahead to the empty tree-lined road, then stopped. His sister slowed beside him. "What?"

"We should stay off the main road."

His eyes once again appeared unnerved.

"Okay. Along the trees then."

•••

The two were quiet for a time in their trek. Allan consulted a scribbled note he'd pulled periodically from his jacket pocket. Vallerie looked back every now and then to survey the distance left behind. The siblings each held to a gun on their way. Allan adjusted the straps of his arsenal, giving a slight groan in the motion when continuing ahead. Vallerie eyed him with concern.

"You know we can rest for a minute." Her brother continued on in silence. "Allan, we can stop—"

"No." His tone was sharp. After noticing her

silence for a time, he looked back. "Sorry. Just… I'm good."

He looked down and away before starting on once more, spitting into the brush with a grimace. Vallerie watched him for a moment, thinking on how best to ease his mind. Eventually, she settled on a topic. As it came to mind, she cracked a smile to herself.

"Trench mouth?"

"Yeah… Need to brush when we get back."

"Yeah, me too."

'It's the cigarettes, you dolt,' she thought. 'So little toothpaste around and you're still smoking. What did you expect?' The words were on the tip of her tongue, but she didn't let them out. She could give him the lecture later on.

"I saw you've been reading."

She paused, looking off to the sky as her ear was drawn by the rapping of a woodpecker. The sound brought her another soft smile. She looked back to her brother.

"Trying to," he muttered, glancing briefly after the noise, himself.

"Thinking for the future?"

"…Maybe. Provided things come together to make"—he paused, stepping carefully over a fallen branch hidden by ferns while warning his sister with an outstretched arm—"one beyond just us. You got it?"

She smiled. "Yeah, thanks… Let's say they

do. Say we've got a small little village. Farms. People. No psychos, just…good, decent people. What would you do? What's Allan's role?"

He shrugged. "Maybe… I don't know, something to do with construction. That's where I'm at now anyway. Like, the houses and stuff."

Vallerie scoffed to herself with bright eyes, following closely behind him while occasionally watching her steps through the forest floor.

"What would they look like?"

Allan pondered for a while before answering.

"I think…something olden. Wood. Stone. Straw. Don't know what you'd call it, the theme or whatever, but…I think that'd look nice."

"I think so too. Something about the horse and buggy thing is…timeless. Charming. Pretty much where we'd have to start anyway, right?"

Allan laughed. "I mean, not really. We've just been hijacking houses left and right."

"You know what I mean. Like if we had to go from scratch," she paused, looking off to the distance. "Hell, maybe it'd be best to just tear it all down and start from there."

Allan smiled. "Sounds like we're going back to the leader idea."

"No. No, there is no leader idea. I'm just saying. If we personally were to start something new like that…"

"And what would your role be? Just being? Helping the people here and there?"

Her cheer faded as she thought on the question.

"Teacher, maybe? A doctor?" he paused, scoffing with a glance her way. "I've got one…an herbalist."

She met his eye before a sigh as they both faced ahead. "We'll see when we get there."

Allan smiled further. "I'm proud of you."

"For what?"

He cocked his head, now in visibly brighter spirits. "Because you didn't say 'if.'"

The two continued on quietly, the surrounding sounds of the wood guiding their way.

•••

"Jesus Christ," Allan groaned as he heaved and set his things atop the dining table. Vallerie followed with an effort as well, standing on the opposite end. They looked onto the small arsenal, catching their breaths as their shoulders seemed to burn. "We need to hide these."

Vallerie looked behind her brother to the cabinet above the counter. She went over, pulling the blind to the screen door on the right before opening it. From inside, she retrieved a single clear plastic zipper bag. She went back to the table, gently placed one of the loaded pistols inside, and sealed it shut, pressing out all excess air. Allan watched curiously.

"Knew it'd come in handy for something,"

she said.

"Where you thinking? Under the dock?"

"Nope." She took the bag in hand and looked to her brother. "Under the rocks and sand under the dock. If someone came to…fuckin'…pillage the town or whatever, they'll be looking under the docks too. Maybe for something under the planks. Maybe in the crack between where the tide slope ends and the dock begins. But not under what's already in the water."

"There's still a chance they'd find it though."

"Well, if you're determined enough, you'll find shit no matter where it's hidden. At least here it's doubling up on the false bottom idea. If they think they've checked a good hiding spot and came up empty handed, then maybe they'll call it quits."

"False bottom as in like with a drawer or something, right?"

"Yeah. Say you're a burglar. You open someone's desk drawer and find it's got a hidden bottom. If that spot's empty, then you're likely to think there's nothing left to find, right? And that… is how you miss the thin little bottom below that with their emergency fund inside, or the false panel on the side with their spare car key behind it, whatever."

Allan nodded, looking to the other guns over the table. "Nice."

"As far as the rest go…" She looked over the table, holding a thoughtful fist beneath her chin. "I say we hide the assault here with the two rifles. There's the one pistol under the dock. Then we keep one pistol each and the shotgun with us to get the rest."

"Here, I'm assuming meaning nearby home, but where exactly? And the ammo? Honestly, I can't think of many spots someone wouldn't check."

"Just give me a minute."

She weighed up several options, each coming with more cons than pros. Eventually one of equal odds crossed her mind. "Well, the assault can't be anywhere too close, and it can't be somewhere worth going through. Only spot I can think of is that taco place across the lake. Maybe a fake wall in the bathroom if they've got one. Or a cleaning closet. Somewhere."

"Taco place. Can't see anyone checking there. Bonus since it stinks like shit."

"Hoping so."

"And the rifles?"

"Well, I have an idea. It's risky, but it might work."

"Let's hear it."

"We hide them in one of the houses. Nowhere nearby looks all that trashed, so we'll have to tear the place up. Camouflage things. A couple other houses too just to make things more consistent."

"Okay. Let's get it done. Then we'll go get the rest. I'm thinkin' we stash the ammo in one of our checkpoints on the way. Maybe number one since it's closest to home. We'll find a better spot later."

"Got it. I'll do the pistol now then meet you for the rest."

"Okay. I'll be at the place with the wide garage. Wrecking the fanciest one should be a good start, right?"

"Yeah."

"Good, because I'd do it anyway. Just seems like too much fun."

The two took their arms and left out the door, which creaked in its swing. Vallerie left with the handgun and the assault rifle, and her brother left with the shotgun and hunting rifles. Allan started down the cabins' lawns toward the edge of the resort, leaving down the driveway. Vallerie stood at the start of the dock, overlooking the lake. The waters lapped calmly as the sun shone overhead. She was still for a moment, listening to the water and savoring the scent in the air. A faint breeze tossed her hair.

In the stillness, a thought came, the very one she'd been distracting herself from for the last few weeks. She attempted to fight back the welling emotion, but the tears came anyway. She wiped her eyes with a sigh and a groan, forcing composure, and headed out onto the dock, holding cautiously to the rail as she stepped down into the water. She set the assault rifle overtop and knelt down with the bagged handgun. She began scraping away rock and sand beneath the waves, pulling with it weeds and an array of sharp shells. She positioned the bag deep on the sand beneath and brushed everything back overtop, setting the heavier of the rocks atop the center of the spot. She took the assault from the dock and hurried up the steps etched into the flood slope, starting briskly after her brother.

Just a few houses down the street was the one her brother had set to target. The home was large and sent a clear message that whoever owned it was well-to-do. A small pond and a patio sat in the elongated front yard. An abandoned boat resided in the driveway, sat before the door of a garage twice the length of any other in the area. Vallerie, strapping her gun over her shoulder, started up the steps of the porch, and headed in the front door. Allan stood in the living room before a dresser with various framed photos sat overtop, holding an envelope in hand. She approached with a curious eye.

"What you got?"

He looked to her briefly before returning to the envelope, pulling several hundred-dollar bills from inside. He held them up to her.

"Found this in a bedroom," he said. "Missed it on my first sweep." He placed the bills back into the envelope and tossed it atop the dresser.

"How much was there?"

Allan paused, then scoffed. "Five grand. They had it under a carpet in the closet. Envelope had the words…rainy day fund…written on it."

"That's one hell of a rainy-day fund."

"Yeah, no shit. That'd take us, what, months to save up? And that's with living off ramen and bologna sandwiches."

Vallerie nodded, looking out to the rest of the room. "Lucky them," she sighed.

"You know, I never really paid much attention when we were clearing the town, but…place is pretty nice."

"It is. Not too big on the décor, but still. Hey, I'm gonna look around for a bit first if that's cool. Won't take more than a few minutes."

"For what? We scavenged for food already."

She shrugged. "I mean, if you found five grand in a closet, then maybe there's something else. Just curious is all."

"Long as you're quick."

"Don't worry, I will be."

She went up the stairs and observed several rooms, eventually starting into one that appeared to have been a teenager's bedroom. It was messy, cluttered with clothes and decorations. In wandering the space, her eye soon landed on a small book set atop the computer desk in the far corner. She took it in hand and thumbed through. It was a journal. She flipped to the latest entry, dated for around eight months ago, and began reading. Her eyes turned cold as she skimmed the writing. After a long sigh, she took it on her way back downstairs.

"What'd you find?" Allan called.

Leaving from the stairs, she started over with a calm stride, her eye to the open page, and read a portion of the entry.

"When I turned him down, he looked like he was deadass about to cry. Honestly, with those shitty wrinkled clothes and greasy hair, I think he deserved to. I've heard rumors that he, as they worded it, fell on hard times, but that just sounds like bullshit. The fact that a man would even think to ask someone out looking like that is an insult. Seriously, go get a job and clean yourself up. Especially before trying to impress someone. Much less a woman with a future and standards." She paused, drawing a breath. Allan looked on, silent. *"I've been told by his friends that I was cruel in what I said to him, but truly I don't think so. They say he'd been working up the courage for weeks, that he was shy and it was a big effort, that he'd hand-scrubbed his clothes the whole night prior, and many other bits of useless information. What is any of that to me? Men are supposed to be strong and successful. Hard times aren't a thing. You either take steps to get better in life or you don't. And there's no excuse to just not care how you present yourself. If he was truly so concerned, then he could've done much, much more than he had, and he didn't. I think I gave him a much-needed dose of reality. Nobody wants a street rat with nothing to offer. How he takes that reality is up to him."*

After a silent pause, her eyes growing ever more furious, she snapped the journal shut and looked to her brother. He stood burning just the same. "What a catch, huh?" she said with a break in her voice.

She tossed the journal across the room. Allan surveyed the space for a moment, then started, a slight quiver in his voice that she knew all too well.

Before, it would worry her, send her running over to hold him back from whatever he was about to do, but not this time.

"So…can we destroy the place yet or—?"

Vallerie smiled.

"Yeah."

She drew her hatchet, and went over to the living room window, slamming the back end against the glass. Allan threw the pictures from the dresser, stomping the frames of each. The violence in their act left shattered glass splintered over the carpeting. Vallerie then targeted the large TV set over the entertainment center, taking hold of the edge and tossing it over onto the floor.

The two ravaged the home. From one room to the next, they smashed windows, tore apart curtains, clothes, and bedding, and crashed décor and kitchenware over the floor. After tiring themselves in the destruction, the two stood before the front door, catching their breath while looking out to the space of the living room, now turned upside down.

"Well, hope they aren't planning on coming back," Allan said, turning to his sister.

"They're probably dead already… Fuck 'em," she paused, returning her blade to her belt. "Let's hit a couple more then figure out where to stash the rifles. Then we'll do the AR."

Allan nodded, starting out the door as his sister took a final look to the room. Her eye caught on the journal, laid open far off against the border of the hallway. She went to it, her shoes crunching over glass and torn fabric, and knelt down, taking the book in hand. She turned it over and flipped back to the first page with a sigh. After tapping her thumb over the page in a moment of thought, she stood, spit aggressively onto the interior, then closed and threw the journal down once more before leaving.

•••

Vallerie replaced the last of the stacked trays on the shelf, concealing the last visible piece of the gun. She pressed them back and evened the display before standing back to look for any sign of what they'd hidden behind.

"Al, you're taller. Can you see it?"

"Nope. Just looks like trays to me."

"Good. Hopefully it stays that way."

"So now we hide the ammo and grab the rest."

"Let's do it."

The two went out from the restaurant into the parking lot.

"So these traps of yours," Allan began. "How many you think we can setup?"

"Right now? A good few. Full roll of that fishing line, we can rig the cabins and our hiding spots."

"Say they get past the tripwire stuff. What keeps them from getting the guns?"

"That's where the razors come in. Like with that top shelf? We can glue them to the bottom of the rack. You and me, we'll know to reach from the side corner, but anyone else... Well, bad news."

Allan nodded. "And we can rig the other spots the same way."

The two entered the truck and Allan started the engine.

"We can probably use that knife you found too; maybe...maybe mount it to a doorframe or something. Maybe rig the roads too. Cover the wire with leaves and debris, someone'll ride right over it."

"Hey, Val," he started before a pause as he looked down the road. "It absolutely tickles me to see you go all commando and shit, but...you know you'll need to be prepared for this stuff actually killing someone, right?" He looked to his sister. She closed her eyes with a shuttered sigh. "You gonna be able to handle that?" She sat silently. "Sis?"

"I'm not losing you too," she replied, seeming withdrawn.

Allan looked back to the road and began pulling out from the lot. Vallerie wiped her eyes before looking out to the passing sights from the window. He glanced back to her, noticing her adjusting her back in her seat with her knee starting to bounce. He looked back to the road.

"I love you," he said.

She continued her gaze over the passing sights of the road, her knee continuing on. An unease was heard in her voice.

"I love you more."

∙∙∙

The room behind the locked gate sat empty. From the outside, the pawn shop sat closed and untouched. Vallerie twirled a keyring, ran through a set of various lock picks in her hand as she tossed a duffle bag into the back of the truck. She stepped back, stashing the picks into her pocket as Allan closed the back window.

They went next to the party store, followed by a final stop at the hardware store, gathering whatever the truck had space for. The shelves of various hairsprays were empty, as were the stocks of fireworks, tape, batteries, and any dried or canned food left behind. Vallerie rifled through the backroom of the hardware store, taking in hand the last package of steel wool and tossing the emptied box aside. She shoved it into a bag and kept on, grabbing a fallen stick of jerky from behind the counter on her way. She tore it open and bit off a piece in leaving out the door, held open by her brother.

"Much thanks, good lad."

"Anytime. That taste as good as it smells?"

"Not bad. There's a few more in one of the bags. Try not to eat it all though, huh?"

"No promises."

Vallerie stopped outside the entrance of the

store, looked back, and started in once more.
"What?"

Allan followed her back inside. She headed off behind the counter and took an American flag from its mount on the wall. Allan looked on, confused. She returned to him and held the flag up briefly by its pole.

"Camouflage," she said, walking past him to the door.

Allan cocked his head with a raised brow as his sister left out the door. He turned to leave, but stopped short himself on catching sight of something behind the counter. A thin white object was on the floor. He went to take a closer look, finding the object to be a single cigarette left behind. He knelt down and took it in hand, briefly looking behind him before twirling it between his fingers and stashing it in the side pocket of his leather. He stood and left outside.

The two entered the vehicle once again, Allan digging into the bag set between their seats and retrieving a stick of jerky before setting off onto the road.

"Now," he started, taking a bite. "Holy shit, that is good. Now, we stash all this, check the snares, set some traps, make a dinner, and then… What's after that, you think?"

"Bed," she sighed.

Allan snickered. "I agree. It's been a day."

•••

The fire crackled softly as the evening took hold. Allan adjusted the height of the mounted stick, set balanced across the pit over cinder blocks on each end. Skewered to the middle of the wood was a crudely skinned squirrel.

"You know, I'm kinda surprised it smells this good. Sorta figured it'd smell like, I don't know, rubber or something." As he tended further to the smoldering coals, the only sound that met him was the soft lapping of the lake. He raised his eyes to Vallerie, sat in the grass at the opposite end with her sight directed back toward the gravel path between the cabins. "Val."

"Yeah, I'm listenin'. Just…just thinking."

"We went over them a dozen times. It's good." She continued her distracted gaze as the evening drew darker. Allan looked back to their dinner over the fire. He continued. "The wires are good… The triggers are good… We covered every way into the neighborhood… No cats or dogs are gonna get caught on it. Maybe a coyote or something bigger, but nothing cute."

He looked back to her. She hesitated in turning back to the fire. She was quiet, looking to him briefly before setting her sights to the coals. The sounds of the evening surrounded them: distant crickets; the tide of the lake; a faint creak of the boat against the dock. Vallerie took her knife from the grass beside her and began digging at the coals.

"It's later," she said.

Allan lowered his eyes to the fire. The two sat quiet as he tried to find the right point to start.

"It wasn't a full day. After you were taken in. Me and—" He paused. "We were in the lobby, waiting to hear back from the doctors. And we turned on the news. Just…just to have some background noise," he paused once more. "Just…background."

Allan fell silent as he watched the fire's glow. Vallerie looked to him. He met her eye briefly before turning back to the coals. He sighed, nervous.

"I can handle it, Allan."

"I—" he started before a breath. "On second thought, sis, I think…maybe you're better off not knowing a lot of—"

"I can handle it," she repeated sternly.

Allan lifted his eyes to her. "No."

His tone was almost desperate. It caught her off guard.

"Al, what—"

"What you need to know about this group, and that's it. Nothing… None of the rest will do anything for you going forward; it'll just—" he paused, clearly upset. "You don't need it."

Her expression softened in watching her brother return to the fire. "Five months," she sighed, setting her knife into the grass and looking off to the distance. "Fine. Just them then."

Allan drew a breath, calming himself for a

moment. He went on.

"The whole world was affected by this. Things…got crazy…here on US soil. Eventually the army got called in. And then there was a draft. More people started to…come back. That on top of everything else. The soldiers did what they could, but it was all just too much. They called for an evacuation. No info on where or for how long. Others stayed to fight off the dead, to try and keep some sort of order. That's where these guys came from. They're the ones that stayed."

Vallerie nodded, turning back to the fire. "And they think anyone that didn't serve could've made a difference."

"Yeah." The two sat quietly in the night. In time, Allan checked on their food. "Well, our little friend here looks done."

Vallerie glanced over.

"That actually does smell pretty good."

"Doesn't it?" Allan took the stick and stood to his feet. "Let's head in and cut ourselves up some dinner. What else did we grab from the party place? Beans?"

Vallerie took her knife and folded it back down before standing.

"Yeah. Two cans of baked beans and one can of corn."

Allan shrugged, starting into the cabin. "Sounds good to me."

Vallerie started toward the door but stopped,

finding herself startled by the crackle of the small pit smoldering behind her just before the slope to the water. She looked back to it. Allan noticed, his feigned cheer fading as he looked after her. He turned and continued inside. Vallerie's sight lifted to the sky, glimpsing the light of the moon from behind the few passing clouds. She turned sharp and hurried into the cabin, passing Allan in the kitchen and heading into her room. She took a calendar from her wall and headed back to the dining table, setting the page beside an array of lit tea lights. She looked to the correct date, observing the moon phase listed in the bottom corner of the block.

"Waxing gibbous," she said to herself.

"Huh?"

She looked up to her brother as he sawed away at the carcass over the table.

"Nothing. Just checking something." She returned the calendar to her room before crouching beside her bed and pulling a bag from beneath. She took it in hand and returned to her brother in the dim kitchen. "Okay, so you're doing the meat..." she started toward the bottom cabinets and retrieved two small pots before taking the cans from the countertop. "I'll go get these."

"Oh, hey, you got the can opener?"

"Fuck. Yeah, that'd probably help now, wouldn't it?"

Already halfway out the door, Vallerie headed back and retrieved the tool from a drawer below the counter. Her brother continued cutting against the carcass as she left out toward the fire. She set everything into the grass before taking a grate from alongside the pit and balancing it overtop the blocks. She started on the cans, pouring each into their own pot and gingerly setting them over the grate to cook. Allan called from inside.

"How long, you think?"

"Few minutes should do it."

"Cool. Come back here for a sec. You've gotta taste this."

"Be there in a sec…"

With a glance up to the moon, Vallerie stood, pulling two stones from her bag, one a smooth and dense black and the other a transparent pink with shades of white, and jogged to the dock. She hurriedly set the stones down over a plank, then made her way back to the cabin. As she and her brother prepped their meal, the two stones sat over the wood, awash in the moon's light.

•••

The crickets sounded alongside the occasional lap of the waters and Allan's snores. Vallerie sat at the table, watching the flicker of a single tea light, captivated by the sway of the flame when visited by the breeze through the window. She sat back in her chair and looked out to the door, observing the sounds of the night. She glanced back to Allan's bedroom for a moment before standing to her feet, taking her pistol from the table, and starting toward the front door.

    She left outside, stepping barefoot into the grass. She holstered her weapon at her hip before closing her eyes and focusing on the softness of the ground meeting her step. She drew a breath of the cool evening's air, held to it, then released it steadily while opening her eyes to the lake ahead. She looked to the moon shining comfortably above. A faint breeze tossed her hair as she started toward the dock. She knelt down and retrieved the stones from the plank, holding them lovingly in hand while rising back to her feet. She stepped to the edge of the dock, seated herself over the plank, and eased down into the shallow waters.

    After an initial grimace in the cool touch of the waves, she adjusted and began stepping forward, careful not to do so too quickly for fear of waking her brother. She made her way out a few feet, with the water's depth no more than just above the ankle, and stood still. She held the stones together in her hands, facing her open palms up to the moon, and focused her sight upon them as they reflected in its light. Her heart began a faster beat as her breaths came unsteadily. She focused intensely, bringing to mind the stones' types and attributes, and then calling upon her intentions for their use. She closed her eyes once more, studying the water's lap against her feet and the soft sand that seemed to hug her skin beneath. She settled herself in the night. After a moment of thought, she spoke.

"Dearest Goddess; dearest God; I ask that you be with me tonight. It isn't as formal as I would like. I don't have an altar. I didn't cast a circle to protect me. It's just me and my will tonight, among the elements. May there be power to that," she paused, drawing a deep breath. As she held to it, the breeze greeted her. An understanding was felt within it, a warmth; it settled her nerves as she exhaled calm. "I hold two stones, black tourmaline and rose quartz, protection and love. I ask that you lend your blessings to them. I ask that you aid me in my intent." She studied the feeling of the stones in her hand, envisioning a light around them, their unique energies. Her tourmaline appeared to mind as an intense red while her quartz came as a bright white. She next envisioned her own energy entwining with the two, emerging from her palms; though no specific color came to mind, it came instead as more of a vibration. It surrounded the energies of the stones as they, too, pulsated with it. They synchronized. She continued. "I know, life being what it is now, asking for outright protection may be asking too much. But I do ask…please…that should anything separate me from my brother, or him from I, against all odds, we'll always find our way back to one another. That's my only request. No bells or whistles about it. Please be with me."

She folded her hands against the stones and

closed her eyes. She focused on their energies as they pulsed in sync with her own and thought hard over her intent. The thing that first arrived was the thought of her standing alone in a field. The thought shook her for a moment, but she continued to hold focus. The field was expansive, the only sight different from the continuous rolling grass being a small hill in the distance. She looked to the hill and imagined Allan approaching over it. She then envisioned the same scenario but in reverse as she approached over the hill in the same fashion.

"May we always find our way back," she thought. She repeated the words in her mind, imagining the scenes another time from both angles, and then a third time, afterwards imagining her vibration bringing her thoughts to the stones. They captured the images in a kind of mist and pulled them within. The images faded into them as she felt a slight heat rise in her hands. A delicate wave greeted her at the ankle, followed by an overwhelming calm. She knew at once that she'd succeeded.

She opened her eyes and looked to the moon as another gust tossed her hair in the night. All of a sudden, the sounds of the water and of the crickets surrounding the grounds, they all seemed different: louder, clearer. Following the guidance she'd read in her books, she attempted to clear her mind to hear for any response from beyond. Any words that came to mind outside of her own thoughts. She waited patiently in the night, a minute or so passing by before three distinct words met her. They came to her in a gentle, reassuring voice, one that she couldn't recall hearing before, an older woman's. The tone sounded wise, experienced, yet with a spark of youth. Her mind raced, pondering whether she'd conjured the voice herself or if she'd truly heard it from another. The question didn't remain for very long though. She decided that, ultimately, it didn't matter. The voice came, and the feeling was true in hearing it. Overwhelmed, she began to cry as a smile crossed her face.

"We've heard, child."

•••

She woke to the sound of a flickering lighter. It started faint, growing louder. Her eyes opened to see Allan no longer at her side. The flickering continued. She sat up and looked to the open door. Her brother was seen sitting at the kitchen table, dressed down in his sleep attire of a sleeveless tee and tattered jeans. He struggled to light his found cigarette, making another failed strike with the lighter.

"Come on, you fucker."

She couldn't help but laugh as he swore with the white stick rising and falling with his words. She stretched and eased out of bed. Allan looked to her starting out from the room rubbing her eyes.

"It awakes." He smiled before striking again. "Still no nightmares?"

"None."

"Healed. Good."

"Wouldn't jump the gun just yet. How long you been up?"

"A while. Might've slept, but I feel like shit."

"Nightmare?"

He scoffed, swearing under his breath as he struck the lighter again without so much as a spark. His sister started over, taking a seat at the table.

"No, no bad dreams," he said, tossing the lighter over the table. "Just nauseous as fuck. Thinking it was the squirrel."

"Well, I feel fine."

"Lucky you. At first, I woke up feeling okay. A little hard to breathe with your drooling mug buried in my chest like that, but otherwise fine," he looked to her. "Seeing you sound asleep, night after night, it's a good start to the day." She smiled, leaning into her hands over the table. Allan looked to the lighter. "I used to be a fucking magician with empty lighters. Must've lost my touch. Fuck, dude. This sucks."

He sat back in his chair and closed his eyes, the cigarette still hanging from his mouth.

"Probably nothing. It'll pass. But… that isn't gonna help." Vallerie said, leaning over and plucking the cigarette from his mouth.

She eased back in her chair, fiddling with it in hand.

"Yeah," he said, now leaning over the table onto folded arms. He sighed. "We should check the snares."

"You mean I should check the snares."

"No, I mean we. Plural."

"Bro, you look like you're about to puke," she laughed. "Don't worry, I got it."

Allan glanced over to her.

"I don't want you out there alone. Day or night. Just…just give me a minute and I'll be good."

She stood from the table. "No. I've got it," she said sternly. "If there's anything out there, you're in too rough a shape to do anything about it."

"You're aware that I'm like, twice your size, right?"

"I'm aware of you looking like shit. You're staying here. Besides, I'll only be gone an hour or so."

"If we caught a rabbit or something you're not gonna like it."

She was silent in retrieving her things from the bedroom, first holstering her gun to her belt, then putting on her necklace and backpack. She patted her pockets, assuring herself of her crystals and her knife before putting on her shoes.

Allan watched with concern. "You know I'm right, sis."

"Yeah, well…it is what it is." She started out to the door, still holding to the cigarette. She looked to her brother while twirling it between her fingers. "One hour. Stay here. Seriously."

He nodded before further slumping over his arms with a sigh. "Fine. Any longer though and I'm dragging myself out there to look."

"Don't worry. I may even be back early," she replied with a smile, starting out the door.

"Hey."

"Huh?"

"Bring back coffee."

"If only…"

"Eggs! And bacon!"

Allan's voice faded as she closed the door, still heard rattling off his list. She smiled to herself after locking the door and went on her way. She looked to the cigarette, twirling it in her hand as she thought.

"Can't leave you in the grass because I don't wanna get anything sick… Can't toss you in the water… Don't even know if I can bury you…" she pondered aloud in starting over to the next cabin. She rounded the corner to the side window and knelt down before the bench, retrieving a small sandwich bag from beneath its foot. She unzipped it and pulled the contents, a handwritten map of the locations for the snares. She unfolded it and studied the layout. After a further moment's thought, she put the cigarette inside the bag and stashed it into her pocket. She looked back to the map. "First one is…ten minutes away. Okay." She started out down the lawns of the resort, folding the page in hand. She knelt down and delicately unhooked the loop of a wire from its mount on a trailer hitch etched into the ground. After crossing its way, she reset the end and continued on.

•••

A chill was felt in the morning air. Before long, she began rubbing her arms in her walk, regretting not taking a jacket. Though she refused to turn back. She looked to the trees on her way, exhaling misted breaths while pondering what they'll look like come the nearing fall. She'd always heard that Michigan had a bright autumn. Imagining the various colors and even just the sight of leaves over the grass brought her a smile as she started out to the street. She looked once more to the map. After a short walk down the winding curve, opening up to another straight road ahead, she consulted the map before cutting across into the wood that lay just past the cluster of homes. The chill came to her further as she caught sight of her breath clouding beneath the shadows of the tree line. She shivered briefly before chastising herself with a grimace. "Come on, you should be used to this. Don't be such a bitch."

Before long, she reached the first of the snares. As the mount appeared to her sight in the distance, she swore to herself with a sigh. It was empty. "Now number two," she said, looking again to the map. "You are…fifteen away." After returning the page to her pocket, she rubbed her arms again and gazed to the trees above. The doves cooed overhead. She called back, soon being met with a response. She laughed with a smile before calling once more. They responded yet again.

After a time, she reached the edge of the tree line and started back to the road. Several minutes passed before she reached a handful of trailer homes along the road, their lawns short and crammed with ornaments, tools, and kids' toys. The next snare was off in the woods beyond, a diagonal shot between the homes and the small convenience store ahead. She stopped just before the wood, shivering once more despite the sun's occasional meeting against her skin.

She started over to the closest of the trailers, entering through the door left unlocked and closing it fast behind her. The small space housed only two bedrooms, one at each end, and the main living area and kitchen set between. They'd been cleared previously, though she decided to rummage through anyway, searching the various cabinets. As she opened the one at the top right, alongside on the fridge, she noticed a can at the top, set behind several dust-covered blenders and pans. She fished it out and smiled. It was an eleven-ounce can of coffee. Half full. She laughed small with bright eyes before setting it over the countertop and looking to the left-hand bedroom, spotting a dark-blue fleece hung beside the window. She went over and took the jacket from its hook. An immediate comfort came in fitting it on and zipping it closed. She raised the collar while fixing her hair behind her shoulders, then headed back to the counter, took the canister, and left outside while stashing it into her bag. She slid her arm through the strap and walked on into the wood, adjusting her pack over her shoulder.

In time, she reached the second snare. It, too, was empty, this time appearing tripped. She sighed before crouching down to reset it. As she made her adjustments over the mount, covering the loop with scraps of brush, a distant thunder was heard. She sprang back to her feet and turned with her hand over her gun. She listened. Tension filled the air as she awaited some other sound among the morning. The moments passed and another thunder came. Her breath came in a shudder as she stood frozen in place. As several pops began to fill the air, two being louder than the others, she found herself running from the wood and down the road toward home. Her heart pounded fast and heavy in her chest. Her breaths came rapid in her stride. Her eyes became frantic as her steps echoed on the littered road. Only one thought crossed her mind, a plea to the forces that be, a desperate call of mercy. "Please don't."

•••

The body of a man lay still in the street, badly burned with one leg missing below the knee. A long black streak crossed the pavement, lined by blood and traces of steel wool still aflame. Vallerie stood with her gun drawn, held tightly in her hand. She looked to the body with shivering breaths, her sight focused on the camouflage of his uniform and the patch over his shoulder. She stepped forward with a slow stride, aiming her pistol directly to the man's head as she nudged the body with her shoe, quickly darting back in her step. He didn't move. She looked forward to the houses before the resort, the calm lake seen lapping just behind. She kept on, her pace quickening as she raised her aim.

On approach, before the driveway to the cabins, two other bodies, both similar in dress to the first, were seen laying still and aflame: one cut off at the leg like the first, the other with intestines laid out from a wide gash reaching up to his sternum. Burns and blood lined the gravel as she stepped forward between the men. She stopped behind the wall of the first cabin, listening close. Nothing was heard aside from the lake and the occasional dove. She continued on.

She undid the trip wire and crossed the lawns with her gun held firm in aim. As she neared her cabin, seeing the American flag swaying softly from its mount alongside the window, she sighted the outstretched leg of another uniformed body peeking out from behind the tree. Drawing closer, her pace slowed and her aim steadily lowered. She stopped at the fire pit before the cabin, lowering her gun at her side with a sigh. A middle-aged woman with long black hair sat beside the tree, clutching tightly to her leg as a deep wound bled from her hip.

"Well, well," Vallerie said. The woman raised her eyes, appearing weak yet stern. "Left behind, huh?

Real patriots."

"You must be Vallerie," she replied in a sigh, quickly grimacing as she returned her attention to her grasp over the wound.

She eyed the woman's hands as blood seeped between her fingers. Her trigger finger tapped against her gun as the lake lapped behind. She drew a breath. It left in a quiver. The woman met her eye once again as she spoke.

"Two choices. Let him go, and I help you. Don't, and I leave you to bleed out."

For a moment, the scene was quiet as the lake lapped calm. The woman cocked her head and squinted.

"You know what he did, right? Or rather, what he chose not…to do?" Vallerie was silent in her stare to the woman's eyes. She continued her tap against her gun. "He could've made a difference to all of this. Just like every other coward that chose to run and hide. But no, no, a juvie kid like that, dropout punk, no, he turned his back."

"You seem to think you know a lot about him."

The woman scoffed. "Not much worth knowing. He fought for you in that shooting. But during the fall, when he really could've saved you, could've saved so many others…he didn't bother. And worse yet, he killed someone that did."

"So, staying behind to look after his sister in the hospital is, what, un-American to you guys?"

"Grand scheme, given this specific set of events, yeah. Yeah, there's quite an argument to be made."

"You know, the military, the…actual…military," she mocked, cocking her head, "told him he couldn't take me along for evacuation. Whoever the hell that was didn't seem to have a problem with him staying behind. Even offered him a chance. The terms were bullshit, but it was a chance nonetheless."

The woman nodded to herself before gradually meeting her again. "They were cowards too," she said. "Many of whom have been dealt with. And a week from now"—she leaned against the tree, closing her eyes with a sigh—"your brother will be too. Might as well accept it, kiddo."

Vallerie stood, near tears, her hand unsteady as it held tight to her gun. Her finger's tapping stopped as it came to a rest against the trigger.

"We took your food. We took your guns: his pistol and shotgun, the rifles in the other house. We took that shitty old four door you had hidden a few yards over. Even took his blade… Seems to me you've got just one choice yourself. Realize what he did was wrong and move on. Soon enough…it'll be back to normal, and you'll be able to put it all behind ya like it was all just a bad dream."

The morning's sounds of the lapping lake and distant doves continued as Vallerie stood furious. Her breaths came shallow and uneven. Her heart pounded in her chest. Her eyes remained still and unable to blink as she glared at the woman through tears starting down her cheek.

"Your two choices," she repeated, quickly being interrupted.

"I'm gonna die anyway. You're wasting your time. Just go."

"I'm changing them."

"Oh? What are they now?"

"Let him go…and have a peaceful death here by the lake. Don't, and I make it worse."

"Oh, yeah? And how exactly do you plan on that?"

Vallerie gestured toward the doors of the cabin. They hung from their hinges, held open by another body lain on the floor amidst a stream of blood. The kitchen knife was also seen beside the body, its blade streaked in blood. The dining table was visible just behind with several small containers set overtop.

"Took our food, but not our seasonings; among which is salt," she said sharply, cocking her head. "I have a knife, a hatchet, and a gun. I also happen to have some steel wool and nine-volt batteries left, which, when connected, spark a flame."

"How vicious," the woman interrupted, smirking with a scoff.

"And…under the floorboards…I have a few extra cans of hairspray…and firecrackers," Vallerie paused as the woman's mocking smile faded, her eyes meeting her sharply. She went on. "That little trick really did a number on your friends. What's to stop me from just…lighting one up and blowing off your other leg? I mean, it's not like you can run away."

"Huh. Didn't peg you for such a sadist."

"Tends to happen when someone kidnaps my family acting like they're doing something heroic."

"Oh, stop acting like you know anything."

"You're no soldier. You're just a goddamn terrorist. Nothing more."

"Listen, you little shit."

Vallerie raised her voice over the woman's, who already sounded weak in her tone.

"No, you listen to me! You…you have got a lot of balls to call me the sadist here. Are you high? You gotta fuckin' be to look me in the eye, me, knowing as much as you do, and say that shit." The woman looked on her with apathy. Vallerie breathed heavily as her gun quivered in hand. Her eyes appeared ravenous as a breeze tossed her hair and the chain of her necklace. She sighed before repeating the woman's words in a mocking tone. "Stop acting like you know anything."

The woman nodded, raised her brows, and fired back. "Know what? Do whatever you're gonna do. I helped cleanse the country for the future; my job is done."

The woman looked away to the lawns spanning the other cabins of the resort. Vallerie stood, still uneven. Gradually, her hand steadied over her gun. She started forward toward the cabin, keeping her eye tight on the woman sat bleeding into the grass, no longer holding to her wound. She entered, stepping past the body cautiously. Her caution waned as she saw the gash torn through the soldier's throat, reaching through to the middle, and the several white splinters scattered around.

    The woman remained, eyes facing now toward the lake. She looked up to the flag swaying gently on its mount. Her focus returned to the lake ahead as the waves lapped. Vallerie exited the cabin, holding her brother's leather in hand. Without a word, she passed by the woman and went down the steps to the water. She set Allan's jacket overtop the dock and crouched down beneath. The woman watched curiously. Scraping away the rock and sand, Vallerie retrieved the bag from the water and began back to the lawn. Before taking the jacket from the dock, she removed the pistol and shook the bag before placing it into her pocket. She gestured the firearm to the woman's view with raised brows and holstered it at her left hip, her other gun at rest in its holster on her right. She slid down her backpack and put on the jacket, her eyes never facing away from the woman as she sat staring back.

    Vallerie adjusted the collar of the jacket before strapping her bag once again over her shoulder.

    "I noticed…of the things you listed off… not only did you miss this one, but you also left out the pickup hid in the forest. And the assault rifle hid across the lake," she paused, standing still as the woman's expression softened, then went on. "And the...not so minimal amount of ammo a couple towns over." The woman exhaled an unsteady breath. Vallerie smiled. "Yeah," she said, starting forward toward the cabin. The woman watched closely as she stood before the window, looking up to the flag while rummaging through the inner pocket of the coat.

"What—What are you doing?"

Vallerie was silent at the question, maintaining her focus toward the softly swaying flag. She retrieved a cluster of steel wool from the pocket as well as a battery kept in a snap-top cigarette box. She took it from inside, returned the box, and touched the items together. Sparks steadily ran through the cluster. After a few seconds, she held them up to the flag's edge and breathed against the sparks. They soon turned into a flame, catching onto the fabric and running upward. The woman was heard breathing heavily and labored. Vallerie looked over to her. In her seat against the tree, she appeared pale from blood loss.

"Judging by that expression I'm looking a little more like a threat. Am I right?" The woman only stared as the flag smoldered before Vallerie's stance, her eyes cold in her attention. "Haven't gone for a radio this entire time either." She leaned forward with a squint. "No bulging on the uniform, which tells me you don't have one." The girl eased back her stance, smirking with a scoff, her eye teeth seen on sharp display. "Let's change those choices one last time. One, let my brother go and I don't go kill your friends in Columbus."

"Please. Listen to—"

"Two, don't, and I kill them all. But like you said…you'll die anyway. So…while you're still conscious…now's your chance to actually be a hero."

"I—" the woman stuttered beneath shaking breaths. "I can't stop it. That isn't up to me. And we moved out from Columbus. Please, just give me a second to—"

"Where is he?"

The woman's face was struck with fear as Vallerie stood completely still. The flag still burned, dropping ashes over the grass.

"I—I can't tell you. Please, let's just talk—"

"Where…is he?"

The woman swallowed hard as she winced, now focused on her wound. She groaned. Vallerie looked on coldly.

"I'm not telling you…until you guarantee you won't hurt them."

Vallerie went to speak, but stopped as a sound caught her attention, a wheezing breath from the approach behind the cabins. It was faint but echoed louder across the space. She glanced to the woman, who then looked toward the same direction. Her eyes flittered back to Vallerie as she gave a gentle sideways nod, a desperate plea, a plea that went ignored. Vallerie sighed, starting toward the woman while drawing her right pistol in hand.

"Yes, you are," she said as the woman attempted to grab her. She was weak in her struggle as Vallerie quickly threw her hands away and slammed the hilt of her gun to the woman's mouth. Her eyes shut tight as she wailed, blood pouring from her lips, attempting in vain to hold her face away. Vallerie struck her again in the same spot before grabbing her by the hair and dragging her onto her belly in the grass.

The second her leg was moved, the woman began a sharp, strained whine. Vallerie led her across the grass as she walked around the cabin toward the approach. The woman's wailing became higher in pitch as she was taken across the gravel, blood streaming in her path. Vallerie then stood before the first fallen soldier, the deceased man having turned and crawled over the road. He was laying in the gravel, still eyes facing up to her as he reached out with another wheeze, his mouth opening slowly.

The woman writhed in Vallerie's grasp, continuing her whine, though it faded in intensity as she saw the body approach. Vallerie tightened her grip over the woman's hair while holstering her gun and wrapping her grasp to the back of her neck. She forced her to the ground ahead, crouching down and planting a firm knee over her back as the body crawled closer. "Where is he?" Vallerie asked in a hushed tone, directly into the woman's ear.

She opened her eyes to the creature, exhaling

into the dust of the gravel as blood poured further from her mouth. "Please," she begged, eyes strained by tears.

The corpse drew closer, opening and clenching its mouth excitedly.

"Where is he?" Vallerie asked again, this time louder as she looked to the body in its approach.

"I can't—"

"Where is my brother?! Last chance!"

"Please!" the woman cried, facing the corpse as its hand neared her face.

"Fine. Have it your way."

Vallerie tightened her grip over the woman as she was about to press her into the corpse's grasp.

"Indiana! Field View Apartments in Fort Wayne!"

She released her grasp over the woman, drew her gun, and fired at the dead. The corpse fell still with a hole through its temple. Matts of hair laced the spatter of blood over the gravel. Vallerie stood up, looking down to the woman as she cried in her position, her tone growing weaker. She eased a breath before facing ahead and starting out across the lot.

"Please. I told you," the woman pled.

Vallerie continued on, silent with her pistol still drawn in hand.

"I told you where he's being taken. Give me your word. That you won't hurt them. They…they can work something out." She raised her eyes to Vallerie as she continued walking out to the tree line across the street. She scraped her nails against the gravel, raised herself, and screamed out. "Don't you hurt them! Think of everyone else that lost somebody they love!"

Vallerie stopped and called back. "If they don't hurt him—if they give him up peacefully and leave us be—then you guys can do whatever you please. At that point, I don't care. But if I don't get him back"—she paused with a glance back to the fallen soldier—"then what happens happens."

The woman's eyes shut tight as she turned herself over with a groan, laying on her back over the ground.

Vallerie sighed a parting word. "Just...just close your eyes and let go. It'll be over soon."

She turned and continued on as the woman's breaths came further and further apart, weaker each time. Alongside them, the only sounds heard were the occasional coo of the doves, the gentle lap of the lake, and Vallerie's brisk steps over the grass fading into the distance as she began into the wood.

5: THE WOLF

He kept his eyes to the road ahead as the truck slowed to a stop. Ahead sat the resort. Several corpses wandered to and fro in the street. He scoffed before shutting off the engine. He turned to Vallerie sitting by herself in the backseat, her eyes focused on her closed knife as she held it in hand.

"This is where it all starts, sis," he said.

She didn't respond, sitting silently. Her sight remained on her knife.

Allan turned back in his seat and watched the bodies closely as they meandered. They didn't approach the truck. He undid his seatbelt, took his sword from the passenger side, and stepped out into the road. He strapped the scabbard over his back and looked ahead with a sigh. He wasn't noticed. He backed away a few steps, gradually turning on his way. He went to the back door and leaned against the open window. His sister glanced over briefly before returning to herself. Her brother reached through the window and rested his palm over her cheek. She looked back to him, her eyes appearing dim. The siblings shared a moment, understanding one another in their silence. Allan took his hand away and stood from the window. "Stay put. It's only a few."

    She nodded, her eyes falling back to her knife. Allan faced the road once more. He drew his sword and started forward with a sharp whistle. One of the undead met his eye and shuffled forward. Another behind twitched slightly before starting a lumbering jog. Allan rushed forward, piercing his blade hard through the first body's stomach, then charging into the second. They toppled over onto their backs. A wet, delayed set of cracking sounds echoed the street in their landing. Knelt down over the skewered bodies, Allan forced the blade deeper and reached for the knife sheathed on his belt. Once drawn, he forced their reaching arms away and drove it through the eye of the body below, twisting the handle fast and with force. Its labored breath halted. He then shifted its head aside and stabbed just the same into the other before sheathing his knife, standing, pressing a foot beside his sword, and pulling it loose. Three other corpses lumbered forward. He readied his blade in a hurried step, pulled his arms to the side, and charged with a growl.

•••

The truck sped fast down the road. Vallerie gripped the wheel with tight hands as her strained eyes, tearful and reddened, looked to the sights ahead. She shuddered her breaths in winding the curve. The restaurant drew closer ahead of her. She slowed the truck to a sharp stop, killed the engine, and left out the thrown-open door, drawing her pistol from her hip and keeping it aimed ready. She started toward the door and kicked hard against it. The chipped wood smacked against the back wall as the distressed girl kept her aim tight in front of her path. In searching the building, nobody was found. She headed to the back of the kitchen and reached around the side of the shelf, delicately retrieving the rifle from its spot behind the array of Styrofoam trays. She strapped it over her shoulder and left back to the truck.

She climbed inside, slamming the door to a close and buckling her seat belt. Feeling nauseous, she hunched over the wheel with her eyes shutting tight. She took a breath and sat back, tears beginning anew as she looked to the road. With her sight fixed ahead, she reached down to the compartment between the seats and took up a large map book. She thumbed through the pages, first looking to the guide over Michigan and then to Indiana. She held the pages open one by one and pulled a notepad and pen from her bag in the passenger seat to take notes on the directions.

Swallowing hard in an attempt to force back

her upset, she then opened the map to a greater view of the states, matching up the main roads. Satisfied, she threw the notepad over the dash and the pen and map to the passenger side before starting the engine. Her grasp held tight to the wheel. Her breaths came strained as her eyes began to burn from the tears. She repeated her notes to herself.

"Mostly full tank. Around four hours. West toward W Lake Road... stay on 127."

She started out, attempting her best to settle herself. Though while progress was made in spurts, calm never truly found her.

•••

She opened the window to the back cabin and set boxes of ammunition inside, the remainder of what was stashed, as well as a small ration of food and water kept in a duffle bag. She shut the window, snapped the lock, and set off once more to the driver's seat. As she pulled away from the house, she stopped, looking the opposite direction, and turned to change her course, heading next to the pawn shop.

Once there, she stopped sharp in the street and exited with her gun held ready. She went to the window and tore down the flyers, starting with Allan's and working her way down. She crumpled them in hand and took them on her way back to the truck, tossing them to the floor of the passenger seat as she climbed inside. For a moment, she questioned her decision, but only for that moment as she recalled the woman's reaction at the cabin.

She pondered. She'd struck fear into an otherwise cocky member of this group just by possessing a few guns and a mission to get a loved one back. She thought back to the other bodies. In passing them, just as with the woman, she'd not seen a radio nor any firearm, which, she reasoned, could only mean two things: they were as disorganized as first thought, and they were as low on supplies as first thought. The others must've taken back what was left from their fallen crew, and any type of soldier, to her mind, would only do so if they were concerned about supplies. Then there's the fact that they walked into the traps to begin with. Regardless of how hidden she'd tried to make them, trained forces would've at least been more cautious. As she weighed the thoughts, at last, a true moment of calm began to set in. She cracked a smile and started on down the road as her eyes settled.

"I'm coming for you fucks," she said sharply. "If one hair on his head—" The truck bounced suddenly on her way, causing a rustle in the chain of her necklace. She looked down to it briefly before shifting her eyes back to the road. "What happens happens."

—What Came Before—

Trisha paced to and fro in the waiting room,

her phone held close to her ear

"Come on. Pick up."

The tone continued until reaching the message.

"Hey. You've reached Allan Sabell. If it's important, leave a message—"

"Goddamnit, Al!" she said, hanging up before dialing again.

•••

Three steady, hard knocks were given to the door. Allan stood back on the porch, his hand sliding into his pocket with a grasp over the hilt of his sister's knife. His stare was fixed to the door ahead, his eyes strained and restless. As a commotion was heard behind, followed by the snap of the lock, he sighed heavily while pulling the blade. The door opened, answered by a police officer. Allan's eyes softened in looking to the man. The officer's eyes looked onto him with concern, briefly glancing down to the knife in his grasp.

"Allan?"

"Frank… Been a while."

"Yeah… What's this about?"

Allan's breaths came unsteady. "Inside… Is he home?"

The officer was silent.

"He attacked Vallerie," he continued. "She's in a coma."

"He called on himself. We're bringing him in."

"He's lucky."

"Allan, I need you to put that away, okay, bud?"

He stood, meeting the officer's eye without so much as a blink, his stare going cold. "He's going away in cuffs. Come down to the station. You're able to press charges."

"I'd rather kill him."

The officer hesitated. "Yeah. Yeah, I can see that."

A second officer appeared behind Frank, standing with his hand at his hip.

"Frank? Whoa, kid. Let's just put that away."

"Hey. Hey. I know him. He's cool," Frank said, forcing his way in front of the other officer.

"Doesn't look cool to me."

"Well, he is. He's Vallerie Sabell's brother. The, um, guy we're taking in… he put her in a coma."

Allan's voice trembled.

"If she doesn't wake up, I swear to Christ I will move heaven and earth to get to him."

"Al. I know it's hard to listen to me here, but…just try, okay?"

Allan started crying, his eyes appearing wild in his rage. "You heard me," he said.

"Kid, drop the knife."

"He's fine. Allan? Just…lend me an olive branch for a sec."

He hesitated, eyes shifting to the second officer. "Fine. But it better be good. I'm talkin' guaranteeing he goes under the jail. No meals. Tortured."

Frank sighed. "You wanna protect her. I know. After—" He paused. "Now this. You have every right to be here right now. You have every right to want his head on a platter. I would too. But you gotta listen, man. When—not if—but when she wakes up, she's gonna want you by her side. Not in handcuffs; not awaiting trial."

The officer behind softened, looking to Allan with his hand now relaxed at his side.

"He's right, kid."

Allan's hand was unsteady in his hold to the knife as another tear fell from his eye. Gradually, he began to settle, closing the blade and sliding it back to his pocket. He sighed with his hand held over his forehead. He looked back to the officers, seeing a third approach alongside the man, standing with his arms held tight behind his back. He never met his eye, though Allan stared at him.

"Frank," he said.

"Yeah?"

"I'm going all the way with this. Whatever I can get."

Frank nodded, placing a firm hand over his shoulder. "You got it. Come on. You can ride with us."

—What Comes After—
—Allan—

He awoke in darkness, a damp sting in his eyes causing him to wince. A loud motor was heard, drowning out his surroundings. He went to sit up but knocked his head against a wall above. He attempted to reach out, finding his hands to be restrained behind his back. He yanked them hard, hearing a soft metallic clank faded beneath the sound of the motor. He breathed fast and heavy as he lay back down, his arms beginning to ache in the position. Through their sting, he was able to open his eyes just long enough to make out his surroundings. All that was seen in the dark was a faint crack of light on his right. His heart began to beat hard in realizing where he was: in a trunk, bound and on the move, the sting in his eyes likely blood from a burning wound felt over his forehead.

He winced again as his senses made a full return. His thoughts went to his sister.

"I'm sorry."

—Vallerie—

The silence over the road struck her, seeming to add further weight to the trek. Her grasp over the wheel was steady, as were her breaths. Her heart, however, was still tense in its heavy beat. She glanced to an approaching sign before hurriedly looking to her notes. As she returned the directions to the dash and her sight returned to the view ahead, her eyes grew wide in seeing a trio of deer trotting to a stop in the road, staring, seemingly frozen in place.

"Fuck!" She turned fast, swerving to the left. She attempted to regain control, but it was too late. Not far from the road, the ground sloped down to a thicket of the forest, exactly where the truck headed with the brakes serving no effect. Thinking fast, she undid her seatbelt and dove out from the driver's side. She tumbled down the hill as the truck barreled forward into a set of pines. The impact that was heard, as well as the sight of the front end as she stood to her feet, caused her heart to sink in her chest.

"No... No, no, no." She started forward, jogging to the front of the truck. The front end was bent in against the trunk of the now leaning pines. She climbed in and turned the key desperately, one attempt after the next, all to no avail. Neither the battery nor the engine gave any response. She sat quivering. One last attempt. No result. She sighed heavily before stepping out. She looked back up to the road, relieved to see the deer beginning to cross, unharmed. Stood alone down the hillside, she looked off to the sky briefly, catching her breaths. She closed her eyes tightly and hunched down, holding her knees as tears began escaping anew. She breathed heavily in looking back to the truck.

She climbed in, took her map, assault, and backpack from inside, and tossed them hard away from the vehicle. She then moved to the back cabin, unlocked the window, and retrieved two duffle bags, one of her food and other possessions, and the other carrying several cases of ammo. With her mind racing, she thought to take everything she could from the truck, looking to her books and other items. The reality set in fast though that, on foot, she may not even be able to take the duffle bags. She sighed, crying further. She slammed a fist against the window to the cabin. And then another.

    She rifled through her things, deciding on what to take on her trek. In the end, she took the loaded rifle onto her back, alongside her backpack. In its back pockets, it contained a light amount of food and water, her secondary pistol, a notebook and pen, her map and directions, and several clips of ammunition. Her crystals resided in a small zipper pouch on the front. Candles, fire starters, and other smaller items were put in the top and side pockets. The textbooks, excess ammunition, and other materials were left behind, including, to her regret, the can of found coffee. She left as the window slammed down to a close and adjusted her things over her back. She fixed her belt in facing out to the hillside. She sighed with a sniff, wiping away another tear as she looked over the empty scene. After gathering her thoughts, she took tight hold to the straps and started her way up the slope.

—What Came Before—

"Goodness, child," the elderly woman said, a baffled look crossing her face. She took the bags from a younger Vallerie's hand as she entered and closed the door. The girl leaned back, straightening herself with a stretch. They met each other's eye. "Vallerie, you know you didn't have to do this."

"Yeah, well, the place needed stuff and I needed to get out for a while. No trouble at all."

"Where did you go?"

"Celia's. Wanted to make sure I got everything in one trip. There are—"she paused, pointing to the bags—"toothbrushes, detergent packs, and a few cleaners in that one, and the other is all canned goods, coffee, and seasonings."

Vallerie stood, stretching again and rubbing her arms, marked by red bands from her hold over the bags. The woman set them over the bench along the wall and looked back with concerned eye.

"Child, you carried all this back here. From Celia's? That's 5th and Mire. That's an hour plus both ways."

She shrugged. "I'm used to it. Good exercise."

The woman nodded as a smile crossed her face.

"Thank you, my dear. Truly."

"Maybe just...don't tell Allan."

"My lips are sealed. Go sit. Used to it or not, your legs are probably burning up."

"Eh. I've been through worse. Here, I'll help

you put that away."

"No," she snapped. "Go sit before you pull something."

Reluctant, Vallerie nodded and eased herself to a seat on the opposite bench. After a moment's rest, she sneered to herself in feeling that her legs were indeed burning.

—What Comes After—
—Vallerie—

She walked slow down the suburban street. The weight on her back and her hips, formerly of no concern, seemed impossible to carry. She groaned while adjusting the straps over her shoulder, pushing on even as a tightness struck the back of her legs with every step.

"Come on, you fucking pussy. Don't … stop." It set in fast that her body couldn't keep up. With her next step, her foot slid, and she fell, just barely catching herself. She sat hunched over on the littered pavement, straining her breaths as they left in a mist from the day's odd chill, a further sign of the coming fall in the northern state. She closed her eyes tightly and swore to herself while slamming the side of her fist to the road. The evening's air greeted her. The sounds of birds settling in for the night and awakening crickets seemed to surround her. She looked out to the abandoned street. Many houses appeared pillaged. Belongings and garbage were thrown about. Otherwise, it appeared empty, not even a single car being present.

As she caught her breath, she forced herself back to her feet, standing unsteadily. She took her time in continuing down the street, wary of the tightness in her legs. She looked to a house coming up on her right. Its front door was wide open. Looking to the inside, it was clear to her that it'd already been searched, the living room appearing ransacked; even the couches had not been spared, torn apart with their stuffing thrown. She held tight to the railing of the porch as she looked out to the sun starting to set. Her mind raced. She thought to carry on, knew she had to carry on, but, too, knew the reality of being tired and left in the dark.

She shuddered a sigh as she looked up to the house. She tightened her grip over the railing and took the first step up. The rest came with great effort, but she managed. At the top, she nearly fell before catching herself against the column. She looked to the inside with hesitancy. Nothing was seen. Nothing was heard. She drew her pistol in hand, its weight feeling three times the norm, and started inside. A bird fluttered down from the staircase on the left. She immediately stumbled against the wall as it flew by her head in leaving through the door. She stood for a moment, observing the quiet as light faded further in the awakening night outside.

With no further disturbance heard, while keeping her eye toward the kitchen ahead, she took a tight aim with her gun and spoke out. "If anyone's in here, let me know and I'll gladly go somewhere else. I'm not trying to steal from anyone. I'm not trying to hurt anyone. Just need a place for the night. So just let me know, and I'll leave. I'm armed, and I don't wanna get scared and end up shooting someone." She listened, eyes going from the kitchen to the staircase and then to the street from the doorway. Every direction was silent. No floorboards creaked. No shuffles sounded. No whispers or so much as a breath found her in the space. She sighed before sliding her bag down to the floor and easing the door shut behind her. An instant relief was felt in dropping the weight. "Alright," she continued, reaching back and snapping the lock. "Gonna assume it's just me, so if you get shot its on you."

    She steadied herself and went into the kitchen, her aim tight. The room was long, but cramped, leading to a back door at the end. She approached it and looked to the yard behind before snapping the lock and pulling the blind. On her way around the corner from the kitchen, she looked up to the staircase with a sigh. The strain was felt in her legs just at the thought. She stepped back and took her bag in hand before checking the locks on the windows. She adjusted the curtains and headed back to the stairs, chucking her bag up to the top with an effort before starting on the first step. She listened once more after its landing. Nothing was heard. She winced, tightening her grip on the rail as the burn came. She looked up with determined eyes and forced herself on.

At the top of the stairs, she was met by a hallway. On the left was the bathroom and on the right was a closet followed by a bedroom sat further down. At the end sat a second bedroom, larger than the first. Each room was quiet, with their doors all left open, even the closet. She was quick to check each room one by one. Each proved easy to clear. Relaxing her aim, she headed back, took up her bag, and went down to the second bedroom at the far end. She set her things down over the bed and unzipped the top pocket of her pack to retrieve a small packet of tea light candles and matches from inside. She took one of each and put back the remainder. She lit her candle and set it over the bedside table, waving out the flame of the match. She checked the lock on the bedroom window before pulling the curtains and heading back to her bag.

From the side pocket, she took a spool of fishing line, a pair of wire cutters, and two thick nails. She cut a length of line and returned to the stairs. She set her gun aside, drew her hatchet, and etched the nails in at a slant, two inches above the floor, each to the opposite posts at the start of the stairs. After returning her blade to her belt, she tied the line tight across. Pulling herself back to her feet with strain, she walked slow back to the bedroom and closed the door. She sat down over the bed and untied her shoes, taking the left off without much effort. Her right was stubborn, however, causing her to swear at it under her breath. She kicked her heel to the frame of the bed and heard a scrape against the floor. The frame had moved, but only the middle portion. It sat slanted under the bed at the edge. After taking off the shoe, she hunched down on the floor to study the frame. It was formed by three long segments of slide-out wooden chests, all blended in seamlessly.

She seated herself back onto the bed and started to take off Allan's jacket, but decided against it, tracing her thumb over the collar and catching a lingering scent of his old cologne. She set her bag and rifle down to the floor and undid her belt to set it down alongside. She then took her pistol and set it over the table beside the candle. She lay down, resting her head over the pillow, and looked to the candle's flame as light faded further from the curtain of the window. She made a plea to the flame before closing her eyes.

•••

Her body was stiff in waking; sore and strained. She'd gotten a full night's sleep, proven in a look toward the light reaching through the curtain. Though it seemed to her as only a momentary rest of the eyes. She sat up, her muscles aching in the motion, and reached for her bag.

"A few minutes," she thought. "A few minutes, then I leave."

From her pack, she retrieved her map and a half-full bottle of water, her last. As her tired eyes adjusted, she held it to the light and sighed heavily, resting the bottle to her lap. Her mouth was dry; annoyingly so. She knew if she didn't drink something soon, she'd only feel worse, though she debated saving it longer. After some thought, she settled on a single sip, likely no more than a cap full. Guarding against temptation, she returned the bottle to her bag. She sat back and studied the map. Despite her best efforts to travel through shortcuts wherever possible, she'd barely reached a quarter mark of the journey.

She forced herself up to her feet, put on her shoes, and gathered her things before starting into the hall, easing her steps as her legs strained. The house was quiet. Nothing stirred apart from the morning outside. She looked to the wire set at the stairs, uninterrupted. She knelt down and untied it from the posts, winding it to a ball and returning it to her backpack.

As she zipped the pocket closed, a sudden noise startled her; the slamming of a door; the door to what sounded like a truck. She stood with a hold over her hip and listened for a moment. She heard distant chatter. And it grew louder by the second. She backed up quietly before making a dash back to the bedroom. She eased the door closed and headed to the bed frame. She slid the front chest over and took off her brother's jacket and her belt, first drawing her gun, before shoving her things across the floor to the back wall. She knelt down and started in, adjusting the chest back. A tense heat ran down her back as she realized she'd forgotten something; the candle. With her heart racing, she moved the side chest and darted out, taking the tea light from the nightstand. She returned, moving the chests back into place as evenly as she could manage. No light entered the space as she stiffened herself beneath the bed. A loud bang was heard from downstairs: the front door. An uneasy breath escaped her at the thought; the lock. The lock gave her away. She was sure of it. She held tight to her gun with eyes focused ahead. Another bang, louder, followed by several metallic clinks and a dull thud. They were in. She tried her best to quiet her unsteady breaths. Footsteps were heard from downstairs, followed by conversation. She listened close.

"You really think there's anything worth taking? Whole street looks like shit."

"There's always something. Especially when they lock the doors."

Vallerie was shaken by another loud bang downstairs, sounding alongside a splintering. A quiet moment passed. The voices continued.

"Huh. Doesn't sound like anyone's home."

"Yeah, that we heard. Watch your back."

"Man, you're so fucking paranoid."

Steady steps traveled beneath her. She lowered her ear to listen closer. In the motion, her necklace drug against the floorboard. She snatched it quickly in hand, holding to it tight. The steps were heard approaching the stairs. They continued up, creaking following their path. Vallerie slid her necklace into her shirt and placed her hand against the other, holding a firm grip over her gun. She locked her eyes forward in the darkness as the men closed in down the hall. The door creaked open. She swallowed hard with an eased breath. Steps echoed the room.

"Wow, they don't have shit."

"I told you it'd be a waste of time. The fuck would you wanna go to the sticks for?"

"We were told to spread out. Thought going where the others aren't would be smart. Fuck, I don't know, man. Get off my case."

Outside, another slam was heard; like the other.

"What was that?"

Steps traveled to the left.

"Oh, fuck. It ain't one of ours."

"Who is it?"

"Soldiers. Three guys."

The Bastion. At once, Vallerie's mind raced.

"Keep your aim tight. We'll ambush the fuckers."

Hurried steps approached downstairs. It wasn't long before they started upward. Vallerie was still and tense, her heart feeling as if it was about to sink to her stomach. As the steps reached the hall, a deafening gun fire was heard, lasting all of a few seconds. Two heavy thuds were heard on the floor, followed by faint gurgling. A set of steps started forward.

"Two more down," one voice said. He spit. "Have fun getting ass rammed by the big man down there."

"Hell Spawn," another laughed. "What a name."

"Yeah," said a third. "Just a bunch of bitches."

"We'll get rid of 'em. Plus these, that makes ten in the last week. Think Esther's gonna be mighty proud."

"Now all we gotta do is bag a deserter. Shit, man, he'd have a field day. You imagine what we'd get?"

"Think we're outta luck there. I heard B Group caught the Sabell kid yesterday."

"They did? Lucky bastards. That one took forever."

"Not that lucky. Lost a few guys. Kid put up one hell of a fight."

"How many?"

"Before I met with you guys this mornin', I heard…like four or five? Somewhere in there. Guy even had the nerve to burn a flag. They found a patch left in the grass."

"He'll pay for it when Es gets back."

Three, at least in this room. At once, Vallerie began thinking of an ambush. Nobody knew she was there. With ease, she could sneak out and take one by surprise. They wouldn't negotiate with a hostage situation, that much she could tell, but she was sure she could learn something before the inevitable. She couldn't let her presence, or her mission be known. The inevitable…

"Think we should search these guys?"

"Nah. Leave em. I don't want anything they touched anyway. Let's go unload then we'll head back."

Vallerie closed her eyes tight as a fire burned in her gut from the realization; it wouldn't work. Three are inside, yes, but how many are downstairs? How many are outside? And worse, unlike the woman at the lake, they had radios. She could hear the static, though it was too faint to make out much of the other ends' conversation. Even if she managed, she dreaded the result if just one word escaped to whoever was out there listening. Perhaps not the only move, but indeed the only smart move, was to stay put and wait. In time, after some further chatter, the men were heard leaving downstairs. Vallerie remained frozen in place. As the steps left the house, a metallic thud came from outside, followed by further chatter. The sound repeated as the men shouted loud.

"Go! Go!"

Their doors opened and quickly slammed shut. The vehicle sped off, the sound of the motor fading into the distance. She continued to lay still, listening. Nothing was heard but the morning doves outside. She reached ahead toward the corner of the front chest, her arm stiff and aching, and moved it aside, revealing the two men dead on the floor with blood spread around. She eased herself out from the bed, dragging her belongings behind her. She got up with an effort and put on the jacket and her belt before throwing her backpack and rifle over her shoulder. She kept her gun in hand. She started out to the hall.

    Reaching the stairs, she heard steps once more and quickly darted to the side wall, holding her pistol at the ready. As the seconds passed and further steps were heard, another sound came alongside: a strained wheeze. Another followed, and then another, and yet one more. She hurriedly moved into the closet, easing the door closed. She held the handle tight as one set of steps lumbered up the staircase.

    "They use the dead," she wondered. "Why? As a trap? To ward off more Hell Spawn?" She held her breath as the uneven steps drew closer. Another thought came to her. "Punishment. Possibly. They don't get a funeral or a burial. They feed the dead." She thought of Allan. Could this be their plan with him? It wasn't long after this thought that she decided against hiding. She was going to throw open the door and take down every corpse out there. As she started to turn the handle, however, a loud wheezing immediately changed her course. She kept the door shut tight. It made it up the stairs. She held her breath as the corpse shambled outside the door in the hall. "I could shoot it," she thought. "Close range, I could just open the door and land a clean head shot." It was an attractive option. And it might've been a smart one. "But the ammo. I only have so much…"

She could get herself out of this rather quickly with a few well-placed shots. She could take out the one outside and then use the stairs as a perfect vantage point for the others; wait for them to funnel in one at a time. It was what happened afterward that caused hesitation. The Bastion. She might need every bullet she had to get her brother back. And then there's the Hell Spawn. What if she ran into them? Perhaps she'd encounter another group as well. The ifs crossed her mind one after the other: the dead; other people; wild animals; too many variables to be worth the risk.

Slowly, she lowered her gun, clicked the safety, and holstered it to her belt, grimacing at the sound. The steps continued down the hall. She hadn't caught its attention. She closed her eyes with an eased breath. "I have to do this quietly," she thought. She took up her hatchet, facing the blade to the door. She listened. The corpse in the hall continued walking into the bedroom, wheezing faintly. The others were heard meandering downstairs, none approaching the staircase. She took a deep breath, readying herself. As her hand began to turn the handle, a second approach came to mind. She stopped and gave a glance down to her blade, barely visible in the crack of light through the doorframe. She shifted the handle, facing the blunt end to the door. She faced forward. The corpse was heard exiting the bedroom, starting back her way. Vallerie stood still and quiet, her heartbeat, while fast, was calmer than mere moments ago. "Maybe I can avoid them altogether." Another wheeze sounded, now outside the door. The stench of the corpse's breath made her wince. It stopped walking. "Come on. Come on, just a little further," she thought.

    The corpse continued on to the stairs, stopping once more just past the door. This was it. Vallerie raised her hatchet and threw open the door. As she exited, the corpse turned to face her. Within a second of meeting its white, glazed-over eyes, she pulled back her arm and struck hard, slamming the blunt of her blade into the corpse's mouth. It tumbled down the stairs, teeth and blood following its way. She ran fast to the end bedroom as quickened steps sounded from downstairs. Once inside, she slammed the door shut and snapped the lock. She looked to a lounge chair in the corner, returned her blade to her belt, and dragged it in front of the door, wedging it to the handle. Wheezing was heard alongside unnerving steps down the hall. She went to the window. She threw the curtains, snapped the lock, and shoved it open. Looking out the screen, she saw an awning beneath. An impact was heard against the door.

    She slid her backpack and rifle down to the floor and shoved up the screen pane. Another impact was heard, immediately breaking the lock and moving the chair. Her heart raced as she took up her pack and rifle and shoved them out the window. They slid down the awning and dropped to the ground beneath. She started her climb through as the chair was heard sliding across the floor. She looked back to see the remaining bodies shuffle inside, wheezing and drooling as they drew near. She forced her torso out the window, propping herself on the awning as she continued pulling through. As her legs began their exit through the window, she felt her foot held back, an aggressive gurgling heard from the room. She pulled forward and kicked hard, feeling something impact against her shoe. She kicked again and found herself free of the grasp. With a desperate groan of strength, she freed herself from the window and attempted to adjust her posture for a safe balance. She was unable to keep hold, however, as she slid fast down the awning. She shrieked in the fall.

She attempted to crouch herself in the drop and landed with her hands and feet pressed forward into the grass. Her eyes having shut as she braced herself for a broken ankle at the very least, as she felt the softness of the grass, she looked out with relief, stunned to find that she'd landed safely. In a hurry, she checked her foot, thinking the worst of what had grabbed her. She found no punctures or blood over her shoe. She sighed in relief before stumbling to her feet, grabbing her things, and strapping them over her shoulder. She looked up to the window as she caught her breath. The dead didn't look out after her, but she could hear them, their otherworldly breaths and echoed footsteps continuing from inside. She backed up a few steps before turning fast and forcing herself to a jog down the street. Her legs still burned, yet she continued despite the pain, grimacing in every step.

—**Allan**—

The uniformed man approached the window with his hands folded behind his back, looking out to the field below. Allan sat in the corner, handcuffed with bruises over his face. He observed the man's stance before looking to the two others stood at each end of the room, silent with pistols drawn in hand. Their sight was locked onto him, steady and cold. The soldier at the window started. Allan's attention went to him.

"You know my daughter used to love baseball," he paused. "You know what it's like … to know you'll never be able to show your kid something like that again? Never…to never have them by your side again?"

He looked to the guards before returning to the man.

"Actually, yeah."

"That so? Who?"

"My sister. Who I can't keep safe right now... because of you guys."

The man scoffed, smirking as he turned. He raised his brows.

"You could've really kept her safe; and my Kaylee; by fighting."

Allan looked sternly to the soldier.

"What… exactly… would I have done? What possible difference would I have made?" The soldier was unmoved. "Even if I chose to risk my life for millions of people that I don't know, during the end of the world, leaving her alone in a hospital. Huh? Lay it out for me."

"Seems I've touched a nerve."

"There's a school shooting survivor out there right now, all alone with the dead; a kid that watched two people she loved die in front of her; alone with the dead. All because some short sighted idiots think one extra guy could've saved the fucking country. Yeah, you've touched a nerve. And you two, guns out like you're action heroes—"

"Careful, kid—", one of the men said.

Allan stared onto him, his eyes never wavering as he leaned in with a whisper.

"You're not."

The man at the window sighed before sitting down in the chair alongside. He folded his hands and looked on Allan, being the next met with his glare. The others stood by, unwavering in their guard.

"History happen to be among the classes you failed? Many situations would've turned out quite different had it not been for that one person deciding to act."

Allan scoffed, squinting at the remark.

"That's nowhere near this scale."

"So…you're in the camp that believes it was hopeless then. Are you really that cynical?"

"Yes."

"Have you thought that perhaps that kind of outlook might've added to our loss? At all?"

"When shit hit the fan, I didn't see many people caring for their fellow Americans… Did you? Didn't see it much growing up either."

"In foster care and on the streets."

"Yeah. Tends to make one grow up pretty fast," Allan sneered. "Tell me, oh holy patriot, have you thought that perhaps we needed a wakeup call? Or are you in the camp that just had too much hope in the masses?"

"Hundreds of millions of lives dead? No, no, I can't say I have thought that. No matter how in disarray things have been, I never thought anything even close to that."

"I don't recall saying they deserved to die. I said a wakeup call; a reset to get things moving in the right direction again. That's what we needed, and that's what we got. We know our mortality now. We know what not to do next time."

The man was silent.

"Look," he sighed. "About your daughter, nobody should ever have to go through that. Same for whatever loss anyone else had too. But I, individually, didn't kill those people. Doing what you're doing here, taking people away from their loved ones…over an inevitable loss, there is nothing right in that. And nothing you pull outta your ass is gonna change that."

The room fell silent for a while, both men eyeing each other coldly, the atmosphere between them tense. In time, the soldier drew a breath and went on.

"There was…a situation…not too long ago. A few of us went out to scavenge for supplies. Three men. A group of the undead came and all three of them were forced to take shelter in a nearby building. They got inside and barricaded the door, but it took two of them just to keep it shut and the dead at bay. The third went upstairs to the roof, likely looking for an exit. On top, he found several planks of wood. Presumably, there was construction planned that never came to be, so the materials were left there. Each plank was long enough to reach across to the neighboring building. It was a sure escape, or at least it could've been, had it not been for the two other corpses milling about; survivors that chose suicide, evidenced by the leftover pills.

"We later sent out a search party, cleared the dead, and found two of the men half eaten inside. The third had fallen into the alley between the buildings and broke his neck. He'd managed to move one of the planks a whole five inches to the roof's edge before, we assume, he got rushed and simply lost his balance." He stood and went once more to the window. Allan's attention never left him. "In that one instance, that one of hundreds or even thousands that took place, one man very much could've made a difference. Especially one of your height and build. But instead, you avoided any sense of greater responsibility. As did the others. And now, in a few days, you'll just be another execution that we all watch down in that very field, as will the others; another of the first few blocks to rebuilding America, and doing it right, without those…hiccups that you mentioned."

Allan nodded to himself before firing back. "Is torturing Vallerie one of those building blocks too? Do you worry at all about what you're doing to her?"

"Those bombs…given the academic record between you two, those weren't yours, were they? Or the idea to hide guns in a house that already looked like it'd been torn upside down? High school dropouts always causing brawls don't usually end up with that kind of creativity." He turned to face Allan's ever more aggressive eye. "You're right about what you'd said earlier; how circumstances like that can force one to grow up fast. Your sister has. Personally, I think you'd only hold her back. So, no. I'm not worried at all."

Allan looked down to his restrained hands sitting clasped over his lap. He paused, then scoffed before looking up to the man as he watched curiously. "You should be."

"Why's that? Seems she's plenty capable to me."

"The question isn't why. It's when."

"So…when…then should I be worried about her?"

The others looked to the soldier with concern as Allan leaned in with a smile.

"When she's standing over you with a hatchet…as you beg for your life."

"Meaning I should go ahead and bring her in too then?"

"You could try. But like you said—"

The Bastion soldier stepped forward, listening at full attention.

"—she's plenty capable."

—Vallerie—

Its hand twitched as she stepped over the body. She reached the foot of the bed and was silent as she read the writing over the wall; penned by blood.

"God, please show me mercy. For that was my only intention on them," the back wall read.

On the bed, two small bodies lay still and decomposed, each with the tops of their heads blown apart, the remnants splayed out over the pillows and the headboard. From what she could tell, the pair were girls, possibly in their early teens.

She closed her eyes, returning her hatchet to her belt, and knelt down, adjusting her knees over the wooden floor with her hands clasped over the foot of the bed. She breathed deeply, exhaled steadily, and began praying, speaking quietly. The slain corpse was still on the floor behind her, blood continuing from the gaping opening in its neck. Its hand continued an occasional twitch between fingers.

"May my spoken word solidify this message and its intent," she continued. "To the fallen that rest before me, may you indeed…be at rest," she paused, shuddering a breath. "I'm sorry for what happened to you. Blessed be."

She opened her eyes and stood, refusing to look further on them. She turned, starting back toward the door, stopping briefly beside the body on the floor. She looked down to the twice-deceased man, observing the kitchen knife plunged into his chest, and slammed her foot down over the handle. A dampened impact was heard as the blade was driven deeper. Taking leave again by the door, she looked to the coat rack on the wall, snatched the ring of keys from the end hook, and left out from the room.

Outside, she walked across the lawn to the rusted four door parked at the curb. She unlocked the door, tossed her things to the back seat, and got in. After some tries, the engine started. She pulled on the seat belt and checked the meters. She had about a quarter of a tank. She sighed and pulled out into the street, eventually exiting the suburb onto a long stretch of road lined by forest and power lines. On her way, the cloud cover overhead thickened. She hadn't thought much of it before, but as the tone changed from its earlier white to an ever-deepening gray, a dread came to mind. She distracted herself in looking to the CD player. Ejecting the tray, she was met by a church record of some sort. She didn't bother reading the label, immediately dragging it in hand, rolling down the window, and tossing it hard off into the grass. She closed the tray and returned her focus over the road with a sigh.

Continuing down the road, in time, no remnant of the town behind remained; the path ahead seeming hauntingly empty. The wind tossed her hair as the clouds above grew darker. She neared a sort of clearing ahead on the left. At first, it went ignored, though a distant sound soon grabbed her attention. Her eye went to the clearing as she came to a stop. She turned off the engine, listening closely. The sound came again, shrill and desperate. She continued watching the space. It was an entryway to a gated trail, marked by sand. Many a thought crossed her mind as she tried to figure out the origin of the sound, though nothing seemed a definite fit. Until it came again, louder and clearer.

In seconds, she was out from the car, starting off to the gate, first at a steady walk, and eventually to a jog down the trail. In hearing the noise again, she shot off to a patch of brush. Ahead, through the tall grass and ferns, she saw two corpses approaching the culprit of the heart-wrenching sounds. She drew her blade and ran forward, driving it through the side of one body's throat and holding its head in her opposite hand. As she forced the blade deeper, the corpse fell fast, landing heavy in the grass without motion or sound. The other turned to face her. She was quick to deliver a kick to its ankle. As it fell to its knees, she slammed the blunt of her blade over its head, knocking it further down as it tried in vain to reach on her. She turned to the blade's edge and delivered the final blow.

Further off, hunched over in the brush, she looked to the frightened life sitting backed against the trunk of a pine. Her eyes softened at once as she holstered her weapon and knelt down in the grass.

"Oh… Not great timing, guys. Really, really, not great timing," she said, looking to the whimpering figure. Ahead, quivering against the tree, was a young dog: a male black lab, emaciated and fearful. It looked to her desperately.

For a moment, she sat quietly, her mind racing. The canine whimpered just before a distant thunder. The pup curled further against the tree as Vallerie looked to the sky, startled. She sighed, closing her eyes tight, and swore to herself. Hearing its whimper continue, she looked back to the lab. As their eyes met beneath the ever-darkening sky, the decision was made.

"Hey," she called, gingerly extending her hand. "You're okay. You're okay, buddy. Come on."

The dog, appearing to her as little more than a few years old, raised its paw and whimpered again.

"That's right. It's okay, sweetie. Come on."

The dog eased itself up as another thunder came.

"Come on, buddy. Before it rains. You're okay."

The dog, after first looking off to the distance, turned and came slowly to her. A faint drizzle began. As the water hit the pup, it quickened its pace, stopping at her hand.

Vallerie didn't move, sitting still with only a slight tilt of her palm. "I know. I know, baby, but it's okay."

He sniffed her and raised a paw. He whimpered once more in a still moment before starting closer, ever cautious in his step.

"There you go." With delicate motion, Vallerie eased her palm beneath his chin. He didn't move away, instead resting against her with urgent eyes as the rain fell harder. "Come on, buddy. Come on, you can trust me."

A loud crash of thunder startled them both. As she looked down from her hurried gaze to the sky, the dog sat huddled against her. She rested her hand over his head. He didn't fight her, only looking upward quietly. She felt an overwhelming sadness in looking to his eyes. It was clear to her that this was no wild animal. "What happened to you, little dude? Huh?" She stroked the pup's head softly. "You gonna be cool coming with me? Huh?" The lab gave a faint whine in response as she grazed further. "Okay. Come on."

She rested both arms around the pooch. It didn't fight, seeming to know her intention. With an effort, it wasn't long before she stood up, carrying the frightened stray in hand back to the car. Its tail began a slight wag as it continued a whine in her arms. She held him close against her chest, trying her best to shield him from the rain. "I know. I know it's scary. I know. Here."

She reached out and eased the pup into the back seat without hassle. She closed the door, then got in the driver's seat. With the doors closed to a lock and the windows rolled up, she looked back to her newfound friend, hunched over the middle compartment and licking at her arm. She smiled. "Definitely not wild." She gave the pup a scratch and examined his belly.

At a glance, and from what she'd felt in carrying him, though he was definitely skinny, it seemed she'd found him before things could've gotten worse. She ran a slow hand over him before turning back in her seat and going to her bag. From inside, she pulled a small rag and turned back, easing her hand. "Let's dry you off a bit, huh?"

Tenderly, the pup lapped at her arm as she ran the rag over him. He wasn't soaked, but she'd rather him not stay wet with the weather cooling off. "Good boy. All done." She turned back, set the rag over her bag in the other seat, and looked to the road with a sigh before starting the engine. She pulled down her seatbelt and rested her hands over the wheel. "Well, buddy, gotta tell ya, I don't really know what I'm doing here," she paused, looking to the canine in the mirror. "But I'll try my best." Now dry and safe from harm, the pup began to relax, starting a cheerful pant in the back seat. Vallerie smiled. "Alright, buddy. Let's go." The pup laid down as she began down the road.

•••

    The wipers swayed back and forth as the rain pelted the windshield. The road ahead, though she knew it to lead into the next town, seemed to stretch on forever. Every so often she looked to the mirror. The dog remained at rest, eyeing her calmly.

    "You know, the highways being blocked felt like some really shit luck at first, but…silver linings." She watched the pup as he blinked slowly. Her focus returned to the road ahead. "Allan's gonna love you." She eyed the meters and sighed, adjusting her hands over the wheel. "So, what's your name? You have one?"

    She looked once more to the mirror. The pup groaned softly.

    "Okay. I'll take that as a no," she laughed. "Huh. We'll have to change that. You'll have to be patient though, okay? I wanna pick a good one." He rested his chin down over the seat and closed his eyes. "Good boy. Get some sleep." She looked down to the map set on the center console. "Just gotta find some more gas and it should be an easy trip from there."

    She looked back to the road. The rain continued with the occasional thunder, followed by a flash of lightning in the distance. In time, she reached the town. It appeared as many others she'd passed thus far: empty. Though she traveled south, the rural sights continued long past where she'd expected them to end. She pulled slowly through the streets, looking to her map on her way. With a sigh, she set it aside and began into a suburb. Down the street, several cars were seen parked in place. Largely, the street seemed untouched. She parked at a distance and killed the engine. Keeping her sight to the road, she pulled her bag from the other seat and rifled through the pockets. From the very bottom, she fished out a small pack of razors and returned the bag to the seat.

    After a moment of looking further on the scene, she pulled her gun and clicked the safety off. She looked back to the pup, lain at rest with warm eyes toward her. "I'll be back, okay?" She turned back, pulled her keys, and started out from the car with a lock of the doors. Rushing the keys and the pack of blades to her pocket, she hurried a tight aim over her gun, standing still with full attention over the street. Nothing stirred. She looked to the doors of several homes and saw that they all had a flyer hung on them. With cautious eye, she made her way to the nearest one, quietly starting up the porch, and began reading. It was an evacuation notice. With an eased breath, she took hold of the doorknob and slowly turned. It opened with ease.

She hurried inside and closed the door behind her while keeping her sight to the living room. She listened for a time before giving three loud knocks against the wall. "If anyone's here, I'm not here to hurt you," she called. "I need gas. A tank. A length of hose. That's it," she paused, listening and hearing no response or stirring about the home. "I'm armed. So…if anyone's here and you don't feel like coming out, just don't sneak up on me, okay? Like I said, I'm not here to hurt you." Again, nothing was heard.

Still holding tight to her gun, she began searching about the living room, rifling through drawers and cabinets and finding nothing but junk and old remotes. She went next to the kitchen, searching the same and finding nothing, not even a scrap of food left behind. She turned her attention to the hallway, standing long and dim, the light from the living room windows barely reaching halfway. She adjusted her aim on her pistol, squinting to see as her heart beat faster. She was slow in her steps, acknowledging the wooden floors.

As she neared the corner, something startled her, causing her to fire. With the flash and the impact of the bullet into the wall, she turned fast round the corner. Nothing appeared down the hall. Though she still squinted to see, the narrow space housed only three rooms, all with their doors closed. Shaken, she pondered for a moment before starting forward.

Perhaps it was the dimness of the space

playing tricks on her. Perhaps it was the doing of all the stress and tiredness she's endured. Perhaps it was just a case of a fast movement and a blink looking like something out of the corner of her sight, though she knew she'd seen something. With her breaths coming heavily, she hurried toward the first door on the left and threw it open, quickly clearing the room and starting to the next on the right, and then to the last at the end with an aggressive kick to the door. Nothing. Relieved, she lowered her gun and began searching about the rooms. It wasn't long before she found what she'd been after, a ring of keys, each with crudely written labels.

    Leaving from the house, she went fast to the garage and unlocked the door at its side. The space, lit by a set of windows at the back, was empty, occupied only by benches full of junk and old kids' toys. She rummaged through the belongings, eventually coming across the very items she'd sought: a length of thin plastic tubing and a couple empty gas containers, all set in a box labeled for recycling. She smiled in reading the label before taking the items out and laying the hose over the floor. She set her gun aside and pulled a razor from the pack before returning it to her pocket and starting on the plastic. She cut two lengths, took a dirtied rag from a bench, gathered her things, and left to the car in the driveway.

    Outside, the rain continued, beginning to fall harder as the air cooled. She hurried to the gas tank, set her things down before it, and started. She opened one of the cans and ran one length of the tube from its opening up into the car's tank. She then ran the end of the second inside and began sealing the open space with the rag. Then, taking up the loose tubing, she blew air through its end. In no time at all, gas was heard filling the can. She took her mouth away from the plastic to listen and smiled with a laugh before continuing with another breath. It wasn't long before she had a mostly full can. She sealed it off and went back to her car, filling her tank before putting her gatherings into the trunk as her pup was heard whining from the back seat. She pulled her keys, unlocked the door, and got inside, taking up the rag from the other seat and running it fast over her as the pup lapped at her arm. "Hey, sweetheart. Told ya I'd be back." She sighed tossed the rag, pulled on her seatbelt, and started the engine before looking to the map once more. She marked her next stop and left down the street.

•••

Looking with sharp eye through the fog of the rain, she spotted her destination ahead on the left; the police station.

"There we go." She pulled over and turned off the engine. The rain continued, though lighter now. She undid her seatbelt and looked back to her friend, laying asleep. She reached back and ran a pet down his back before taking the keys and exiting the car. "I'll be quick, little dude." She pressed down the locks and closed the door, turning toward the station. She stood still, listening for a moment as she pulled her gun from its holster. Things seemed quiet. Starting forward, she made her way up the steps to the doors. She tested the handle. To her surprise, the doors were unlocked. She stepped inside with caution, easing the door shut behind her as she kept her aim tight on her gun. Ahead in the small room sat a reception desk between two hallways; one to each side. She stopped just before the desk, standing behind the walls to each hall.

"Hello?" she called. A disturbance was heard distant down the left hall. She held her aim and darted down the way, rounding the corner and stopping in seeing a man heading into the room on the right. "Stop, or I shoot!" Her tone was fierce.

The man, holding a gun of his own, stopped in place. His back faced her. He was tall, standing with ragged clothes and a shaved head, riddled with marks.

She eyed him, watching his hands closely. "Drop it," she said.

The man replied, his voice a hoarse rasp. "Okay. Just…please don't shoot me. I'm…I'm just trying to survive."

He sounded clearly shaken. Vallerie remained firm in her stance. "Drop the gun, kick it over to me, and I give my word I won't hurt you."

He clicked the safety, let go of the pistol, and

slid it back to her with the heel of his boot.

She was fast to grab it from the floor and holster it at her side. "Thanks."

"I ... I have your word?"

"Yeah. Turn around."

With hesitation, the man turned to face her. An uneven beard surrounded several marks over his face. His eyes were fearful in facing her, though his expression soon shifted to one of shock. She studied him for a moment. She was unable to tell about the marks: perhaps they were scars, perhaps they were a condition of some sort. She held tight in her aim.

"Okay. Here's the deal. I have somewhere to be, and I need gas. That's the only reason I'm here. Not to hurt you. Not to hurt anyone. Just need to know if there's any around and I'll be on my way."

The man hesitated. "I ... I saw some cans, yeah, but ... they're behind a gate. It's locked."

"Padlock?"

"Yeah."

"Show me where. But keep your distance. Like I said, I'm not out to hurt anyone. But if you give me a reason to, I will."

The man shuddered a breath and nodded. "Before I do ... what, um ... what happens to me after?"

"Nothing. I take what I need and go. I'll leave your gun in the street for you once I feel safe."

"Do ... do you maybe have any room to spare?"

She stood silently.

The man continued. "I've been on my own for a while. And it's … it's honestly getting really hard. I don't want any food or nothing. I just… I'd rather not travel alone. If … if you need help where you're going or even if I only tag along for a while. Just some company." The man sighed. "And not…like that. Just…just traveling company."

Vallerie pondered for a moment before replying. "Show me where the gas is. And I'll think about it."

He nodded, gesturing to the room he'd just left. "Right down here."

"After you." Vallerie gestured her gun toward the room. The man turned and went inside. She followed a few feet behind, her aim remaining tight. Her arms began to tire, but she never let them rest. She surveyed the room as the stranger started ahead, rounding the corner. It was an office cubical with a narrow path between the rows of walled-in desks. At the end sat a caged door, padlocked as the man had said. As they approached it, she looked to find very little inside. Three canisters of gasoline sat on a shelf. Various boxes were housed inside as well, labeled by packing stickers; ordered-in supplies at her best guess. The man stopped before the gate.

"What, um… What do you want me to do?"

Across his shoulder, a set of pins on a keyring was thrown, landing at his feet.

"I'll guide you through it. That's my last set,

so go easy."

Without argument, he took up the ring and began on the lock, following her instruction. Though he soon found himself stuck. "I'm feeling for it, but I'm ... I'm not sure I'm doing it right."

"You'll get it. Sometimes it takes a few tries. Just keep at it."

As the stranger continued with the lock, Vallerie stepped back to a nearby desk. With her eyes tight on the man, she slowly opened a drawer before glancing back at its contents. Inside were several notebooks, pens, a stapler, and two pairs of handcuffs. She reached back while returning her sight to the stranger, still fiddling with the gate.

"There. I think I've got it. Yup."

The lock clicked. He pulled it from its latch and opened the gate.

"Take two cans and walk them back. Don't face me. I'll tell you when you can set them down."

"Okay."

He stepped back toward her as she stood still, her aim to his head.

"Stop. Set 'em down." The swish of gas was heard in the cans' landing over the carpet. The man stood up, keeping his palms open at his side. "Good. Now go back to the gate. I need one of those boxes." The man nodded and started forward. After his second step, he groaned in feeling a blow to the back of his leg and fell to his knees. Vallerie pulled his arms back and locked the cuffs over his wrists. He went to look back but felt a force over his arms. He winced from the pain. "Eyes forward. Stay right there."

The man scoffed. "You ain't kiddin' around."

Vallerie took one can and backed up toward the door, setting it at the entrance whilst holding her aim in her opposite hand. She started back to grab the second. "You know, for transparency's sake I'd like to point out what just happened here, if you don't mind."

Vallerie took the can in hand and stood, eyeing him curiously as he looked back to her. "What?"

"I'm a man in my thirties. Don't take offense here, because you're no imp or nothing, but I'm guessing I'm about twice your size. You might've gotten the jump, but if I wanted to resist, there's no way you would've gotten those on me. You know that, right?"

Vallerie walked back the second can of gas and set it at the door.

"You're Vallerie, right?" the man continued, seated in place. "That was national news, you and your brother."

She watched him with an unwavering stare. "Valuable context."

"It is."

"So what's your point? I'm in a hurry."

He paused, looking back to the contents of the cage.

"The Bastion."

Vallerie squinted in her stare.

"I saw the wanted posters," he continued, looking back to her with concern in his sight. "That's where you're going right? To get him back?"

A quiet moment passed. Vallerie's voice was gentle but anxious as her emotions took over. "Yes."

"I can help. I can—"

"Why?"

"Because you're a kid that's been through hell; going through more…on your own, and I'd rather that not be on my conscience when I could've done something to help."

"But…why else? I can't offer you anything. I'm low on food, I'm not set up anywhere."

"Like I said … I just don't wanna be alone."

Vallerie lowered her gun.

"That's it. No secrets. No hidden agendas. You don't wanna go after them on your own. You can trust me."

She looked on him quietly, mulling over her next steps.

"Please."

"What's your name?"

"Daniel. Daniel Evens."

"Well, Daniel, I'm half and half on this one, but…truth be told I'm not in any position to turn down help, so—"

The man smiled. "I get it. Tell you what… I so much as breathe the wrong way, and you have my permission to put a bullet between my eyes."

"That's quite a bargain." She paused. "You sure on that? Because if you do anything—"

"I'd deserve it."

She eased a breath in looking toward the door. "Mind helping me with those cans?"

"Do you one better. I'll take both and come right back for the third."

She nodded, starting forward while pulling a key from her jacket pocket. "Sorry about these," she said, undoing the cuffs.

He rubbed his wrists, looking up to her as she stepped back. "Never apologize for being safe."

...

The two started out from the room, Daniel leading the way. Despite his offer, Vallerie carried one of the cans herself while he walked with the remaining two. She still held to her pistol in the other.

"Just so you know, I have a dog."

"Fine by me. But just so you know, dogs don't usually like me, so I hope that isn't a big trust gauge."

"Well, I just got him, so I'm not even sure how he'll react to me when I come back."

"You found a pet in the end of the world?"

"I was driving by and heard him crying. If I hadn't gotten there in time, the dead would've got him."

Daniel gave a nod.

"I see. Ever have any pets?"

"I'd run into a stray or two, but never any that stayed. And never any dogs."

"Must be exciting."

"Yeah, but…also terrifying," she sighed.

"Have any names in mind?"

"Still working on it." They reached the entrance. Vallerie stopped. "Did you…by chance see an evidence locker? Or something like one?"

"Yeah. Actually, that's where I got the gun."

"Was there anything else?"

"Far as weapons, no, not anything I'd take. Couple small camping knives. A ring of brass knuckles. That's about it."

"Brass knuckles?"

"Yeah. Just…standard. Exactly what you think they'd look like. I guess they'd be worth taking if you want, but I wouldn't advise fist fighting those things."

"Where?"

"Down the right. You really want those?"

"I don't plan on getting stuck like that, but if I'm ever cornered, they…might be useful, yeah."

Daniel smirked, setting the cans on the floor. "Well then, follow me."

•••

Vallerie started down the steps, watching Daniel closely as her hold remained tight on her gun. As her and Daniel descended, her dog looked on silently from inside the car.

"I don't know if I should take that as a bad sign or what," Daniel said.

"Oh boy. Um, just wait here a sec. It's better if I get in first. Here, when I hold him, put these in the trunk, then get in. But be quick about it."

"Got it."

Vallerie walked forward and unlocked the door. The pup began wagging his tail with a low whine. She set the gun on the dash, and removed her jacket, setting it on the center console.

"Hey, buddy. We've got some company, so be chill, okay?" She unzipped her fleece and took it off, setting it gently around him in the backseat. "There you go. Here, just stay still for a bit." She closed the door, and hunched over toward her pooch, stroking his back while talking in a soft voice. Outside, Daniel hurried down the stairs and opened the trunk, setting the cans inside. The pup whined anxiously, turning toward the back window. "It's okay. It's okay, sweetie. Eyes on me. That's it."

Daniel closed the trunk and entered the passenger side, closing the door. The dog backed behind the driver's seat, wriggling free of Vallerie's hand and whining.

"Oh, baby, it's okay. You're okay."

"You're safe, little guy. You're good."

"Well, we're inside, so he'll have to get used to it."

With Daniel's eyes to her pup, Vallerie eased

back into her seat while taking back her gun, her sight never leaving him. Gradually, he turned, relaxing while pulling on his seatbelt.

"He's looking pretty rough."

"Yeah, that's how I found him. We'll have to stop somewhere so I can try to feed him. Doubt he'd eat right now."

"What do you have? Hopefully not a chocolate bar or something."

Vallerie scoffed. "No. I've actually got a couple cans of dog food. It was meant for me and it's actually for seniors, but…not many options."

"That isn't all your own food, is it?"

"No, no, I've got some other stuff. But definitely not much."

"Wherever we stop, I think I'll look around and see what I can find. That way you can be with him."

She looked to him, unsure of the comment. "Thanks."

He nodded before observing the road. Vallerie followed suit and locked the doors before retrieving her map from beneath Allan's leather.

"So, where we going?"

She looked over the map for a moment, setting her gun in the door's pocket before starting the engine.

"Fort Wayne."

—**Allan**—

He landed on his shoulder, a shock overtaking him as he looked to the concrete floor. He groaned to himself as the gate shut behind him, the snap of a lock sounding at its end. A wetness was felt down his nose as blood began to drip onto the floor.

"If it wasn't for our orders, you'd be going through worse," a deep voice called.

He sat up and looked back to find he'd been locked in a cell. He didn't know its location or what the room might've been before. A muscular soldier stood behind the bars, clean shaven with hair buzzed at the sides. He snickered at the man.

"Talk about a stereotype."

"Says the punk in ripped jeans and a wife beater."

Allan sensed it in the man's reply, his tone impatient and sharp. If given the chance, he'd walk right in and beat him senseless; utterly convinced of his mission. He sighed, standing to his feet, and faced him through the bars. "You're not going to convince me. In fact, you're better off staying quiet."

Allan looked on his anger, seeing himself targeted by his worn eyes. He turned from the bars and sat at the back wall, feeling a soreness rise in his arm. He faced the man again and gestured to him.

"Know what? You're right. Rational discussion was shunned years ago anyway," he paused, cocking his head with a smile. "Despite our, you know, first amendment."

The man nodded, turning away from the gate. He took a folding chair from its rest against the wall, opened it, and sat facing the bars. He pulled a small notebook from his uniform pocket, along with a pen, and gave a final stare before beginning to write.

He studied the man for a time before speaking. "I remind you to work out the kinks?"

"No kinks to work out. Just doing crossword puzzles to kill the time."

Allan squinted. He couldn't rationalize it, how they could be so laid back about it. Doing crosswords before killing two kids? It enraged him. He kept his eyes on the man behind the bars.

"I just need a minute's worth," he thought, resting his hand over the lining of his jeans at the hip. "You can't sit there forever. Just give me a window."

The soldier continued on in his notepad, the scribbling of his pen the only sound to fill the silence.

Allan looked to the end of the gate, held shut by a padlock, large and heavy, but still a simple padlock. The longer he looked on it, the more he wanted to smile, the more he wanted to laugh. How ill-equipped and naive they were. He forced it back and kept watching the man, sitting with himself in complete seriousness. He pondered. Just one small window.

—**Vallerie**—

Her eyes were gentle in her kneeling over the floor.

She looked to the pup, approaching slowly.

"You've got it, buddy. Come on." Before long, he came up and began eating from the plate. She sat back on her knees and smiled, speaking softly. "Good boy. I know it's not a lot, but we need to ration it out," she sighed. "And it's definitely been a while since you had anything in there…"

As the pup continued picking away at the food, she wrapped a rubber band around the closed can, sealed by paper towel. "Not sure how long this'll keep for, buddy. Let's just go on hope, okay?" She sat with him in the bedroom, the door closed and Daniel having gone to scavenge.

Gradually, he finished and made his way to the small bowl of water, the last of some rain she'd collected on the way. "I tried filtering it for a while. Hope it doesn't taste too bad." He took several laps and looked to her before delicately approaching. "Hey," she said, sitting still. "You feeling better now?" She extended her hand beneath the pup's chin. He rested into her palm. "I think it's time you had a name. Now I think I've got a good one, but I'll let you be the judge, okay? How about… Bullet? That sound good?" He looked on her with a gentle sway of the tail, resting further into her hand. She gave him a scratch and smiled brightly. "Bullet then." He gave her a brief lick. Her heart melted at once. "I like you too, little dude."

She got to her feet, taking the remainder of the food in hand, and went over to her bag and placed it inside. Before zipping it closed, she noticed an item she'd forgotten was there, never having moved. She took it from the pocket, and, in the following moment, a racing began in her chest. Quickly, she snapped her eyes closed and forced herself back to her feet, away from the thought. She looked over with her eyes heavy and gestured to her pup. "What say you, little dude? Purple your color?" Bullet sat with a warm eye toward her. She approached with the collar in hand. He began wagging his tail once more, sitting patiently. "Well, you're not running away," she sniffed. "That's good."

Gently, she wrapped the collar up around the pup and adjusted it just enough. He didn't resist. She smiled, stroking his back. "Good boy. Not your first rodeo, huh?" Bullet began an excited pant. His front paws began a tap on the floor. "What? Well, what's up?" Vallerie asked with cheer. "Oh, I see. You remember the *W* word, don't you? Well, sorry, buddy, but it may be a while before we take one of those." Bullet whined, dancing further, and, for the first time, spoke his mind fully, an excited bark. "Hey, you found your voice! I know. I know, but we can't right now. Gotta lay low for the night, okay?" She affectionately rubbed his neck, the collar jangling along her motion. A spaced-apart set of knocks came at the front door. Bullet looked, sitting quiet and still. "It's okay, buddy. Just stay here." Vallerie stood, pulling her gun, and went to the bedroom door. "I really hope we can trust him…"

She gave a glance to Bullet before leaving into the hall and closing the door behind her. She made her way to the front and looked through the peep hole to find Daniel standing with a hefty duffle bag. She undid the lock and opened it.

"T'was a good hunt," he said with a smile.

"That's not full, is it?" she asked, stepping aside and ushering him in.

"To the brim."

As he hurried in and set the bag over the floor, Vallerie kept her eye to the outside as she closed the door locked and checked the already drawn curtains. She looked back to Daniel unzipping the bag.

"Several houses, all untouched. Soup, canned pasta, dry goods, even some bottled water."

She looked on him with excitement. She'd been rationing only for a few days now, but it felt like a lifetime since she'd had a proper meal. She could see Daniel felt the same.

"Anything for him?"

"Five cans. The good shit too; high protein, that kinda thing."

"Thank you. Seriously."

"Just trying to help."

"Well, you definitely earned first pick at the stuff."

"Nah. You're younger. You need more than

me. Have at it."

"Well, you found it. And you're taller and bigger, so you need more."

"Vallerie, I don't know if we're quite on joking terms yet, but…if you don't start grabbing cans, then I'm gonna pelt one right at your dome."

She snickered.

"Fine. But don't get mad if I pick the good stuff. No take backs."

"Knock yourself out. There's some pots and a can opener in there too."

She knelt down to look through the bag. She plucked two cans of ravioli and a box of crackers from the pile. She held them up to Daniel's sight.

He scoffed. "All yours, kid. Never been a fan of ravioli."

"What? But that's like the quintessential shit. You think canned pasta, you think ravioli."

"I usually think rings and franks."

"Well, more for me then." She took her food and went into the kitchen.

Daniel eased down to a seat on the couch and sighed.

"Lot of weight?"

"Just a bit. Would've been worse if the rain didn't let up."

"Next time just come get me and I'll help."

Daniel looked to the kitchen and smiled to himself. He heard Bullet whine from the other room.

"Nothing for him yet?"

"No, he just ate. From the looks of it, he's been out there a lot longer than me, so he can't have too much just yet. I don't want him getting sick." With an excited pace, she shook the can out into a pot. She went to turn the knob on the stove, failing to realize until the second try. "Goddamnit…"

"Yeah, I was waiting for that," Daniel laughed.

"Guess I'm eating it cold."

Irritated, she scraped the food out onto a plate and started searching cupboards, pulling seasonings out and slamming the doors. Daniel listened, his smile fading. He hunched over with folded hands.

"So what's the plan after Fort Wayne?" he asked.

Vallerie, after a final dash of salt, crumbled some crackers overtop, took her plate and a fork, and left back to the living room.

"Not sure," she started between bites. "My brother and I, we started talking about how we could restart things. Mostly just daydreaming, but…possible. What with the world being over and whatnot, who's to say we can't?"

"That's a big mission."

"Yeah, well, not so big now when you think about it."

"So like what the Bastion's trying to do or what?"

She looked to see Daniel sitting fully attentive.

"No. No countries. No boundaries. No bullshit." She paused, starting back on her food. "This time, we're gonna get it right. People shouldn't be separated like that. We shouldn't be at each other's throats because of where we come from, what we look like, what's between our legs, anything superficial."

"So you're hoping for a utopia?"

"There's no such thing. But…with the right mindset, we can get close enough."

"Did…your past experience have anything to do with all this?"

"Every bit of it. We need a world where people aren't stepped on every day of their lives. I mean, we'd still need commerce, currency and shit, but not as, well, frankly, not as sadistic as before. Like, okay, say you don't have enough for a certain meal. Should that mean you just don't get food? Or maybe you're short on rent. Should you be kicked out into the street? Your partner too? Kids? Pets?"

"More empathy."

"Yeah. That's the core of it. Doesn't stop someone from being crazy, but…it can still lessen the blow. Not sure on the details of everything, but…that's sorta where I'm standing right now."

"And Fort Wayne."

Vallerie stopped, looking to him.

"What's your plan? Getting him back?"

She returned to her food until she found the words. After a time, she did.

"Go in armed to the teeth and give an ultimatum. Everything I've seen so far, these guys aren't as well put together as they let on. They're disorganized. They're low on supplies. And, unsurprisingly, they're childish. Simple. Give him back, and we go our separate ways. Don't, and you all die."

Daniel was shocked at her tone. "Just kill them if they don't listen?"

She looked to him. "I don't want it, but… yes."

Daniel nodded, returning to his hands. "You've been through a lot, haven't you? To come to that." She was quiet. Daniel looked back to her, his sight drawn to the pendant of her necklace. "What's it mean?" He pointed. "The star?"

"For me… protection… and do no harm."

"Second one; that's a conundrum these days."

"Yeah." She sighed. "Yeah, it is." She finished the last of her food and set the plate down over the table before taking a seat in the chair opposite. "There's something in my faith. It's called the rule of three. Or the law of thirds. The name depends on where you look, but it all means the same thing. Basically, whatever you put out into the world gets returned to you three times greater. So you do good, then you get good back. You do bad, well, then you might as well be cursed. I'm just, um…trying to hope that it's on my side here."

Daniel nodded, listening silent.

"I mean, my brother was the last person I had in my life. Taking that away…causes pain. So that would invoke the law against them. Following that logic, getting him back, whether I fire a shot or not, I'm hoping…it still brings good my way. Stopping them from killing an innocent person; stopping them from bringing back something that might not be for everyone's benefit. It, um…it's—"

"Complicated."

"Yeah." Bullet whined again from the bedroom. Vallerie got up. "Hang on, buddy!"

"He gonna be okay out here with me around?"

"He's gonna have to be."

She went off down the hall. Daniel remained sat with himself.

"You've really been through a lot," he said quietly.

—Complications—

The crickets sounded steadily in the brush. Accompanying their song was the soft turning of pages. Three uniformed men stood in the night, the center among them hovering his flashlight over the open book set on the tailgate.

"Smart kid," the left man said, seeming impressed. "Saw the opportunity and got some free college. Shame. We could've used her."

"We have our orders," the center man broke

in. "She's a threat."

"Never said anything against our orders."

The man on the left was facing toward the road with his gun ready in hand. The other on the right stood the same, finishing a cigarette. The center continued thumbing through the textbooks.

"Well," he began. "We've got her trail. Let's take what's here and head further down the road." He was met by silence. "You guys hear me?" Again, no answer. He closed the book, tossed it toward the back of the cabin, and dropped his flashlight over the tailgate before turning. "You know I hate it when—"

He stopped at once in being met by a deep red laser sight. His hand slowly moved to the pistol at his side. Four figures approached from down the road, the one on the left and the end two on the right all carrying laser sight rifles. The one in the center walked unarmed. As they entered into view, the flashlight offering some clarity in the night, the center figure stepped ahead of the others. A handsome man in his early thirties, standing tall with his hands in the pockets of his bomber, looked onto the soldiers. His eyes were still as he smirked through a thin beard. The night's breeze tossed lightly through his mid-length blond hair. The three men were silent, hands over their guns.

"Evening, gentlemen," greeted the center man. "Why don't you put the guns down."

The men stood just the same. The center spoke up.

"What is this, Grahm? You're in breach of contract right now."

"Relax. I'm merely here to talk. And they"—he gestured to his companions—"are here as insurance. You guys do tend to…ignore…differing viewpoints, so—"

The three men glanced to one another. The center among them nodded. He eased his hand away from his hip. The others holstered their guns.

"Okay, let's talk then."

"Hey, what a guy! I appreciate that. I'm sure you know why I'm here, so I'll be brief. I want him back. Tonight. Our deal goes on uninterrupted from there."

"You know that's not how it works. According to the terms, any and all dodgers are to be taken. We made that very clear."

"Yes, you did. And I kept my mouth shut at the time because I wasn't aware of any in my group. Then, Thomas went missing. And more than that, his mother came to me in tears. Now, that eighteen-year-old boy is one of my people. He has a parent and friends that very much think what you're doing is wrong, as do I. He's coming home. Tonight."

"You know the terms of breaching contract like this."

Grahm's smile faded. "And you know I much prefer peace."

"Let's just kill them, man. You're wasting your time."

Grahm held a hand up to his man on the right, then cocked his head, staring at the soldiers.

"You see that? The kindness I just extended to you?" The men stood silent, the center speaker appearing impatient. Grahm eyed the truck. "Before we continue, just out of curiosity, what's all this?"

"Tending to another matter. Seems there's a threat coming our way."

"A threat with college books?"

"An…associate of a dodger we recently brought in."

Grahm scoffed a laugh, his smile returning. "Well, well. You boys practically just started and you're already making enemies. It starting to sink in yet as to why?"

"As it happens…this matter is time sensitive. So I'm going to propose a compromise."

Grahm watched as the man came forward.

"Vallerie Sabell: red hair; blue eyes; scar on her forehead; age nineteen. You share anything you might know, and we'll consider giving Thomas a pardon."

"Well, that just doesn't work since, unfortunately, I've no idea who that is. Though I am curious how a teenage girl can be a threat. That true or…are your boys just lonely? Going the way of all the other savages these days?"

"So you break contract, and now you insult us?"

"Careful. I'd take your hand away before you

lose it."

The man's grip fell on his pistol. "No, I don't think I will. I'll be brief. Thomas betrayed us; you, me, both of our people, our country as a whole. That's grounds for termination no matter who or what circumstance. So you and your people accept it, you go home, and our deal remains intact. Or…it looks like peace won't be an option."

Grahm was quiet. The man continued, pulling his pistol. "We don't have time for this. Men, draw your guns. Keep your aim tight."

"I have sights locked on all three of you. Are you sure this is what you wanna do?"

"Far as I'm concerned, you're standing against the future right now, so yes. I'm going to count to three."

Grahm sighed.

"One," the man began.

"Open fire."

The soldier's eyes went wide and before long, all three of them, with only three separate shots, were on the ground, blood pouring from their heads collapsed on the pavement.

"Told you," the right gunman said.

"Well, fuck me for trying."

"They don't budge, my friend," the gunman continued. "They're too stuck to hear anything else."

"That girl they mentioned," started the woman on the left. "Think I heard of her before."

Grahm started toward the bodies, his people

following.

"All ears," he said, kneeling down beside the fallen leader and observing his vest.

"Survivor of a school shooting a few years back, her and her brother. Lot of kids died, her boyfriend among them."

Grahm looked up to her at once. "What the hell would they want with her?"

"This dodger they mentioned; guessing she's not too happy about losing them."

"Maybe the brother?"

"Could be."

Grahm looked back to the body, rifling through the pockets of his uniform. From the inner, he retrieved a small notebook. The word "wanted" was scribbled over the cover. He opened it to see a list of names, many having a line drawn through them. He looked to the most recent name, scratched out like the others.

"Allan Sabell," he said in a sigh. He snapped the notebook shut and returned to his feet. He turned to his people, all three, two young men and an older woman, waiting attentively. "Looks like our mission just got more complicated."

"You wanna help them," the third boy started, having been silent until now.

"We need people. And we owe it to the next world to save as many as we can from these guys," Grahm paused, starting toward the tailgate. "And if their background is true, then I think those kids have been through enough."

He looked to the textbooks and other items left behind.

"I'm in," the woman said.

"Me too."

"Me three," the men agreed.

Grahm continued perusing the books. The woman walked over to his side.

"What?" she asked.

"Dental, nursing, biology, politics, engineering, carpentry, all these notes; seems we share a goal with this girl."

"I'll pull the van around," the brash boy said, starting off down the road.

"Yeah, do that. We take everything. You two, search them real quick; their guns, any food, everything right down to a flask or a pack of smokes." The others did as instructed as Grahm continued observing the belongings, the flashlight illuminating the warm brown of his eyes from its rest on the tailgate. He pondered to himself. "If you're a threat to them, then you're someone I want to know."

—Vallerie—

An angered scream was heard before the corpse fell from the shattered window. It landed heavily onto the driveway. Daniel stopped from his jog, standing before the still body. He looked up to the window of the house to see Vallerie stood looking out, breathing heavily with blood spattered over her shirt.

"Is it down?!" she called.

"Yeah! Smacked its head pretty hard."

"Get away from it!" She left from the window, disappearing back into the room. Daniel looked down to the body and stepped back. Before long, Vallerie jogged out from the house, her hatchet in hand, and looked cautiously to the corpse. It remained still. She stood over its back and plunged her blade down into its head before propping her foot over its neck and pulling it free. She looked to Daniel. "Just in case," she said, still breathing heavily.

"You hurt?"

"No. Just…more of a fighter than I expected."

"You should've waited for me."

"Yeah. Yeah, I guess I should've. House after house with nothing; then there's one. I got cocky," she groaned, rubbing her shoulder. "Lesson learned."

"We've been out for a while. Think your pup is starting to miss you."

Vallerie nodded. "Yeah, I think we've got a good stock going now. We'll go get him and start out."

"On your lead."

Daniel stepped aside. Vallerie looked to him with a smile and a nod and started back down the road. He watched as she cleaned her blade down against the grass before returning it to her belt and walking on, giving another rub over her shoulder. He looked down to the body, formerly an older man that had to be at least five foot ten. He then looked to the window, its frame hanging from the wall with glass and blood spread down over the awning below. He turned to follow as Vallerie walked briskly down the road, stopping for a moment with a groan and a tight grip on his inner thigh. She looked back to him.

"You okay?"

"Yeah. Just a muscle cramp. Something I get here and there; had it since forever."

He regained his footing and started slowly on.

"You take any medication for it?"

"I did. Not so easy to come by anymore." She nodded and continued on. "Were you on anything? After, um, after the shooting?"

She hesitated before answering. "Several. Mostly for sleep."

"Insomnia?"

"Nightmares. Sometimes every night. Sometimes every other. Sometimes just here and there."

"You still on those? You seem to sleep like a rock."

"No. Haven't even thought about them. I got into a bit of a, um, scuffle before all this. Took a good hit to the head. I was out for a few months. Then, next thing I know…this. Probably saved me from withdrawal."

"You woke up in this?" he asked, shocked.

"Yeah."

"… And did the injury stop the nightmares, you think?"

"No. I had them for a bit after, but less intense. It was always the same dream. Always remembering looking the guy in the eye and then the gunshot. But since I woke up, I can't remember his face anymore. Or his voice. I'm sure there's other stuff, but that's just what I've noticed so far."

"For a bit after as in…they've stopped since?"

"Yeah. Yeah, they've stopped."

...

Bullet whined in the backseat, huddling into the corner as Daniel entered.

"I know, buddy. I know." Vallerie gave her pooch a kiss and rubbed his head before turning back in her seat. She reached to start the engine, and a strain struck her shoulder. She winced. "Fuck."

"Here. Go sit with him. I'll do the driving."

"I've got it."

"No, you don't. Come on, hop back."

Seeing his insistence and feeling the throbbing in her shoulder, she reluctantly climbed into the back seat, guiding Bullet to sit beside her.

"Come here, buddy."

Daniel looked to the map and started the engine. "Should be mostly highways soon."

"Yeah. Past the suburbs. Then one long

stretch of rural road. Then onto the highways. Provided they're not blocked. Wasted enough time going around."

"We'll get there."

Daniel pulled on his seatbelt. Vallerie rested her head against Bullet, who was still wary of her companion.

"Hear that, little guy? You're gonna have a nice little family soon. Yes, you are."

Daniel smiled as he pulled off down the street. "It's Wiccan, isn't it?"

"Huh?"

"Your faith. I've been trying to remember the name and it just hit me."

"Yeah, that's the one."

"I remember seeing this thing—I forget where—mentioning something called a familiar. That's all I'd ever heard about Wicca before: why witches are so often depicted with pets; how there's a unique, like, link between us and certain animals; odd behavior when they come to us; that kinda stuff."

Vallerie looked to Bullet, who promptly rested a paw over her hand.

Daniel glanced back in the mirror. "Yeah, I think you've found yours."

Vallerie planted a kiss to her pup while scratching his neck. "That you, buddy? Was I meant to find you?"

Daniel rolled down the window a few inches as they drove out from the suburb.

"Get us some of that breeze." Vallerie looked out, watching the sights pass. Bullet rested his head over her leg.

"Gonna be fall soon. You and your brother do anything for the season? Traditions?"

"No, nothing much. Well, compared to other people at least. No hayrides or pumpkin patches; no trips to the cider mill. We had one, but"—she laughed in recalling—"it's gonna sound poor as shit. For breakfast, we always bought store-brand cereal, trying to save money, and our go-to was this one with cornflakes and raisins in it; well, during the fall, and only then, no matter how much I begged him to keep it going, he'd buy this special, like, grade-A gourmet pumpkin spice stuff, and we'd mix it in our cereal. So good. Never told me where he got it from; probably because he didn't wanna tempt me. But I'd know it right away if I saw it; Granny Del—something."

"You know, that does sound quite poor."

Vallerie snickered.

"But it being so simple's why it's so special. Can't imagine having a whole to-do list like those other people. Seems more chore than fun."

"Did you do anything?"

"Sit outside with some coffee and watch the leaves. Usually grab a pumpkin pie on the weekend. That's about it though. Kept it simple."

Vallerie nodded briefly before turning away from the window and reaching over Bullet to her backpack on the floor. She retrieved her notebook and pen from the pocket, opened it, and began writing. "What's that?"

"Just some ideas for the future."

"*Things To Bring Back:*
Coffee
Cornflakes
Raisins
Pumpkin everything
More fucking coffee..." the page read.

She looked to it, tapping her pen overtop in thought.

"Hey, how'd you know they were in Indiana? I thought the posters said somewhere else."

Vallerie continued facing the page. After a moment, she clicked her pen shut and set it and the notebook down to the floor. She looked briefly to Daniel through his reflection in the mirror and directed her sight back out the window.

"Long story short, I, um... I met one of them. Rather not talk about the how or why, but...they told me."

Daniel adjusted his position in his seat and looked out to the long stretch of road.

•••

After driving a while more, they seemed to wince in unison, quickly grabbing their noses. Daniel rolled up the window. He snickered in looking to Vallerie in the mirror.

"You smell it too, huh?"

"Yeah, what the fuck is that?"

Bullet remained nestled at her side, at full attention, but quiet.

"I don't know. I can't see anything. Maybe road kill or—" He paused in looking to the distance down the road. "Jesus Christ."

"What?" Still holding to her nose, Vallerie eased Bullet aside and hunched over the seat for a better view. Daniel slowed the car to a stop as they both looked on what was ahead. Bullet sat up in the backseat, starting to whine.

In the distance, a large gathering of corpses was seen. Some twitched their heads in their stride. Most seemed to either shamble aimlessly or stand idle. As he turned off the engine, amid the rustling wind outside the car, a faint hum was heard, even with the windows closed: the collective sounds of the dead.

"We can go through it," Vallerie said, her voice unsteady. "We could just plow right through the middle."

"No. No, we can't. Look at the ones there with their heads cocking to the side. Don't know if you've ever encountered one like that, but they ripped me right out of my car before." She looked to him in disbelief. "If we go plowing through and get stuck, we're dead."

She looked back to the road, her breaths becoming uneven. "There's no more time for delays.

He can't keep waiting for shit like this."

"Vallerie," Daniel called sternly. She remained focused on the road. "We can't go through. Just...just let me look at the map for a sec, okay? I'll find a way around."

Feeling defeated, tears began to well in her eyes as she nodded, easing back in her seat. "He doesn't have time," her voice quaked. "He doesn't have time."

Daniel examined the routes on the page. "There. A little ways back, there's a trail that branches off. On the way there's some sort of private property before it opens back up to the main road. If we go down that, we can wait it out and maybe...maybe they'll move on overnight."

Vallerie rubbed her forehead and smacked her hand over her knee.

"My brother can't wait for a maybe! We can't— There's no more fucking time for overnight!"

"I get it. Okay?" Daniel said, turning back to her. "But this road leads straight to the highway. One more night, and we'll be there tomorrow afternoon. You said it was a week, right?"

"Yeah, so they said. He's probably fucking dead already," her voice cracked as she began crying, her heart beating out of her chest. "Stop for this. Stop for that. Stop for food. Stop because it's dark. Because I can't fucking walk—"

"Hey. Hey. He's not dead. Okay? You're not losing him too. Vallerie. Look at me." She faced him through tears. His eyes were firm. "He's not. Dead,"

After a moment's pause, she nodded, wiping her eyes. Daniel turned back and started the car. He turned and began back toward the trail. "It should be just a few minutes back on the left here."

"I'm looking."

Bullet looked to her, continuing to whine low as he rested his chin over her leg.

"I know. I'm okay, baby. I'm okay." She kept her eyes out the window while giving him a scratch on the back.

"There we go." Daniel slowed and pulled off down the trail, the car bouncing over the rough dirt on his way. "Sorry, little guy," he called to the anxious pup nestling further into Vallerie's lap. The shadows of the overhanging trees alongside the road darkened their path. Vallerie kept her eyes front, holding tight to Bullet as the car continued unevenly down the winding path. Daniel pointed ahead. "There. See it? Up there on the right?"

"Yeah."

"Overnight and wait it out. They'll move on." She nodded.

"Overnight."

The rumbling of the car subsided as Daniel slowed beside the old cabin, appearing to Vallerie's eye as a run-down hunter's stop, no larger than the place she'd had by the lake, the only difference being a heartier structure. Daniel turned off the engine and threw his seatbelt up.

"Stay here. I'm gonna check it out."

"Here."

She reached into her bag on the floor, retrieved a pistol and handed it his way. He nodded with warm eyes and took hold of the gun. He stepped out from the car, eased the door shut, and started inside the cabin, the door having been left open. Vallerie watched intensely, doing her best to calm her pup who remained on edge. As she sat in silence, it was a welcome relief that the hum was no longer present. The scent, however, remained; thin, but present nonetheless. Her thoughts wandered from best case to worst in pondering the next day, though she tried her best to think toward the best.

She'd wake up, and the dead would be gone. Her, Bullet, and Daniel would make it to Indiana with no further obstacles. She'd meet with someone from the Bastion, and they'd show mercy. They'd see her desperation and they'd let Allan go. He'd come to her unharmed. He and Daniel would get along. He'd fall in love with Bullet as she had. They'd move on, somewhere, somehow, and build a life for themselves, eventually leading to a life for others as well; one where everybody, from all walks of life, would be welcome. A new world where peace and understanding took precedence over division and chaos, over anxiety and pain.

As she envisioned this, she took hold of her necklace and began a prayer. Upon finishing her request, Daniel was seen stepping calmly out from the cabin. He gestured for her to follow.

"Okay, buddy, you've gotta work with me on this." Bullet eyed her and put up no struggle as she took him close. She eased the door open and led him out by his collar, careful in her stride. She then hoisted the pup into her arms. He whined mildly, but did not fight her, his eyes locked toward the tree line, in the direction of the dead. "Don't you worry," she said, starting to walk.

She rested a kiss over his head and held tightly while approaching the cabin. She stepped inside and Daniel directed her to a nearby bedroom.

"You can put him in there while we get our stuff. It's clean. Little dusty, but he won't get hurt by anything."

She nodded to him and started into the room. Daniel left outside as she set Bullet down inside the room.

"I'll be back in a sec, okay? I promise." He tried to follow as she closed the door, but stopped as she reassured him once more. "I'm coming back. Just gotta get my stuff."

She closed the door and hurried outside. Daniel was already on his way back with several of their belongings, her backpack included. She took what she could carry from the car, closed and locked the doors, doing so delicately while looking out to the wood, and followed back inside. Daniel barricaded the door and helped her organize the packs. She still appeared tense.

"There's a fireplace in the other room. I'll get us some food ready. Go sit with him."

"I can help—"

"Vallerie. Please."

Bullet whined from the room.

"Go rest your mind."

Feeling an ache in her head from the stress, she agreed, and went off. Bullet happily swayed his tail upon seeing her.

"Told you I'd be back." She knelt down and held him close as he licked her chin. "I know. I know."

Daniel watched, retrieving some canned goods from the duffle bag. He had an uneasy expression, smiling for a moment before it gradually faded. He lowered his eyes and started off to the fireplace in the other room.

•••

She woke to Bullet lapping at her cheek.

"Hey, hey. Good morning to you too," she laughed, rolling away from his barrage to no effect. She rubbed his neck before guiding him away and sitting up. He climbed down to the floor, his tail wagging alongside the jangle of his collar. Vallerie rubbed her eyes. The sound of waking birdsong accompanied the rush of wind. She looked to the window to see the trees swaying softly. It was early, the sun still rising. She looked out to the room as

Bullet panted excitedly on the floor. The door was closed. A candle was lit in a caged holder atop the corner desk. Alongside it resided a foil-wrapped plate and a folded note. She stretched, wincing with a groan from her shoulder. She pressed on with the motion regardless. The pain dulled after its initial strike. After settling for a moment, she sighed and stepped out of bed. Bullet began a prance on the old wooden floor. "I see you, buddy. I see you."

She headed to the desk, first looking to the plate. Ravioli. Still warm. The candle beside looked to be dying out. She looked to the letter, her name written overtop, and unfolded it in hand.

"Well, kid, this is where we part ways. When I first saw you in that police station, I was sure you'd blow my head off. And when you didn't, I knew in that moment that I'd been given a gift. A chance to repent.

I won't try to explain or justify what I did to you or to those you love. Whatever context there is doesn't matter. It was an evil act. An act I have no right nor desire to ask forgiveness for. All I'll say is this.

You learn a lot when you're behind bars. When you have time to sit with yourself. When you're faced with how rotten you've become. You learn even more after being beaten. And yet even more than that when the world ends. In traveling with you, I see the true damage I've caused, and for that, whether you believe me or not, please know that I'm sorry for it all.

The highways are clear. I know so because that's how I ended up around here to begin with. I'm going ahead to clear the way for you as much as I can. I meant what I said. I truly didn't want to be alone. Not after realizing exactly what I did. Not after knowing I could bring some sort of good back to you. Providing a safe route for you to find your brother seemed like the best I could do. There are more dead than I thought, but I'm sure I can get rid of most of them. Any stragglers I'm sure will be no problem for you though if they get the best of me. If you don't find my body among them, for your own sake, please do not go looking. You have a present and a future to focus on and I don't deserve a place in any of it. I hope in time you can find peace.

Be safe. Goodbye."

Nausea overtook her as the letter became crunched in her fists. Her heart began to race, all while feeling like it was about to sink to a stop at the same time. She dropped the page to the floor and headed to the bedside table, retrieving her belt in silence. Bullet became uneasy, watching her intensely while whining low. With unsteady hands, she fit her belt through her pant loops and gathered her things before starting back to the desk. She blew out the dying candle and left for the door. Bullet's whines became louder. As she stood gripping the handle, the nausea caused her to stumble. She caught herself with a hand propped against the frame and looked down to her necklace as it swayed from her neck. She settled for a moment, standing straight with a deep breath. Upon its release, she closed her eyes and took off her necklace, tucking it away in her pant pocket. Bullet gave a desperate bark. She looked to him.

"I'll be back."

She took her hatchet in hand before leaving the room and easing the door to a close.

—What Came Before—

The siren blared as the ambulance raced down the street, guided by several police cruisers. Inside, Vallerie sat beside him as the vehicle bobbed over the road. The paramedics talked amongst each other while tending to his wounds, though she paid no attention to what was specifically said; their conversation was more like background noise. She trembled, crying quietly as blood ran down from her forehead over her gown. She held tightly to his hand, her eyes never leaving his despite their strain. Allan sat on the opposite bench, his head resting over folded hands. He was silent but shaking much the same as his sister. Jaxton, growing ever weaker, looked to her through heavy eyes. He traced his thumb over her hand and spoke softly, barely managing the words.

"I... love you."

Completely lost, she closed her eyes as her tears came harder. Her voice broke as she met him. "I love you more."

The chatter from the paramedics gradually faded as they looked briefly over to her, quickly lowering their eyes as if in defeat. Her focus remained on Jaxton. "I don't want you to go. I…I don't want you to go. Please don't go."

Jaxton quietly traced her grasp once more, his eyes never leaving her.

She lowered her head and kissed his hand. "I don't want you to go."

—What Comes After—

The rotted eyes of the corpse stared intensely as it lumbered forward with a reaching arm. She ducked beneath its hand and slammed the blunt of her blade up against the undead man's chin with an enraged scream. The body lost balance and collapsed onto the road. She was quick to drive the sharp end down into its skull, planting a foot and retrieving her blade as a spatter of blood followed its path. She looked ahead, eyes blazing through tears, and slashed hard, her screams seeming from another world as the neck of another corpse split open. It tried to grab her, baring its jaws, but found itself stopped as her hand reached up into the wound. She dropped her blade and gripped the back of the man's head with her opposite hand. With a hard motion, a snap echoed the street and the body fell.

Three others began her way. She grabbed her hatchet from the blood-soaked road and readied a strike, but found her arm caught in the grasp of a taller woman. The body wheezed as it tried to ready a bite. Vallerie used her other hand to grab her arm and pulled down hard, driving them both to the ground. She shifted her position, planted her foot over the woman's stomach, and bent the arm back as hard as she could manage. It broke, and she freed her hand from the undead's grasp, raising her blade and driving it down several times into the woman's throat. Gradually, her motion ceased.

    Another of the two remaining ducked toward her. Fueled by anger and pain, she was hyper aware, looking to the corpse's eyes and rolling away just in time. After falling to the ground, it made another grab, a low strained breath calling menacingly. She kicked hard, knocking the body onto its back, and scrambled to her feet, quickly having to grapple with the next deceased figure as it took hold of her. Its strength prevented her from following through with any pull or twist. She stared onto it, eyes hateful and strained as she breathed fast and heavy. She made a kick with her foot but missed her timing. She nearly stumbled but regained her footing before a second attempt. It landed, and she knocked the body off balance just long enough to overpower it, throwing them both to the ground.

    Overtop the undead, she held its arms down to its chest and drew her gun from her hip. Viciously, she slammed the hilt against its forehead as the previous corpse regained its footing, starting to rise from the ground. She aimed the barrel to the disoriented body as its arms weakened, no longer fighting against her, and fired. A hole was driven through its head and blood sprayed over the pavement as the shot echoed the road. She took aim to the body lumbering her way and fired another shot, ending its breath as soon as it began and knocking it down to the ground as blackened blood and mats of flesh and hair sprayed from its head.

    A breeze blew through the surrounding trees as she breathed heavy, sitting up on her knees with her hair tossing. She took her hatchet from the gore-painted pavement, wiped the blade over the closest body's shirt, and returned it to her belt. She stood, brushing her hair away from her face, and looked down the road with her hand still tight on her gun. With her heart racing and breaths still heavy and uneven, she screamed out to the distance, her voice a piercing roar.

    "Cale!"

    No response came. She could see nothing but death in the distance as several bodies lay still, though the low hum of the dead continued. She listened closely, adjusting her stance in facing the open road. Gradually, a familiar voice was heard groaning faintly further down the way. As the hum of the dead became more erratic, their putrid scent hanging heavy in the air despite the breeze, she smirked. Her finger moved to a rest against the trigger of her gun and she began walking down the road.

—Allan—

The soldier sat guard outside the cell was deep in thought, reading a book open in hand. Allan watched, his hand resting over his hip. A tray of bread, barely touched, sat against the bars. The man briefly looked to it before returning to his book with a smile and a scoff.

"Go ahead and starve. Makes no difference to me."

Allan remained silent, intensely focused on the soldier as he sat in a dark corner against the wall. As the man turned to the next page with a sigh, a voice was heard calling urgently over his radio.

"Brian, we need you out here! Asap!"

He set his book down over his lap and impatiently grabbed the radio from his vest, eyeing Allan closely.

"What's going on?"

"Twitchers! At the gate! Sal almost got bit and we're having a hard time getting it under control!"

"The fuck— What do you mean having a hard time?! Just shoot 'em!"

"Knocked 'em right out of our hands, and now we can't get near either one! We're holding the gate, but they're putting up a fight trying to get through!"

"I'm guarding a dodger here, don't you have anyone else?!"

"Negative! We're shorthanded, and it's gonna get worse if you don't get out here!"

An erratic breath and metallic banging was

heard behind the man's shouting over the speaker. The soldier sighed.

"Goddamnit. Fine! Hold tight!" he said, returning the radio to his vest and standing from his seat. He slammed the book down over the chair and pointed to Allan. "Don't try anything. Orders or no orders, you do and you die today, slowly. Got it?"

"Yes, sir."

After a moment's stare, the soldier took his leave past the bars, his footsteps echoing heavily down the way before the distant open and close of a loud door. A click came soon after.

Allan, with his pulse beginning to race, began etching his fingers against what appeared to be the lining of his jean pocket. After some effort, his fingers pinched hold onto two ends of thread. He pulled hard on them, revealing a hole in the fabric. He delicately fished inside and removed a small plastic bag containing a keyring with various pins run around and a single razor blade held in a cardboard guard. He got up and hurried to the gate, etching each pin one by one into the hole of the lock. "Come on, baby. Come on, work with me here."

—Vallerie—

Another groan was heard, closer, followed by ever more strained breaths. She walked calmly toward the wood at the road's edge, stepping off into the grass as the stench of decay hang heavy all around. She scoffed a laugh to herself in looking ahead toward a small clearing between the trees. Off in the grass, Cale laid pinned beneath a heavy branch with wide-reaching limbs, holding it close as two of the dead were held at bay overtop, reaching toward his face while gaping their jaws.

    He heard the crunch over the grass as she approached. He leaned his head back and was met with the sight of a pistol barrel pressed firmly above his eyes. Vallerie stood, looking down to him, her eyes reddened and vicious as she held a slightly quivering hand over the gun's aim. He met her eye briefly before directing his attention back to the dead. He sighed a quivering breath. Vallerie spoke, her voice sounding exhausted.

    "Why?"

    He didn't respond. Another steady gust of wind brushed through Vallerie's hair, though she stood firm, her eyes never leaving him. The dead continued their reach, their attention never facing her, as if she weren't even there. She pressed the barrel harder against his head. "You owe me a reason."

    Cale looked up to the swaying trees. The morning sky was clouded gray. He drew a breath and closed his eyes.

    "I was alone. No family. No friends. Every day it was the same thing. Get up. Get ready for work. Rarely take a shower. Rarely even brush my teeth. Go to a job I hate that barely paid the bills.

Come home, eat dinner and watch TV, then go to bed and start it all again the next day… And then I met someone. On my way home from work one night; this girl; teenager. She was alone too. Didn't take long before we became friends," he paused, shifting his arms over the branch as the dead continued to reach.

Vallerie stood listening at full attention.

Cale heaved several uneven breaths and went on. "One night, she met me after work, and we cooked dinner together. She hardly ate any of it, which for her was a bad sign. When I asked why…she got…really quiet. Eventually she told me she'd been raped by her teacher. And it'd been going on for a while. She told the counselor. She told the principal. She told classmates. And it kept happening." He looked back up to the trees swaying in the wind and began crying. "I told her she could stay the night, that I'd try to help. The look she gave me, how she hugged me tighter than anyone ever had," he paused, closing his eyes tight. "And…when I woke up the next morning…I found her hung by an extension cord in the bedroom closet."

Vallerie adjusted her grasp over the gun, seemingly stoic to his story.

"That's why I did it. For what happened to that innocent girl, I just wanted to hurt the world back. And it was the worst decision I've ever made. What I did, what it took from you, from your boyfriend—"

"Shut up."

She pressed the barrel harder against his head, her hand quivering further as her eyes blazed with pain and hate. She'd heard his story; she'd heard every word, finally getting an explanation, but it brought no form of relief, it eased no pain in the wound. This fact made no difference, only angered her further.

Cale was still, a tear running down from his closed eyes. "I'm sorry," he said.

Vallerie looked on him with her pulse racing as her hand trembled. The sheer emotion made her nausea seem almost unbearable, yet she remained on her feet. Tears welled in her strained eyes as she rested her finger against the trigger.

—Allan—

Three soldiers walked down the outdoor hall, spattered in blood and gore, all seemingly exhausted. Two eased down to a seat on the benches while the other continued back to his guard. He pulled a ring of keys and unlocked the door ahead. As he walked through the open door, Allan slammed it shut and grabbed him from behind, hurriedly pressing the razor against his throat and tearing across. Blood sprayed across the wall as the man gasped, struggling to no avail to fight back as Allan held his head back with the wound opening further. Shouting was heard from outside the door as a banging started against it.

Allan lifted the soldier's pistol from his hip and tossed him aside against the wall. He darted down the hallway as the man continued gasping in a desperate flail over the floor.

The door opened, slamming against the wall as the other two men charged in, armed with assault rifles. Allan, stood behind the corner wall, held tight to the gun, and waited with his heart racing. As one man rounded the corner, he fired a shot into his foot before aiming another to his throat, silencing him mid-scream. The bullet exited, striking the wall just beside the other soldier's head as his friend's blood caught in his eyes. The dying man dropped his gun in a struggle to hold to his wound. The second tried to open his eyes but was soon met by gunfire as Allan unloaded the last of his pistol clip into his chest. He slid slowly down the wall. Allan tossed the pistol aside and went out, taking up one of the rifles. He fired a final head shot to each of the fallen soldiers before looking to the open door and starting outside.

—Vallerie—

"I'm sorry," he repeated.

Vallerie's unsteady hold over the gun remained. Her finger started further against the trigger but stopped as a loud crack sounded. She looked to the branch holding the dead away. It was split in two. They leaned heavily against it, reaching closer to

Cale's face as he strained to hold the broken branch in his hands. She looked back to him, his eyes fearful, watching his struggle.

Gradually, he felt the barrel ease back from his head, and looked back to see her stepping back with a stoic expression. He went to speak but noticed her gesture up to the nearest tree. He looked to it, spotting the broken end where the branch had snapped. He returned his sight back to her as she glanced up just the same.

"Looks like the universe cast judgment already," she paused, looking back down to him. "Why should I meddle?"

Cale nodded, closing his eyes as the dead continued an excited fight against his hold on the branch. Eventually, his arms gave way, and they came upon him.

A sharp scream echoed through the wood as Vallerie watched, another gust tossing about the clearing. The pitch of the screams reached higher above the slow tearing of flesh. She turned with closed eyes at feeling the spatter of blood against her face. However, she remained in her stance, never stepping away. Slowly, her eyes opened back to the feast. She watched as the man's life faded in the moments that followed. In time, his screams turned to moans, and the moans faded almost as soon as they started. As he fell silent, Vallerie rested her eyes with a deep breath, hearing nothing but the wind and the subtle scraping and following swallows. She turned and began back to the road, looking out down the way as the events settled in mind. Her eyes glistened through further tears as her breaths came shuddering.

As she left the wood and the sounds of the dead behind, a dam within seemed to break, and from it flooded a host of memories. She stopped, snapping her eyes shut as the tears and uneven breaths overtook her. There, stood alone in the road, she recalled every bit of time she'd shared by her love's side. She remembered his shy approach when he'd first asked her out at lunch. She remembered the feeling that washed over her that day, the butterflies, the excitement, the fear. She remembered the night he'd gotten jumped as her and Allan snuck into the track field to settle a bet on who was faster. She remembered how Allan didn't hesitate to beat his attackers senseless. She remembered how she held him as he cried, sensitive as he was, and reminded him that it was over and that he didn't do anything to deserve what they'd done. She remembered how she'd kissed him then; their first. She remembered it all. As she stood among the flood, she wished she could tell him the same thing now. It was over, and that he didn't deserve it. Though it wasn't long before a sudden thought snuffed out that wish as she opened her eyes. Allan.

Thrusted hard back into reality, she walked briskly on. In making her way back to the cabin, she reached into her pocket and retrieved her necklace.

She held it briefly in hand, tracing the pendant with her thumb, then planted a kiss over the star and returned it to its place around her neck. As it fell over her shirt, swaying in her step, a distant sound caught her attention. She stopped with a wipe of her eyes and listened as it drew closer. In the distance ahead, two large vehicles came her way: a black van and a military truck. She held tight to her gun, holding her stance at the road's edge. As the vehicles came into clearer view, still at a distance, they slowed to a stop. She watched, laser focused, her finger resting on the trigger of her pistol.

    The driver's side door to the truck opened, and a man in a dark-blue bomber jacket stepped out, his boots landing heavily onto the pavement. He stood with gold hair swaying as the breeze picked up yet again, the sky growing darker. He looked on her with his own gun drawn in hand. Vallerie's eye lowered to a glare at the distant stranger. He raised his opposite hand, holding it still while holstering his gun. He then glanced to the truck and nodded, looking back to her and lowering his arm. A woman with black hair pulled to a ponytail stepped out from the passenger side, standing unarmed. Following her, two younger men with short brown hair left the van, holding no weapons of their own, though the taller of the two kept his hand close to his holster. The man in the bomber, stood in the center of the group, raised his brows with a smile, and called out, warm in voice.

    "We come in peace!"

Vallerie was silent, looking upon them with confusion. Her hand was steady over her gun at her side.

He gestured toward her and called out once more. "You're Vallerie, right? You can relax. We're friends."

"Don't recall making any."

"Nor do we. Yet it seems destiny led us to each other. That's quite the mess you left back there. You do that all by yourself?"

She stood quiet, heavily confused by the stranger's friendly tone.

He looked to the woman, who in turn looked to him. His smile faded as he looked back to her eye. "Point taken. I'll trim the fat. You want The Bastion, right? About your brother? They took one of ours too. We're on our way there ourselves. Happened on a small band of 'em and heard about you. We'd like to help. And…we're always open to some new blood back home; especially someone of your... talents."

Vallerie, nerves on edge, softened her expression, but remained in her stance.

"You," she called out. "You're the leader?"

He gave a nod. "I am."

"Put your gun on the ground and walk over to me. Just you. Then we can talk."

"I take it you're not willing to extend the same courtesy."

"No. No, I'm not. Think I'm plenty justified too."

He cocked his head and sighed. "Very well."

Carefully, he took his gun from its holster and set it on the pavement. The others looked to him nervously. He gave each a reassuring glance and looked ahead, starting slowly with hands raised. After several steps, with a few feet between them, Vallerie gestured for him to stop.

"Good enough. Name."

"Grahm Floyd. My companions back there are Tammera Stevens and Jason and Bill Collins; Jason's the taller one."

Vallerie cocked her head with a curious brow. "Awfully open."

"When I have a good feeling about someone, yes."

"Even to a stranger covered in blood?"

"When that stranger is the survivor of a tragedy, holds a pentacle around her neck, and leaves a brutal slaughter of the dead behind on her way to rescue her brother from deranged army men…yes. And yes again," he nodded with a smile.

"What else did you find back there?" she asked, eyeing him coldly.

"A dinky old shack with an anxious pup inside. He's okay. We never stepped foot inside the room. Just looked through the window from outside. If he's not there when you return, you're welcome to blow my head clean off. And in front of my friends."

She studied his expression for a while, keeping deep focus on his eyes. He never looked away from her, remaining calm. With hesitation, she holstered her gun.

Grahm lowered his hands to his sides. "We found your books," he continued. "We're of like mind it seems. Regarding a future." Vallerie's eyes seemed to brighten toward the man. He smiled further at the sight. Keeping his eye her way, he took a step back and nodded toward his people. "Let's go get your brother back."

•••

She held Bullet close in her seat on the van's floor. He shivered slightly, sat nestled against her and refusing to look to the others. Grahm sat on the seat before her. Tammera sat behind, massaging her shoulder.

"How's that?" she asked. "Any better?"

"A little. Thanks."

"Doesn't feel like you tore anything. You get that from them?"

"This was earlier on."

"What happened?"

"There was a big one. Tall, older guy. Put up more of a fight than I thought. Should've known better."

"How'd you get him?"

"Threw him out a window."

Grahm snickered. Eventually Tammera laughed too.

"Geez, kid." She eased off of her shoulder and sat back in her seat. "Just take it easy for a while. We'll get a better look at things back home."

Vallerie rested a hand over Bullet's head. "You're okay, buddy."

Grahm glanced over with bright eyes as Tammera's greens seemed to shine right back.

"That reminds me," he started, looking back to Vallerie. "Looking at your shadowy friend there. There's this thing I do with new people where I kinda—ugh, this is gonna sound so stupid—where I think about what animal they're like; just this little comparison thing like people do with zodiac signs. So far I've met a few lions; a bear; some others. But yours…yours is a first."

Vallerie sat quietly, softly stroking her pup.

In finding the right words, he looked on her with concern. "You okay?"

"I'm listening. Just…thinking."

He smiled. "That makes me all the more sure."

She met his eye.

"You, my dear, strike me as a wolf. Specifically a black one, a runt."

She snickered, returning her attention to Bullet.

"Don't let that last bit throw you. A runt wolf is still a wolf. And a runt wolf is one you underestimate."

"The color have a meaning?"

"Always thought black wolves looked more…threatening."

Vallerie nodded, cracking a smile.

"Just a second back, when you said you were listening, I swear I could see your ears perk up."

"We're pulling in," Jason called, looking back from the front window. Vallerie noticed his eyes, a warm brown, just like Bill's. Unlike his brother, they didn't seem to fit his demeanor at all.

Grahm turned his attention to Tammera. Both appeared nervous.

Vallerie looked on him, studying his eyes for a moment.

"Mind if I try yours?"

His cheer returned as he eased back in his seat. "Shoot."

After a moment's gaze, she returned to her pup. "White wolf. Mature. But not old."

Grahm scoffed. "Consider me flattered. Usually I'm told I look older than I am." He paused, meeting Tammera once more before a sigh as the vehicle came to a stop.

"You're sure it was the best approach? Sending him to the checkpoint first?" Vallerie asked.

"We've got a good rep, and Bill's the innocent one, so…sure as can be, given the circumstances."

She nodded to herself as Tammera brushed her hair from her face.

"Your way could've worked too, but, like I said—"

"I look threatening."

"Scars and those blues, yeah, they might feel a little on guard. No offense, obviously."

"None taken."

"Good," Tammera said. "Because you're a rather striking young lady. With gorgeous hair, I might add, especially for the end times."

Vallerie shied away a smile.

Grahm's attention turned as the truck came.

"He's back, guys. Nobody with him from the looks of it," Jason said.

"That was too fast."

Both Grahm and Tammera tensed up, their hands going for their guns.

"Think something happened?"

"Probably the expected response."

Vallerie sat silent, looking between them as her hand, too, reached for her weapon. The echoed slam of a door came before hurried steps as Bill approached with heavy breaths.

"What? What happened?" Jason asked.

"It's empty. Left their radio and their documents."

"Passways are always at least five and there wasn't one?"

"They left in a hurry. Something must've happened at base. Whatever it is, they're distracted. Now's our window."

"Let's go then."

Jason exited the van as the two were heard

talking further. Vallerie looked to Grahm.

"And now we get our people back." Taking his rifle from beside the seat, he stood and met her. "I think you should stay here with him. You've been through enough."

"You might need help. I'm coming too."

"Really, I'd rather you not be out there. We've got this."

"I'm coming. Besides, if anything happened…it's gotta be me."

Tammera stood from her seat, hoisting the strap of her own rifle over her shoulder.

"Well, if you're insistent, then I'll get out of your baby's way here so he doesn't bolt when you get up."

She left out the door and closed it on her way.

"When we get close, stay in the center. We'll keep a tight formation so you won't get in trouble."

"Okay. I'll be out in just a second. I wanna talk to him for a minute."

Grahm nodded before opening the door and stepping out. He looked back before closing it.

"You picked one hell of a name for him by the way."

"Hear that, buddy?" Bullet looked up to her as she roughed the fur around his neck. "I'll be back, okay? Mommy's coming back." She stood, taking up her own rifle, and gave him a final pet before opening the door. "Mom's coming back." With a stern eye to her pup, she left out and closed the door. Grahm took her by the shoulder and guided her into the center of the group as they started down the road, himself leading the way. "How far to the stadium?"

"Not far. Stay sharp."

Vallerie, nervous in eye, surveyed the sights around the street. "I'm assuming all this concrete takes stealth out of the running."

"Unfortunately, it does."

•••

Nothing was seen in their trek toward the parking lot, every building on the way having stood as if abandoned, the scene unnaturally quiet. On their approach, before the entry gate, the group, all with guns aimed steady, looked to a truck parked with the engine still running. Nobody was seen.

"Think it's a trap?" Tammera asked.

"No. No, this is something else," Grahm replied. "Looks like they got caught off guard."

Vallerie was silent as they met the opened gate.

"Gentlemen? You guys see anything at the back?"

"No. All clear," Jason responded.

"What the hell happened?" Bill chimed in. "They would've been on us already."

Grahm entered, cracking a smile and a laugh. "Well, look at that. The Bastion fell."

Ahead, before the ticket booths, several fallen

soldiers lay on the ground. The group, under Grahm's nod, spread out, observing the scene and looking to the path ahead of the gates. Tammera stepped forward as he nudged one of the bodies with his foot.

"Looks like there's more ahead. The dead too," she said.

Vallerie went ahead of her, holding her rifle at a firm aim.

"Vallerie," she called out.

"Vallerie!" Grahm followed hurriedly in her path.

She stepped into the hall overlooking the field and observed the bodies, anxiously eyeing each one. She looked to each end of the hall before standing still with a shout. "Allan?!" she cried out, her voice desperate.

Grahm reached her side. The others caught up. "Jason, Bill, you go right. Vallerie, you're with me on the left. Tam, stay here and keep watch."

"Got it," she said, turning with a tight aim back to the entry.

The boys went down the hall. Vallerie, standing with anxious breaths, was comforted by Grahm's hand over her shoulder.

"We'll find him. Come on."

With guns held forward, they started down the hall, listening closely. They rounded the corner, starting down a long stretch with shops organized alongside. As they walked on, Vallerie slowed her stride, lowering her gun as she squinted with a look to the distance ahead. Grahm stopped, looking in the same direction. At the end of the hall, before the staircase to the upper floor, two men were seen, one in camouflage, sat still beneath a shop's window, and the other sat on the first step of the stairs—with brown and silver hair.

Vallerie rushed ahead, Grahm following close behind as their steps echoed the hall. As she reached the stairs, she stopped, dropping her gun and crouching down before him. Allan sat seemingly asleep. She rested her hand over his cheek and called out softly.

"Hey. Hey, sleepy head. Wake up."

Allan opened his eyes and raised his sight to her. He smiled. His voice was weak. "Hey."

As she looked on him, she felt a dread starting in her chest. Something was wrong. This wasn't what he looked like waking up.

"Allan?" she called.

He sighed. "It's okay, Val. Everything's gonna be okay."

"What—" She looked to Grahm, confused.

He knelt down beside her, setting his gun down to the floor. Allan looked to him.

"You've gotta take care of her," he said in a daze.

Vallerie rested her opposite hand over his cheek, holding gently to him as she directed his eye to her. "Allan. Are—" She paused, the dread continuing as tears filled her eyes. "Are you okay?"

Grahm hunched forward, looking to his back.

Vallerie glanced to him. Allan took his sister by the hand, closing his eyes with a sigh. "What?"

Grahm sat back with a heavy breath, turning away from her. "Fuck," he said to himself.

She looked to her brother.

"Allan, what happened?"

He met her eye.

"I got out. On the way…one bit me."

Her heart plummeted hard.

"What—What does that mean?"

"It's okay, sis. It doesn't hurt. I'm just…tired," he paused, closing his eyes again.

"Grahm, please tell me he's…not—" Her voice shook as she continued crying. She looked to him desperately.

He met her sight, his eyes telling all. "If it was his arm…a leg," he started, "but the neck…"

She turned back to her brother, lowering her sight in disbelief. "No."

"It's okay," Allan said, near a whisper now.

"Allan," Grahm asked. "Can you tell me if anyone else was taken here? Anyone else that dodged?"

"…One of yours?"

"Yeah. Yeah, one of mine; a boy, younger than you."

Allan nodded. "He was down before I could do anything. The dead, they…were just on him. In the field."

Grahm nodded, lowering his head and clutching his brow.

"So—So that's it?" Vallerie asked, becoming increasingly off balance. "I go through all that just to…to…to, what, find you and you fucking die? I survive all that just to lose my brother too?"

He looked to her once more, managing strength to hold her hand tighter. "No. No, don't do that. You…survived…because you're meant to. You made it." He looked to Grahm. "And you met friends."

"But I'm losing you." She looked to her brother with pleading eyes. "I…I can't lose you too. Allan, I can't deal with that. I—"

"You can. Vallerie, you can. You—" He struggled, meeting her gaze sternly. "You…don't…need me…anymore."

"Yes, I do."

He smiled, closing his eyes. His grasp on her hand became weak. "I…love—"

"Allan?" He fell from the stairs, caught in his sister's arms as she faced him toward her. "Allan?!" she cried.

"—love…you," his voice faded.

"Please. Please, not you too. Please, not you. Not you! Come on, wake up! Allan, please wake up!"

"Vallerie," Grahm plead, sitting beside her with a hand on her shoulder.

"Allan, brother, I need you! You hear me?! I fucking need you! Wake up!"

"Vallerie," Grahm urged, holding back tears of his own.

She was unable to compose herself, hyperventilating as she held Allan close. A cough echoed around the hall from the shop on their right. Vallerie and Grahm look to the soldier sat beneath the window, bleeding from a gunshot in his abdomen; the same one that met with Allan in the hotel room. A trace of blood fell from his mouth as he began to smile. He looked to them.

"Karma," he said. "From everything he could've done. He had it coming. They both did."

They looked on him with hate in their eyes. Vallerie remained holding her brother in her arms.

Grahm looked to her as she closed her eyes, her breaths settling as reality dawned. He guided her to let Allan go. "I've got him. It's okay, I've got him. Just breathe. Focus on calming your breath."

She sat on her knees as Grahm took hold of her brother, resting him down over the floor. Her sight was fixed to the small trace of blood on the stairs, feeling utterly lost.

"Yup," the soldier said, sighing with a look out to the field. "Little Mr. Badass. Taken out by a corpse. Fitting end for a coward. Not sure why you guys are so upset…" He closed his eyes, stretching out his legs as he coughed again.

Vallerie slowly turned to him, her eyes glaring.

Grahm looked to her. "Val?" he asked. He was ignored, her attention remaining fixed on the soldier.

He drew a strained breath and opened his eyes, turning over to her. "Huh. So you're the one he meant. You killed our men…just because of him?"

His mocking tone enraged her. She no longer trembled. Her tears have stopped. She sat still, glaring at the man.

He began to laugh. "All that for some coward that chose not to fight for us, or for you."

Vallerie turned back toward the stairs and closed her eyes. She took a deep breath, reaching up and holding to the pendant of her necklace. She exhaled slowly.

"Vallerie?" Grahm was again ignored.

The soldier looked out to the field once more. "Allan Sabell…" he mocked. "What a waste."

Vallerie took her hand away from her necklace as it fell back down over her shirt. She stood to her feet and opened her eyes, glaring at the man as she drew her pistol from her belt. She started over to him as Grahm watched with concern.

The soldier looked up to her as she stood before him. He cracked a dismissive smirk and shook his head, laughing. That laugh soon turned to a shrieking scream as she fired a shot into his groin. He doubled over immediately as she stood looking down to him, watching him writhe and gasp for breath amid the agony. She tossed her gun away and drew her hatchet from her belt. She grabbed the man, forced him up, and threw him down to his back over the floor. He continued gasping for air amid high-pitched groans, looking up to her with a raised hand. Vallerie, silent, with a cold expression, knelt down and etched her blade deep into the bleeding wound. He begged, soon screaming higher than before as she tore upward. Blood sprayed over her face as her blade ran into his abdomen. She pulled it free and sat back, watching as he struggled for air, dying before her eyes.

Grahm looked on in horror. Vallerie, stricken by pain and rage, swiftly raised her blade and drove it down into the man's face as he lay fading. She pulled it free and did so again, and then again, slamming violently over and over as blood showered every part of her—her face; her hair; her shirt; her pants. She began a scream unlike anything Grahm had ever heard as she continued hacking into the body. It wasn't long before she lost her voice.

After a final strike, Grahm stood and ran over to her. Without hesitation, she picked up her gun and stood, pressing the barrel up to his forehead as she gripped the weapon tight in her hands. She stood breathing heavily with eyes that looked to him like they belonged to hell itself. Slowly, he raised his hands, giving a desperate look to the girl.

"Vallerie. Hey. It's okay." As if coming out of a trance, her breaths slowed, and her eyes began to soften. "I'm your friend. Okay? I'm your friend," he said with a gentle voice, pleading for her to calm down.

She lowered the gun, dropped it down at her feet, and averted her gaze, closing her eyes tightly as tears began again. Grahm pulled the girl into a tight hug, holding her head against his chest as she cried. He closed his eyes and rested against her. He shed a tear of his own as he tried to comfort her. It seemed to no avail as Vallerie, covered in death, continued a violent cry against him. "You're gonna be okay," he said. "You're gonna be okay."

Made in United States
North Haven, CT
23 July 2023